D0776750

"I'm an old-fashioned girl, Mr. Fraser."

"What does that mean?"

"It means I am not promiscuous," Cassie declared and lifted his hand off her leg.

Weighing her through shuttered lids, he took a sip of coffee. "I'm impressed."

She gave him a skeptical glance. "I just bet you are."

"Why would you doubt it?"

"Do you have any idea how many times some passing cowboy has tried to get me to climb into the hayloft with him? Why do you think I prefer to dress in men's clothing?"

Colt burst into laughter. "Are you saying that beneath that men's shirt and pants lurks the heart of a frightened female?"

The amusement in his eyes was as compelling as his contagious laughter. "Hardly frightened," she countered good-naturedly. "Merely bored with men who think I can't tell what their intentions are. Yours, for instance."

"Mine are very clear, Miss Braden. I only have a week to get you into that hayloft before I leave town."

Also by Ana Leigh

THE FRASERS: CLAY

Published by Pocket Books

THE
LAWMAN
SAID
"I DO"

The Frasers

ANA LEIGH

POCKET STAR BOOKS
New York   London   Toronto   Sydney

An *Original* Publication of POCKET BOOKS

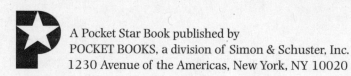 A Pocket Star Book published by
POCKET BOOKS, a division of Simon & Schuster, Inc.
1230 Avenue of the Americas, New York, NY 10020

ISBN 0-7394-6143-5

Cover design by Anna Dorfman

Manufactured in the United States of America

I dedicate this book to Micki, Nancy, and Edwina. It was a long, hard journey, gals, but my love and gratitude for making the trip with me.

Chapter 1

Colt Fraser had been raised to appreciate God's gifts, and he was gazing appreciatively at one of them right now—the curvaceous backside of the passenger climbing into the stagecoach ahead of him. The sweet hips and long legs encased in those pants clearly belonged to a woman.

When the couple had arrived at the stagecoach relay station in New Mexico, Colt had assumed they were both men.

Now he realized that this one was definitely a woman, even though she was dressed in a shirt, vest, jeans, boots, and hat.

They were the only passengers who boarded the stage, and he sat down in the seat opposite them and offered his hand to the man.

"How do you do? I'm Colt Fraser. Looks like we'll be traveling together."

"Jeff Braden," the man said and shook his hand. "This is my sister, Cassie."

Colt tipped his hat. "Miss Braden." He had already noticed she wasn't wearing a wedding band.

She nodded and asked, "You a drummer, Mr. Fraser?"

"No. I'm California bound."

"That accent sounds southern," Jeff Braden said.

"I'm from Virginia, sir."

The "sir" was from habit; Braden looked like he wasn't dry behind the ears yet.

"Most folks heading west stay on the Oregon Trail," the woman said. "It's unusual to cut off onto the Santa Fe Trail. You picked a good time for your sight-seeing; right now the Apaches are quiet. Of course, that can change from day to day."

"I managed to dodge Yankee bullets all through the war. I figure I can do the same with Indian arrows," Colt said confidently.

"You'd find it more difficult than you think. The Apaches are skilled warriors and you'd be fighting them on their ground. I imagine you were in the Confederate army, Mr. Fraser."

"Yes, ma'am, the cavalry. I had the privilege of serving under the command of General J.E.B. Stuart until he was killed."

"Sorry, I never heard of him."

"No other cavalry officer can compare to his skill and courage in battle. Confederate or Yankee."

"However, I *have* heard of that illustrious Confederate officer William Quantrill and the merciless raid he led on Lawrence, Kansas." Her tone was bitter. "It must have taken a great deal of skill and courage to order the slaughter of innocent women and children, along with the men."

"That raid was not sanctioned by any officer in the regular Confederate army, Miss Braden. and those were not

regular Confederate soldiers in his command, but rene-
gades and drifters. Neither I, nor any of my fellow officers,
held any respect for the man. He was a mad killer in the
guise of an officer, and a blight on the Confederacy and
the brave and honorable men who have served it."

"My apologies, Mr. Fraser." She turned her head and
stared out of the window.

He couldn't blame her for what she said. Others had
said the same. Seemed like since that incident, every
soldier or civilian south of the Mason-Dixon Line had
borne the scorn for that son of a bitch's actions.

Colt studied her. Cassie Braden was intriguing. Despite
her masculine clothing, she had an attitude that made
him think of finishing schools and liveried servants.

She certainly was as pretty as any woman he'd ever
met, even without all the powder and stuff some women
put on their faces to beautify them. Her eyes were the
blue of a summer sky against the smooth, sun-deepened
bronze of a face shaped with high cheekbones, a straight
nose, and a wide mouth with full, kissable lips.

These features, combined with a curve of determination to her chin, gave her face both delicacy and
strength. The same characteristics he had noted in her
bearing—a vulnerability when she asked about the
war, along with a rebellious boldness.

And the way those pants hugged her hips and long
legs didn't hurt, either.

Back home in Virginia, females didn't dress in pants
that clearly outlined their hips and legs. And those legs
of hers were long, all right; she was easily eight inches
above five feet.

From the time he'd crossed the Mississippi and headed west, he'd noticed a lot that was different from the rolling green countryside of Virginia. And the sight of her in those pants had certainly improved the view.

The thought of how they'd feel wrapped around his legs in bed invaded his thoughts, and he couldn't help grinning. His brothers would agree, especially Garth.

Lord, how he missed Garth and Clay. They'd rarely seen one another during the war, and they had no sooner gotten home then Clay and Garth headed west to California.

As if reading his mind, Cassie Braden suddenly asked, "Do you have family in California, Mr. Fraser?"

"Two brothers and a sister."

"So they were in California during the war?"

"No, they came West right after it ended. Our sister Lissy eloped with a Yankee soldier, and Clay and Garth headed West to find her."

Her mouth twitched in amusement. "Imagine that! Eloped with a Yankee!"

He didn't miss the sarcasm; so she was more cat than kitten. "Truth is, Miss Braden, at the time, I couldn't understand how a born-and-bred Virginian like my sister could run off with a Yankee."

"Does seem outrageous, doesn't it?"

"But, since she's happily married with a baby and all, seems it all ended well, and I'm happy for her."

"Even though she married a Yankee. You have a tender heart, Mr. Fraser. So, unable to bear the shame of failure, your brothers remained in California, too."

Colt raised his open palms. "Okay, so this is all amusing to you. I'll shut up." He nodded toward Jeff Braden, slumped and asleep. "Your brother didn't find it entertaining, though."

"You mean you're going to stop without telling me what happened with Clay and Garth. Why did they remain in California?"

"I really don't think you want to hear more."

"Why not? It helps to pass the time."

"My folks had six sons and one daughter," Colt continued, "but my youngest brother perished during Pickett's charge at Gettysburg. Other than our older brother Will, Clay had always been the most level-headed among us. That's why it was so perplexing when he up and married a Yankee woman the same day he met her. And now they have a baby boy, too."

"He didn't!" she exclaimed. "And a Yankee, too! Tell me, Mr. Fraser, is marrying a Yankee a hanging offense in Virginia?"

"Forget it. You've had your laugh."

"What do you expect! You talk as if marrying a Yankee is a disgrace. I happen to be a Yankee, Mr. Fraser, and I resent the implication."

"I can assure you, Miss Braden, that unlike my siblings, I have no inclination to wed—so your spinsterhood is not at risk with me. And I recommend that instead of sarcasm, you begin using that kissable mouth of yours for just that—or it's unlikely your spinsterhood will ever be in jeopardy, even with a damn Yankee."

Colt opened his newspaper with a snap. As always,

the news was bad. People dying from cholera in the East, and an Apache Indian chief by the name of Cochise was conducting murderous raids on settlers and the cavalry in Arizona.

He glanced over the top of the paper at the couple. Jeff had awakened and was sitting in a stupor staring into space. The flame in the firecracker had gone out, and she was gazing out the window.

They bore a deep resemblance to one another. The woman appeared to be in her early twenties, a few years older than the man. Besides having auburn hair and blue eyes in common, their facial features were similar—but looked a damn sight better on her than they did on her brother.

As Colt studied him, Braden took a silver flask out of his pocket and took a long draught from it.

"Jeff, please stop drinking," Cassie Braden said. "You've had too much already."

"Hush up, Cassie. I don't need you for a mother." He took another drink and returned the flask to his pocket.

Braden's speech was slurred, and Colt had to agree: the man had had enough to drink already.

He resumed reading an article about the rise of outlaw gangs. Since the war's end their number had increased dramatically, and they were as much a menace as the Indians, who were resisting the influx of settlers on their hunting grounds.

Of special note was the James Gang, led by Jesse and Frank James, two brothers from Missouri. Another gang gaining national attention was the Younger Gang, four brothers named Cole, Jim, Bob and John.

According to the newspaper, these two gangs had joined together and were now robbing trains and banks in Missouri, across the Kansas plains, and as far west as Colorado. God help the poor people in their path.

Apparently there was even a female outlaw named Belle, riding with a gang led by an outlaw named Tom Starr.

Female outlaws, bank robbers, wild Indians, and long-legged, slim-hipped women dressed in men's pants—the West truly was wild.

Colt put the paper aside and stared out the window. The countryside was as wild and startling as the people who rode it. Erosion and extinct lava flows had carved out shallow canyons and craters around the narrow, mountainous trails, with stretches of colorful mesas abundant with forests, white-blossomed yucca, and deep-colored wildflowers. Trout streams, rivers, and cold-water lakes were everywhere.

Restless, he leaned back and reached for the newspaper again. The coach jostled and rocked like a cradle in a windstorm, which soon made reading too much of a challenge. Braden must have had a cast-iron stomach to keep that liquor down, with all the rocking going on.

As the hours wore on, Jeff Braden drank himself into a stupor. His sister had closed her eyes, but Colt could tell she wasn't sleeping.

Suddenly the blast of a gunshot broke the silence, and the driver pulled up sharply on the reins, sending a cloud of dust into the air. The woman was thrown forward and ended up in Colt's lap.

"I'm sorry," she gasped, her blue eyes wide with embarrassment. She quickly shifted over to her seat.

"No problem, Miss Braden. The pleasure was all mine."

Jostled awake, Jeff slurred, "What's going on?"

Five men with drawn pistols rode up to the stagecoach.

"Everybody out," one of the men ordered. "Get those hands up and grab some air."

Colt wasn't about to argue with a man holding a drawn pistol. "Just stay calm, Miss Braden," he advised.

She looked at him with contempt. "Practice what you preach, greenhorn." She raised her arms and climbed out.

Colt followed, and Jeff Braden staggered after him.

Gus, the driver, was out of the box and stood with raised arms. Buck, who had been riding shotgun, was lying on the ground, wounded.

"Get them gunbelts off."

The order came from one of the men who was still mounted: he appeared to be the leader.

There were five outlaws, and Colt figured he could only take out two before they took him down. That would probably get the Bradens killed, too. The fact that the outlaws hadn't shot the driver probably meant they didn't intend to shoot the passengers, either. He unbuckled his gunbelt and dropped it to the ground.

A couple of the outlaws tossed down a box from the top of the stage. As one of the other bandits shot off the lock, the piercing blare of a bugle sounded nearby. The sound was music to Colt's ears.

"Dammit!" the leader of the gang snarled. "Hurry up before that damn cavalry gets here."

One of the men stuffed the box's contents into a black bag, and the men all mounted.

To Colt's horror, Jeff Braden snatched up his gun.

"No, don't try it," Colt yelled, but Braden shot at the riders as they started to ride away.

Colt shoved the woman out of the line of fire and dove for his own gun as the outlaws fired back. He felt the sting of a bullet on his left shoulder but got off a shot, and the man holding the black bag fell from the saddle just as the cavalry arrived and thundered past in pursuit.

Blood oozed profusely from the wound to Colt's shoulder. Feeling woozy, he slumped down and leaned back against a tree. He pulled the bandanna from his neck and awkwardly tried to make a compress with his good hand. Cassie hurried over to help him while Gus went to the aid of Buck.

"Here, let me do that." She folded the bandanna into a thick pad and pressed it against his shoulder. "I'm going to have to take your shirt off."

"Why, Miss Braden, I'm shocked. You must control yourself; we've barely just met."

"Do you men ever have anything but sex on your mind?" she grumbled in disgust. Quickly but gently, she slipped the shirt off him.

"You did that quite speedily. Have you had a lot of practice removing a man's shirt?"

"Yes, I have." His mocking look changed to surprise, and she grinned. "In case you haven't noticed, I wear men's shirts."

"Oh, I've noticed," he said. "And so appealingly that I can barely keep my eyes off . . . ah . . . it."

"So I've noticed," she countered as she studied the wound.

"Will I live, nurse?"

"Not if you don't hush up," she said. "Or I'll finish the job for that guy who tried to kill you."

Cassie pressed the bandanna against the open wound again "Now, hold the compress tightly against it to stem the bleeding."

"I'm quite aware of what to do. I've been shot before."

"By a cuckolded husband, or some no-good, low-down Yankee, Fraser?"

"The latter, Miss Braden. But for now, can we cease refighting the war and get this over with before I bleed to death?"

Gus approached with the canteen and set it down beside her. "Figure you'd be needing this."

Cassie looked up fretfully. "How bad is Buck?"

"Still unconscious. He's hurt bad, Cassie; he's got a bullet in him that has to come out. How's Fraser here?"

" 'Fraser here' will be just fine, but I prefer 'Colt,'" Colt said good-naturedly.

"I think it's just a surface wound," Cassie informed him. "I couldn't see any sign of an entry or exit hole. You've lost a lot of blood, though, so I'll have to get a bandage on it."

"What about the fellow I shot?" Colt asked.

"That sure was one hell of a shot, Colt. That fella won't be holdin' up no more stagecoaches."

"He's dead?" Cassie asked.

"Yep. He'll soon be pushin' up posies on Boot Hill. Bank'll be happy to get the money delivery that these hombres tried to get away with. You sure picked the right one to take down, young fella."

"I didn't pick him, Gus. He just made the mistake of being last in line."

Gus nodded, and then frowned. "Cassie, I've been thinkin' that we shouldn't try movin' Buck. It's 'bout ten miles into town, so I'll unhitch one of them horses to ride in and bring back the doc."

"I think you're right."

"Trouble is, there's no tellin' if them outlaws are gonna show up again, so I hate leavin' you alone with all these wounded men."

"Why don't you send Braden?" Colt asked.

"He's drunker than a hoot owl and passed out cold."

"That figures," Colt said. "Well, once I get a bandage on my shoulder, I can handle a weapon if those outlaws come back."

Cassie returned to the task of bandaging his shoulder. "I don't suppose you have a nice clean, white handkerchief in your pocket."

"Never carry one."

She thought for a moment, then ordered, "Close your eyes."

"What?"

"Just do as I say." Cassie turned her back to him,

removed her shirt, and pulled off the white camisole she was wearing. Quickly donning the shirt again, she buttoned it and turned back to him. His eyes were wide open. She might have known he'd ignore her request.

With a strong tug, she managed to rip the garment in half, then tore a smaller piece off and wetted it from the canteen. She began to cleanse the wound gently, washing away the blood and dirt with light strokes.

"I just thought of something," she said. "Hold this compress on the wound until I get back." Hurrying over to Jeff's sleeping body, she dug into his pocket and found the flask, then returned to Colt.

"There's enough whiskey in here to sterilize your wound. I'm afraid this is going to hurt, though," she cautioned, and gingerly poured the liquid on the wound.

Colt sucked in a deep breath when the whiskey hit, but the shock gave him something to concentrate on besides her nearness.

She folded the other piece of torn camisole into a compress, poured the remaining drops of the whiskey on it, and then pressed it against the wound. Pulling the bandanna from around her own neck, she looped it around his shoulder and underarm to hold the compress in place.

Satisfied, she bent down and looked him in the eye. "What do you think?"

Those kissable lips of hers were temptingly close, but before he could carry out his thought, she straightened up.

"You can use a little cleaning up." Wetting the cloth again, she began to wash away the smeared blood on his chest.

Cassie's strokes gradually slowed as she became more and more aware of the warm flesh beneath the thin cloth. She'd never felt this funny tingle when she'd rubbed salve on Jeff's or her father's chests when they had colds.

With an open palm she slowly ran the cloth across the corded brawn of his chest and shoulders. Her hand itched to toss aside the cloth and run her fingers through the cluster of dark hair that trailed down his flat stomach and disappeared into the top of his pants.

She'd never experienced this feeling before, and it frightened her as much as it excited her.

What was she thinking of? She barely knew this man, and didn't much like him, to boot.

Cassie quickly stepped back. "That should do it. Do you need any other help?"

"I'll say. Now that you've got that camisole of yours tucked tightly against my chest, I can't help thinking of the last place it'd been. And that thought's causing a powerful pain . . . elsewhere. Don't suppose you'd consider healing that area, too, Miz Cassie?"

Cassie bolted to her feet, her face flushed in fury, her eyes blazing in contempt. "You, sir, are indescribably rude—and depraved!"

His warm chuckle followed—as warm as the hungry gaze that regarded the sway of her hips as she stormed away.

Colt got up slowly and tested his legs. They seemed steady enough, so he started to move to where Cassie was kneeling beside Buck, to offer her an apology. His teasing had gotten way out of hand, which wasn't like him.

Jeff was sitting up looking around groggily. "Where in hell is my flask?"

"Over there," Colt said.

Jeff staggered over and picked up the flask. "What the hell; you drank it all!"

"He didn't drink it, Jeff," Cassie said. "I used it to sterilize his wound."

"You wasted my whiskey on a stinking Reb," he snarled.

Still feeling embarassed and frustrated, Colt turned on him.

"You drunken fool! They were riding away. You could have gotten us all killed!" He clenched his hand into a fist and punched the drunken idiot in the jaw.

The force of the blow shot directly up to Colt's wounded shoulder, and the last thing he remembered before blacking out was Braden staggering backward and falling to the ground.

Colt slowly fought his way through the darkness into a gray haze. When he groped instinctively at his aching shoulder, his hand encountered a thick wad of gauze. He opened his eyes to discover he was lying on a cot, but when or how he'd gotten there was a mystery to him.

Colt closed his eyes again, and slowly the picture

materialized: the stagecoach, the holdup, and that damn kid setting off the fireworks. Then the burning sting of the bullet.

He sat up slowly and swung his legs over the edge of the cot. For a long moment he fought off the dizziness. When his head cleared, he looked around and gaped in shock. What in hell? He was in a jail cell!

Through the bars, he could see a man sitting at a desk across the room. "Hello," Colt called out.

The man got to his feet and approached the cell. Middle age had set in, in the jowls of his face and the thickened waist of his tall frame. His mouth pursed in a grin as he ran his fingers through thin, sandy-colored hair generously sprinkled with gray.

"So you're finally awake, Mr. Fraser. How are you feelin'?"

"Like I've been shot. How long have I been out?"

"Slept through the night and most of the mornin', son. Doc Williams gave you somethin' to keep you still."

That meant this was Thursday. Perplexed, Colt asked, "Where am I?"

"In Arena Roja."

"Arena Roja?"

"Red Sand, if you don't speak Mex."

"How far is that from Santa Fe?"

"'Bout a hundred miles. Name's Jethro Braden. I'm the sheriff here."

That came as no surprise, since a shiny silver star was pinned to his shirtfront. The bad news was his name—especially if he was related to the drunk Colt had socked in the jaw.

Colt's expression must have betrayed his thoughts, because Sheriff Braden grinned. "Yep, I'm his pa. You in the habit of throwin' punches, son?"

"Only with drunks who start gunfights. He could have gotten us all killed—your daughter included."

Braden nodded. "Yep, Gus said the same."

"What happened to the wounded guy riding shotgun?"

"He wasn't as lucky as you. Doc Williams had to dig a bullet out of Buck, and he'll be laid up for a couple weeks. The shot you took only peeled off some of your flesh. Trouble is, you bled like a stuck pig. You'll have to take it easy for a couple days."

"Did the cavalry catch up with the robbers?"

"No, they got away. But thanks to you, the money was recovered."

"Then why am I locked up?"

"Door to the cell ain't locked. We ain't got no hospital in town, and the doc only has one cot in his office. Buck needed it worse than you did, so we put you up here for the night."

"Then I'm free to leave."

"Soon as you get your legs under you. You're lookin' shakier than a newborn colt."

"I'm fine." Colt sat down on the edge of the bunk and pulled on his boots, then got up and shoved the cell door open. "Where's my hat and gunbelt?"

"Hangin' on them pegs over there. You can claim your traveling bag at the stage office."

Colt tried not to stagger as he walked over and strapped on the belt.

"You're welcome to bunk in the cell 'til you're up and around. Bed and food are on the house."

Colt plopped his hat on and shook his head. "Thank you, Sheriff. I appreciate your offer, but I think I'll be more comfortable in the hotel." A horrifying thought crossed his mind. "You do have a hotel, don't you?"

"Yep, with clean sheets and no bedbugs." The sheriff opened a drawer and pulled out a sheet of paper. "Want to sign this receipt, Mr. Fraser? There's a fifty-dollar reward on the head of each of them robbers—dead or alive."

Fifty dollars was a lot of money. Considering the fact that he'd only gotten a grazed shoulder out of it, it was worth having taken the bullet.

"This is an unexpected surprise," Colt said, tucking the money into his shirt pocket. "When does the next stage come through?"

"Depends where you're headed."

"Santa Fe."

"Pulled out this mornin'."

Dammit! Just his bad luck. "When's the next one?"

"Not for a week, son. But the hotel's got hot baths and the grub's good, too. It's even better at the restaurant, if you like steak."

"Sounds like it's just what I need." Colt headed for the door.

"You take care, son." The sheriff's ruddy face split with a wide grin. "I hear you're quick with that iron you're packin', so keep it leathered. I don't want no trouble in my town."

"I'm not looking for any trouble, Sheriff."

They shook hands and Colt stepped out into the bright sunlight and paused to look around.

Arena Roja was typical of the other towns he had passed through—small, compact, and dusty. A dozen wood-and-adobe buildings stretched for a couple of blocks on each side of an unpaved main street. Scattered houses boxed in the business buildings from the streets behind them.

As Colt walked along the wooden sidewalk that lined the main street, a rider astride a magnificent black stallion rode up on the walk and blocked his path. Colt glanced up and recognized Cassie Braden.

He tipped his hat. "Miss Braden." He might have known she wasn't the type to ride sidesaddle.

She scowled down at him. "Mr. Fraser, I'm grateful to you for saving my life, but I don't figure I owe you anything. I can take care of myself."

"I'm sure you can, Miss Braden. But I don't understand your animosity. Your brother could have gotten us all killed."

"He didn't, though, did he?"

"Thanks to the timely arrival of the cavalry."

"Keep away from my brother, Fraser, or you'll have me to deal with."

"Is that a promise, Miz Cassie?" He grinned broadly. "As much as I would welcome the opportunity of dealing with you, I settled my differences with your brother with my fist. I have no further quarrel with him. If he has one with me, I suggest you offer your advice to him."

His remark brought amused chuckles from the spectators that had been attracted to the scene.

"He's sure got your number, Cassie," a male voice
shouted from the crowd.

Her growl remained fixed on Colt. "Consider yourself warned, greenhorn."

When she started to leave, Colt grabbed the reins to
halt her and said softly, "It must be painful, Miss Braden,
to ride with that thorn you have up your . . . posterior."

Her darkened glare pierced through him like a saber
thrust. Wheeling the horse, she rode off.

Colt watched her ride away. That trim little ass of
hers could sit a saddle admirably, but she sure had no
sense of humor. Wonder what it took to get a smile out
of her?

Two young boys and a girl with a battered hat
pulled over her red hair stared at him intently as he
passed the livery. He nodded and smiled at them. The
youngest one grinned back, and the other two glared
at him. Colt figured they must have Braden blood, although, in all fairness, the sheriff seemed to be a very
affable fellow.

Colt stopped at the stage office and claimed his lug-
gage, then continued on to the two-story hotel. Its
sign promised clean sheets and a hot bath for a dollar
a night.

Several men sat in chairs in front of the hotel, and
they nodded and offered a "Howdy" when he drew up
to them. It became clear that his reputation had pre-
ceded him, because they all knew who he was and introduced themselves to him. After chatting with them

for several minutes, he excused himself to go register.

Colt liked the feel of the town; maybe hanging around here for a week wouldn't be so bad. He'd get well rested, and the people all seemed pleasant—except for that termagant, Cassie Braden, and her red-headed kin.

He paused when the object of his thoughts and another young woman came out of a store across the street. Both women were slim and tall, but there the resemblance ended.

A straw bonnet was perched on the other woman's long blond hair, and she wore a bright blue dress.

Cassie must have seen him, because she said something to her companion and the woman turned her head and glanced in his direction. She made a comment to Cassie, and they broke out in giggles. Arm in arm, they walked away.

Good looking or not, Cassie Braden was a pain in the ass, probably as untamed as the mustangs that ran wild out here.

By nature, he was an easygoing man who got along with most people. He rarely started an argument, but it would be a cold day in hell before he'd run from one. And apparently Cassie Braden intended to stir one up. The wisest thing to do was give her a wide berth, but her unruly streak intrigued him.

"She just needs some loving and domesticating," his brother Garth used to say about a wild mare they'd had on Fraser Keep.

Yeah, Arena Roja was looking more and more interesting. A man needed a goal to focus on, and what better motivation than an intriguing and feisty female? His mother hadn't raised any sons who couldn't charm the skin off a snake, and Miss Cassie Braden wouldn't be the first filly he'd gentled to his touch.

Grinning, Colt entered the hotel.

Chapter 2

His room was on the second floor overlooking the main street. Colt unpacked his suitcase, then opened the window and climbed out on the balcony that circled the building. A staircase at the rear offered a way of reaching the balcony from the outside.

All things considered, he'd been in far worse hotels than this one. It had a nice lobby with comfortable upholstered furniture, a barroom, and a dining room adjacent to the lobby. In addition, the hotel boasted an indoor privy and bathroom on the second floor. That, and the promise of a soft bed and clean sheets, was well worth the cost to a weary traveler.

Colt's gaze swept the dusty street, which was practically deserted at the moment. The sudden growl of his stomach reminded him that he hadn't eaten since yesterday, so he climbed back inside and headed for the dining room downstairs.

A waiter had no sooner taken his order for a steak, fried potatoes, and a cup of hot coffee, than Cassie Braden came in with the woman he'd seen her with earlier. He stood as they reached his table.

"Miss Braden, we meet again."

"It's a small town, Mr. Fraser." She started to move on.

"Would you and . . ." He looked at her companion with a questioning smile.

"I'm Cathy Braden—Cassie's sister," the woman said pleasantly.

"My pleasure, Miss Braden."

Cathy was a lovely young woman. Her features were similar to those of her sister, her eyes the same light blue. Cathy Braden's blond hair hung freely to midback and was topped with a perky bonnet, while Cassie's auburn tresses were woven into a single braid that hung below the wide brim of the Western hat she wore.

Grinning, Colt waved a finger from one to the other. "Twins."

"What gave us away?" Cassie said.

Colt let her tone bounce off him and responded instead to Cathy Braden's delightful light laughter and smile.

"I was about to ask if you two young ladies would give me the pleasure of joining me for a meal."

"No thank you, Mr. Fraser," Cassie said, rejecting the offer immediately. "We only came in for a lemonade. Come on, Cathy."

Once again Colt was subject to Cathy's sweet smile. "Thank you for the offer, Mr. Fraser. It was a pleasure to meet you."

"Perhaps another time, Miss Braden."

Her eyes twinkled with humor. "Perhaps, Mr. Fraser." She followed her sister to a nearby table.

Colt sat back down and drank his coffee. The sheriff

seemed pretty levelheaded, so how could he raise a son with the sense of a gnat, one daughter with the sweetness and delicacy of a rosebud, and another daughter who was a doom-threatening Valkyrie?

After finishing his meal, he tipped his hat as he passed their table.

"Have a good day, ladies."

"My, he's a handsome figure of a man, isn't he?" Cathy said when Colt moved on.

Cassie glanced in his direction. She'd forgotten how tall he was, and she had to admit Cathy was right.

"The bigger they are, the harder they fall," she grumbled.

"What is your problem with Mr. Fraser, Cassie? He's handsome, mannerly, and very charming."

"Don't tell me you're smitten with him."

"Of course not; I just met him. And I don't understand your obvious resentment toward him."

"He had no call to punch Jeff the way he did."

"Jeff's the one you should be angry with. I heard Gus tell Dad that Jeff's rash action could have gotten all of you killed. If Mr. Fraser hadn't punched Jeff, Gus said he would have done it himself. Mr. Fraser was wounded protecting you, and you owe him an apology, not angry scowls. I think there's something else that's bothering you about this stranger. What is it?"

"He made a very suggestive remark to me when I was bandaging his wound."

Cathy's eyes widened in shock when Cassie told her. "He said that to you!"

"He started to apologize but then Jeff woke up, and you've heard what followed."

Sighing, Cathy said, "I'm sorry to hear that. Mr. Fraser seems like such a gentleman. Perhaps he was feverish from his wound."

He was feverish all right, but it had nothing to do with his wound, Cassie reflected. Recalling her own feelings at the time—the tingling excitement of his nearness, his warm, muscular chest—her pulses quickened, and she realized her thoughts had been just as heated.

Cassie swallowed hard and lifted her chin. "But that isn't my major concern, Cathy. I'm afraid for Jeff, Cathy. You know how foolish he can be at times, and he might bear a grudge against Mr. Fraser now. Something tells me Mr. Fraser's not the kind to run from a fight, and Jeff is the kind who starts one. I think some cowboy would have shot him by now, if Dad weren't the sheriff."

Cathy looked concerned. "I think you're right. What are we going to do?"

They sat in deep concentration, with worried frowns, their chins cradled in their hands.

Raising her head, Cassie exclaimed, "I've got it! Fraser will only be around for a week. Why don't you cozy up to him while he's here? That will keep him and Jeff apart."

"Me? Why should I be the one? It's your idea."

"Because you're the sweet one. Besides, I'm spoken for. As soon as Ted comes home, I'll be getting married."

Cathy reached across the table and squeezed her hand. "Hon, we've been through this before. The war ended over a year ago," she said gently. "You've got to face the fact that Ted was probably killed, or he would have been back by now."

"I won't believe that. I know he'll be back." Cassie took her sister's other hand. "So it's up to you to keep Mr. Fraser entertained for the next week."

"Are you forgetting that I'm working at the stage office this week?" She glanced at the timepiece pinned to her bodice. "Oh, my, I'm due there now. Remember what I said: be nice to him, Cassie." She hurried off.

Darn! Cassie had no patience with feminine wiles. Charming a man? She wouldn't know how to begin.

Deciding to ride around the area, Colt paused in front of the livery.

Jeff Braden and several others were leaning against the wall when he approached; the doors were closed and locked.

"Looking for something, Fraser?" Braden asked.

"I was hoping to rent a horse."

"Livery's closed for the next two hours—siesta time. But you can take that horse."

Braden pointed to a black stallion tied in front of the Wells Fargo office, the one Colt had seen Cassie Braden riding earlier.

"It's already saddled and wearing a Lazy B brand," Braden continued.

"Lazy B?" Colt questioned.

"My family's spread."

"I thought your father was the sheriff."

"We had the ranch before he was elected sherriff. We own the livery stable, too, so feel free to borrow that horse."

Colt was surprised, having thought Braden would bear a grudge against him.

"I appreciate the offer, but wasn't your sister riding that horse earlier?"

"She told me to unsaddle it because she won't be needing it any more today."

"Well, thank you. That's very considerate of you."

Braden shrugged. "Figure I owe you that much for what you did during the stage holdup. Horse answers to the name of Midnight."

"Thanks." Colt crossed the street and started to adjust the stirrups.

"What do you think you're doing, mister?"

Colt turned around. The query had come from the young redheaded girl he'd seen earlier, who looked eleven or twelve years old. Her red hair was cut to her ears in a short bob, and her freckled face wore a hostile frown. The same two boys were with her.

"I beg your pardon?" Colt asked.

"You heard her, mister. Where are you going with that horse?" the older boy inquired.

Perhaps a year younger than the girl, his blue eyes scrutinized Colt with suspicion behind spectacles that made his eyes look too large for his face. The other boy, considerably younger, was eyeing him just as suspiciously.

Good Lord! What next?

The redhead folded her arms across her chest. "Petey, run to the stage office and get Cassie. Tell her somebody's trying to steal her horse."

"Don't waste your time. She's eating lunch at the hotel." Colt finished adjusting the stirrups and untied the horse.

"What should we do, Sam? He's gonna get away," the older boy said.

"That's what he thinks, Bowie. I wouldn't do that, mister, if I were you," she shouted when Colt mounted the horse.

The children scattered as the horse reared up and began to buck. Caught unexpectedly by the sudden motion, Colt was unseated but managed to land on his feet when he slipped off. The horse immediately came to a stop and stood docile.

The three children looked at him with big grins.

"Warned you," Sam said.

"Yeah, warned you," her smallest minion echoed.

"How do you expect to steal a horse when you can't even stay in the saddle?" Sam asked.

"I was not trying to steal this horse." To Colt's consternation, a crowd began to congregate. Where in hell had they come from? They were supposed to be taking siestas now, such nonsense.

"Bet you won't try that again," Bowie taunted.

"Yeah, bet you won't," little Petey added.

Colt centered his frustration on the three children. "Don't you have someplace to go?"

"We are some place," Sam replied.

"Here's ten cents. Go to the store and buy yourself some candy sticks."

"Ten cents? Boy, mister, are you cheap! We don't sell out a friend," she informed him with righteous indignation.

Colt couldn't tell if her objection was to the amount of the bribe or the suggestion of disloyalty.

As a stagecoach pulled up, Colt glanced over and saw Jeff Braden and his cronies holding their sides, laughing, and everything became vividly clear to him.

The stage driver climbed down and peered at him, then the passengers piled out of the coach and did the same.

"What's the trouble?" the driver asked.

"This fella's trying to steal Midnight," Bowie said.

"Oh, you don't want to do that, mister," the driver warned. "That horse don't let nobody but Miz Cassie ride him."

The driver's words produced murmurs and nods of agreement from many of the spectators, and snickers of amusement from others. To think he had once thought these people were friendly.

"What's going on here?" Sheriff Braden asked, joining the crowd.

"We caught him trying to steal Midnight," Sam quickly volunteered. "Should I get a rope so's we can string him up?"

She turned to Colt and stuck out her tongue at him. "We hang horse thieves here, don't we, Uncle Jethro?"

Why me, Lord? Colt wondered. "Despite what this little busybody claims, Sheriff, I was not stealing this horse. Your son gave me permission to ride it."

"Gave you permission, did he?" Sheriff Braden said.

The three children started poking and laughing in amusement.

"You kids go home. I'll handle this," the sheriff said.

"But we're witnesses to the crime, Sheriff," Sam protested as he began to herd the children away.

Sheriff Braden gave her a stern look. "Samantha, I said go home."

His no-nonsense tone must have finally convinced them. As she left Samantha gave Colt a chilling look. "You ain't seen the last of us, mister," she warned.

"The rest of you folks move on, too," Sheriff Braden said. "Everything's fine."

Colt moved to the shade of a building and waited until the sheriff succeeded in dispersing the crowd.

Peace and quiet at last. Colt closed his eyes and heaved a sigh of gratitude.

Then Cassie Braden came out of the hotel and walked over to them. "What's going on, Dad?"

"I guess Colt here tried to ride Midnight."

Frowning, she turned to Colt. "Why would you do that, Mr. Fraser?"

"Because your brother suggested I use this horse since the livery was closed."

"Jeff told you that!"

"Cassie! Cassie!" Shouting her name in unison, the three kids raced up to them.

They huddled around her and began to relate their

version of the incident. Sheriff Braden threw up his hands in disgust and walked away.

Cassie looked up at Colt with the three children before her, encompassed in an embrace. "Have you met my three buddies, Mr. Fraser?"

"Don't you mean buds, Miss Braden? None of them are bigger than a sprout."

"You mustn't judge them by their size; I couldn't ask for three more devoted friends. The little lady is Samantha Starr, and the boys are Bowie and Petey James. Children, this is Mr. Fraser."

"Yes, we've met and I have no doubt they're related to the outlaws by the same name," Colt said, recalling the newspaper article he had read.

The three children were smiling with friendliness and innocence, and Cassie was actually smiling, too. By the amusement in her eyes she had put the pieces together and figured out that her brother had made Colt the brunt of a joke.

"I'm sorry about Midnight. Jeff should have warned you that my horse doesn't let strangers ride him."

Colt enjoyed a practical joke as much as anyone, and he'd always been able to laugh when the joke was on him. Growing up with a house full of brothers had taught him that lesson.

But jokes that could get a person injured were not amusing; getting thrown from a bucking horse could get a man killed or maimed.

"Luckily, no harm done, Miss Braden," he said coldly and walked away.

Chapter 3

As she watched Colt Fraser walk away, Cassie could tell he was disgusted, and rightfully so. Underneath that Southern charm was a man of steel, and Jeff was a fool to push this man too far.

And she was as much a fool as her brother for threatening Fraser earlier. Whatever had she been thinking?

Maybe she should voice her fears to their dad, get him to order Jeff back to the ranch until Fraser left town. It would be a much better idea than her trying to charm him; Colt Fraser clearly wanted nothing more to do with her. She headed for the jail.

Her father was dozing off in his chair when she burst in on him. He listened patiently to her fears, then shook his head.

"Honey, you and Cathy have got to stop lookin' out for your brother. He's never gonna grow up until you do."

"Do you want to see him hurt, Dad? Or even killed?"

"Of course not, honey, but we can't be protecting him every minute. Jeff's the only one who can make a man of himself—we can't do it for him. I've tried, and Lord knows you and your sister have tried. 'Bout time he tries."

"But I have a feeling about this Colt Fraser. I'm afraid for Jeff."

"You're wrong, honey. I've stayed alive this long by bein' able to judge a man when I meet him. Colt Fraser's a good man. I'm even thinkin' of askin' him to wear a star while he's here."

"Are you serious? You're going to ask him to be your deputy?"

"Since Ben's run off, I could use some help this comin' weekend."

"What do you know about the man? For all you know, he could be a smooth-talking murderer."

"He ain't no murderer, honey."

"How can you be so sure?"

"By his handshake, and the set of his head on those broad shoulders of his." A spark of cunning glittered in his eyes. "Don't suppose you've noticed what a fine figure of a man he is. He'd be a fine catch for a young gal like yourself."

"No, Dad, I haven't noticed."

His mouth drooped in dejection. "I was afraid of that."

She walked over and hugged him. "Furthermore, you old schemer, I'm already spoken for. You should be telling Cathy this." She kissed him on the cheek and departed.

Jethro watched sadly as she walked briskly up the street.

"You ain't ever gonna see the light, are you, gal?"

On the way back to his room, Colt stopped at the desk and ordered a hot bath. It would feel good to soak off some of the ache and trail dust. The jolt from slipping off the horse had added to his already existing pains.

Once in his room, Colt carefully removed his shirt without disturbing the bandage on his shoulder. His boots and socks followed, then he lay down on the bed and waited for his bath. He'd almost dozed off when there was a knock on the door and a voice informing him the bath was ready.

He grabbed clean underwear and went down the hall to the bathroom, where he lowered his aching body into the hot tub. It was a squeeze, but the water felt damn good. Leaning his head back on the rim, he closed his eyes.

Suddenly he felt something brush his foot under the water, and he jerked upright. Whatever was in the tub was on his right foot now, and it was moving.

Don't let it be a snake. Please, Lord, don't let it be a snake.

He had always hated snakes, even harmless grass snakes.

Colt jumped out of the tub, and the encroacher followed and hopped across the floor. The frog leaped into the bucket used to fill the tub, and Colt checked the tub for any other uninvited critters. Satisfied, he climbed back in, resumed his position, closed his eyes, and remained that way until the water cooled. Then he soaped up the sponge and bathed himself.

He climbed out of the tub regretfully, dried off and dressed, and return to his room for a short nap, after which he would head to the barbershop for a shave. He had just lain down when a knock sounded on the door. He opened it and gaped in surprise at the caller.

"I'm sorry to bother you," Cassie Braden said. "May I come in?"

"What now, Miss Braden?" Leaving the door ajar, he turned and walked away.

She entered and closed the door, then stood with her back against it. "I came to apologize for my threat to you this morning."

"I'd already forgotten about it, so you could have saved yourself the trip."

"Well, I want to apologize for Jeff's actions this morning, too."

"I imagine you spend a good deal of your time apologizing for him."

"That's beside the point. You could have been seriously hurt."

He crossed his arms and leaned against the wall. She was squirming with uneasiness, but he didn't intend to make this any easier for her.

"After what your brother pulled yesterday and now today, I figure if I can avoid him for six more days, I'll make it out of here in one piece."

She groped behind her for the doorknob. "Well, I've said what I came to say. Thank you for listening." She turned to open the door.

"Miss Braden . . ."

When she turned back to him, he said, "I owe you an apology, too. My remark yesterday was extremely crude and uncalled for. I never thanked you for what you did for me, and you were undeserving of the re-mark."

Her blush was so appealing Colt found it impossible to sustain his displeasure with her. She was such an innocent.

"I guess I overreacted. I've had a lot worse proposi-tions from men passing through the town."

He chuckled. "Don't be too critical of us poor males, Miss Braden. We're just frail creatures at the mercy of our passions."

"The next time I get propositioned, I'll try and keep that thought in mind and offer Christian charity in return."

"If it's the kind of charity I have in mind, there's a bed right here waiting for us."

She threw her hands up in frustration. "Feverish, indeed! Cathy is naïve for believing there's any hope for you, Colt Fraser. You really are depraved!"

"You told your sister what I said?"

"Of course! Twins don't keep secrets from each other." She slammed the door on her way out.

Colt climbed out of the window and waited until she appeared in the street below. Leaning over the railing, he shouted, "You left without saying good-bye. Does that mean no?"

Grinning, he watched her stride angrily down the street. She was sexier than hell when she was mad. And that luscious ass of hers a sweet sight to behold. Damn sweet!

And she was driven by passion: her outbursts of temper, her love for those three annoying sprouts she nurtured, and her loyalty to a worthless brother, were all evidences of the passion she brought into relationships.

He couldn't help imagining all that passion unleashed in bed. And he sure as hell intended to find out what it would be like.

Yep, this was shaping up to be a real interesting week.

He went back inside and stretched out on the bed, but his attempt to sleep was again interrupted by a knock on the door. He opened it to Samantha Starr and the two little James brothers.

"What are you doing here?" he asked, suspiciously.

"We live here," Bowie said. "My folks own the hotel."

"And what about you?" he asked Sam.

"Me and my mom live here, too. She's the cook. My mom told us to apologize, seeing how you're wounded and all."

"Well, thank you. Your apology's accepted."

"We ain't given it yet," Sam said.

Why me, Lord?

"Don't you have school, or chores to do?"

"Most days we don't have school, and we've done our chores."

Things became real clear to Colt. "And I bet one of those chores is filling the bathtub."

"Yeah, how did you know?" Bowie asked.

"And why don't you have regular school?" Colt asked.

"We ain't had any regular school since Mr. McBride went off to the war. He ain't come back yet, and Mama says he most likely was killed," Sam said.

"We had a couple new schoolmarms for a time, but

they didn't like it here and left town," Bowie added.

"I can't imagine why," Colt said and began to close the door.

Samantha and Bowie started to leave, but Petey lingered, staring at him.

Colt smiled at the boy, who was the most appealing of the three. "What is it, pal?"

"Are you gonna be the deputy sheriff?" the youngster asked.

The question took Colt by surprise. "Wherever did you hear that?"

"From Cassie."

Bowie yanked on his arm. "Come on, Petey. Cassie said you wasn't supposed to say anything."

Flashing a belligerent glare, Sam turned around and looked at Colt.

"Well, as long as Petey's blabbed, are you and Cassie getting married?"

"Good heavens, whatever gave you that idea?"

"Mama says you'd make a good husband for Cassie. So are you gonna ask her to marry you?"

"When mules fly," Colt mumbled under his breath. How did people come up with crazy notions like that? He started to close the door again. "Nice seeing you all again. Good-bye."

"Yeah. See ya." Bowie grabbed Petey's hand and headed down the hall.

Samantha hung back.

"Is there a problem, Belle?" he teased.

"My name's not Belle," she declared. "What did you do with Leaper?"

"Who's Leaper?" Colt asked, as if he couldn't guess.

"Petey's pet frog."

"I don't know what you're talking about."

She eyed him suspiciously. "You know. The frog we put in the bathtub."

Colt feigned innocence. "You put a frog in the bathtub? Why would you do a thing like that, Belle? Now run along and catch up with Jesse and Frank. Maybe you three can find a bank to rob next."

"Their names are Bowie and Petey. And my name ain't Belle!" She raced to catch up with the James brothers.

Colt watched until the three disappeared down the stairs. They were a mite heavy on the annoying side, but he and his brother hadn't exactly been angels, either. Grinning, he closed the door.

Then he remembered their purpose for coming. Deputy sheriff! What in hell was that all about?

Sheriff Jethro Braden was behind his desk reading the newspaper when Colt entered.

"Howdy, son."

"Sheriff Braden, I just heard a rumor that I'm going to be your deputy."

Jethro glanced over the top of the spectacles perched on his nose. "I might have mentioned that I could use a deputy, and Gus said you was fast with that Colt on your hip. Ever think of becomin' a lawman?"

"I intend to become one, Sheriff Braden."

Jethro's eyes gleamed with pleasure. "So you're volunteerin'."

"No, I am on my way to California. I'm only here until the stage arrives next week."

"Son, that stage will only take you as far as Santa Fe. Then you'll have to change to a different one. And several more after that. You've got a long way to go, and there'll be a lot of delays along the way before you get to California. No sense in hopin' to rush it. You gotta have the patience to do one stage at a time."

A gleam of amusement sparked his eyes as a chuckle rumbled from his chest. "One stage at a time. Get it? A little humor there, son.

"You're gonna need a lot more than that fifty dollars in your pocket to get all the way to California. The town'll pay you ten dollars, and the cost of your hotel room. So what have you got to lose?"

"The offer's tempting, Sheriff, and I won't deny I could use the money. But what do you need a deputy for? The town appears to be pretty quiet."

"Now and again we get some bad hombres passin' through town. And come Saturday, a lot of the cowpokes from neighborin' ranches come in and get themselves likkered up. I can use a helpin' hand roundin' them up when they do, to keep them out of trouble."

"What happened to your last deputy?"

"Ben and one of the gals from the Alhambra took off for Santa Fe. Town don't have too many young men. We lost a few in the war, and the ones that came home settled down to ranchin' and startin' families." Jethro grimaced. "I ain't gonna try and fool you, son.

Arena Roja is a peaceful enough town, but in the past year there's been a lot of stragglers come through lookin' for trouble. They join up and form outlaw gangs. And there's always the Indian threat. Just ain't too many young men who want to pin on a badge. It warms my heart to hear one like you say you want to be a lawman."

Nothing was going to keep Colt from going on to California and joining his brothers. The plight of Arena Roja was not his problem. But as long as he was stuck here for a week, he certainly could use the money.

"All right, Sheriff Braden, you've got a deputy for a week. Come next Thursday, I'm getting on that stage."

Jethro pulled a badge out of a desk drawer and stood up. "Raise your right hand, son. You swear to uphold and defend the laws and citizens of Arena Roja?"

Colt raised his right hand. "I do."

Jethro handed him the badge. "You don't have to start wearin' this 'til tomorrow. Take the rest of the day to get your strength back, Deputy."

"I appreciate that, sir. In the meantime, I'd like to read the manual on the local laws I just swore to uphold."

"Won't take much readin'." Jethro opened a drawer and pulled out a sheet of paper yellowed by age and bearing more than one coffee stain—or was it whiskey?

"We ain't got too many laws to obey. There's ordinances against killin', robbin', drunken brawlin', horse stealin', spittin' tobacco on the walks, firin' a weapon on Sundays, rapin' women, abusin' horses, and kickin' dogs."

"What about fist fighting, Sheriff?"

"Man's got a right to protect his honor, son."

"Even on Sundays."

Jethro nodded. "But there's no sellin' beer and alcohol on Sundays. Don't much matter, though. The boys get so likkered up on Saturday night that the next mornin' they don't want no more of the snake that bit them."

Upon leaving the sheriff's office, Colt decided to take another look around at the town he had just agreed to defend. Granted, Arena Roja was just one of the many small stagecoach stops on the route to Santa Fe, but it offered most of the amenities a traveler would hope for.

The Santa Fe Trail had been the main route linking east and west for five decades, and caravans of wagons had traveled the eight-hundred-mile route between Independence, Missouri, and Santa Fe, New Mexico, carrying everything from calico and denim to sugar and whiskey, returning with Mexican silver and gold, furs and wools.

What surprised Colt was the length of time the town had been in existence without its citizens making any effort to improve most of its buildings and streets. The bank was the only stone building; even the church and its bell tower were wooden.

It came as no surprise, however, that his acceptance of the deputy's job had already spread swiftly through the town. As he walked through the streets, merchants came out of their businesses to introduce themselves and offer their welcome.

Colt figured by the time he reached the hotel that he would have shaken hands with most of Arena Roja's citizens.

The clang of a bell caught his attention. He saw Cassie Braden pulling on a bell rope in front of a small building at the far end of town, and several children headed in that direction.

Curious, he meandered down the street to check it out.

A sign bearing the words School House hung above the door. Peering through the only window of the small building, Colt saw that it was a single room consisting of five rows of desks, four deep. Twelve of the desks were filled.

A brick fireplace filled most of one wall, and well-stocked bookshelves lined the opposite one.

Colt was amazed to see the number of books. Apparently someone had taken great care to see that the children of the town were not denied a broad education. Cassie was at a chalkboard at the front of the room. As she reached up to write an equation, her shirt stretched tightly across her breasts. It made him wonder how willing she'd be to go another round with a different camisole—only this time, he'd be doing the ripping.

Little Petey sat in the front row with a full view, including her bodacious, pants-covered derriere.

Some kids had all the luck, even though they were far too young to appreciate it.

Colt returned to the hotel a short time later, wondering how he'd let himself get talked into becoming the deputy sheriff in this sleepy town.

Well even so, one thing was for certain: that other town rumor was totally false. Hell would freeze over before he'd ever marry Cassie Braden.

He took off his boots and lay down to take that nap he'd been looking forward to all afternoon.

Darkness had descended by the time Colt awoke. He had no idea what time it was when he stepped out on the balcony. From the sound of music and voices coming from the nearby Alhambra, it would appear that many cowboys were already in town.

As Colt stood enjoying the evening breeze, he heard an angry voice coming from below and recognized it as Cassie Braden's.

Now who was the firebrand chewing out?

"You're making fools of us, making the family look ridiculous to the people of this town. Can't you consider anyone but yourself? How do you expect Dad to keep the people's respect when his son is stumbling around most of the time like a town drunk?"

"Everybody loves him, and Cathy, and you. I'm the only one they're laughing at."

"I didn't see Colt Fraser laughing. That childish trick you pulled on him today could have gotten him hurt or killed. The man is recovering from a bullet wound! You're lucky he didn't shoot you on the spot. If you don't care about your welfare, have some consideration for those of us who love you. Do us the favor of growing up."

She spun on her heel and strode down the road toward the schoolhouse, dust puffs kicking up at her heels.

You could have saved your breath, Cassie Braden, Colt thought when he saw Jeff Braden cross the road and enter the Alhambra.

But Colt was glad he'd been wrong about Cassie: She hadn't been a party to her brother's practical joke.

Furthermore, she thought enough about the children of the town to make some attempt to educate them. So she wasn't as irresponsible as he once thought.

The Braden twins were both attractive, but as sweet as Cathy was, Cassie was the one who fascinated him.

The prospects for the next week became very promising again.

He glanced down the road and saw a glowing light coming from the schoolhouse. Why had Cassie gone back at this hour?

He decided to walk down and find out.

Chapter 4

Cassie finished sweeping the floor and looked around at the schoolroom. She never entered this room without being reminded of Ted. The books that lined the shelves, the round globe of the world that sat on her desk, the dictionary on a pedestal in the corner of the room—so much of it bought with his own money.

Her gaze swung to the message he had written on the corner of the chalkboard, which she had insisted remain there until his return.

Good-bye. I'll be thinking of and missing all of you. I'll be back as soon as the war is over.
    —Mr. McBride

You promised to come back to us, Ted. You have to be alive.

Cassie stared out of the window, her memories whisking her back five years to the day she had kissed Ted McBride good-bye. Her young heart had ached that day when Ted had left to go off to war. He had looked so handsome in his blue uniform, with his tanned face and blond hair, that she'd thought her heart would burst. He'd held her hand as the mayor had extolled his praises and wished a safe return for Arena Roja's beloved schoolmaster.

The clock chiming on the wall jolted her out of her musing, and Cassie was amazed to discover that it was eight o'clock. She blew out the lamp and rushed from the room, slamming into a figure about to enter. The force of the collision threw her back, and her head struck the door.

Gasping, she slumped to the floor. Giddy and light-headed, she sat as a kaleidoscope of color whirled around her head.

"Are you all right, Miss Braden?"

Responding to the warm timbre of the deep voice, she smiled. "I've never been struck by lightning before. I didn't even know it was raining."

"Miss Braden, I think I should get you to the doctor," the deep voice said worriedly.

The voice began to sound suspiciously like Colt Fraser's as she drifted blissfully between awareness and a sensation of heavenly languor.

The strength in the muscular arms that swept her up was a marvel to her. As she snuggled contentedly against a firm chest, the pleasant, musky scent of male and shaving soap teased her muddled senses. She burrowed deeper against the firm chest, and to her delight, the strong arms tightened protectively.

She groaned in protest when those strong, warm arms relinquished her to the hard indifference of a chair. From somewhere she heard a voice shout, "Doctor, in here."

Her dark lashes flickered repeatedly until she finally managed to force them open. The whirling array of color converged into two luminous, brown spheres. Dazedly, she saw that the center of each sphere contained an even darker circle of deep-brown velvet. They reminded her of the eyes of a colt she once had.

Cassie blinked several more times until her vision cleared. Focusing on the man who hovered above her, she saw a strong, masculine face with a broad forehead and forceful jaw that signaled determination.

His nose had been broken at one time; there was a small crook at the bridge. Smile lines inched from the corners of his eyes. Why hadn't she noticed that before?

When his frown changed to a smile she shifted her attention to his full lips, a disturbingly sensuous invitation at such close range. Clearing her throat, she brought a shaking hand to her head. "What happened?"

"Well, Teach, I'm afraid you had your bell rung." He flashed a sheepish grin that launched another missile at her defenses.

"And I just bet you're the bell ringer," she murmured. "Are you driven to knocking down members of my family, Mr. Fraser?"

The mouth above her slashed into a lethal grin, and she was relieved when Dr. Williams appeared.

The good doctor leaned over her, his countenance grave with concern. "How are you feeling, Cassie?"

"I'm fine now, Dr. Williams. Just a mild headache."

She tried to sit up fully, and Colt's strong hands immediately assisted her. Dr. Williams examined her eyes and tested her reflexes.

"Everything appears normal, my dear. I'm afraid you'll probably have a headache, though." He handed her two pills. "Here, these should give you some relief."

Colt handed her a glass of water, and she swallowed them.

The doctor closed his bag, then patted her on the shoulder. "Come and see me in the morning, Cassie." He turned to Colt. "I have a patient next door who's in labor and I must get back to her. My carriage is right outside; will you drive Cassie safely back home?"

"Of course, Doctor."

"That's not necessary. I'm fine now," Cassie said.

"It could take all night for this delivery, and I hate to see old Willie hitched up to a carriage all night. When you're through, Mr. Fraser, will you take him back to his stall at the livery?"

"No problem, Doctor," Colt said.

"Thank you. And, Cassie, you'll be fine."

"I am fine," she declared again, but the doctor had already left.

Cassie decided to make her own departure, as well, and rose to her feet. "Thank you for your help, Mr. Fraser."

She had not taken more than two steps when he caught up with her. "Miss Braden, I think you shouldn't attempt to walk. I insist upon driving you home."

"That's really not necessary. My head is cleared now."

"It's settled. I owe you that for the inconvenience I've caused you."

Nothing was *settled* as far as she was concerned.

Particularly her climbing into a carriage with this persistent man.

"Mr. Fraser—"

"Colt," he corrected.

"Ah . . . Colt, the accident was my fault, as much as yours. It's not necessary for you to feel any obligation—"

"The matter's settled." That forceful jaw she had rashly admired had settled into steadfast determination. He grasped her elbow in a firm grip.

Cassie soon found herself ensconced on the seat of the carriage. She felt more intimidated by this intimate proximity than she did by the size of him, even though he had to be several inches over six feet and almost two hundred pounds of muscle and hard flesh. The pure male essence of the man was overpowering.

He turned his head and studied her with a slow, sensual perusal.

"Well?" he asked.

"Well, what?" she challenged. Her belligerent tone dared him to make one suggestive remark. That's all she was waiting for; it would give her a good excuse to get out of the carriage.

As if Colt had read her thoughts, he inquired in a concerned tone, "Feeling any better?"

"I'm fine." *Darn it, Cassie, why are you making a fool of yourself?* "The pills helped," she added in a conciliatory tone.

"I bet you haven't eaten any dinner."

"You're right." Now tired and hungry, she realized the day had slipped away from her.

It took her a moment to realize the carriage had stopped. They were in front of the restaurant that was much more exclusive than the hotel's, and Colt was reaching up to lift her out of the carriage.

"Let's go, Miss Braden. I don't want you to faint on me."

His pleasing, musky fragrance tantalized her nostrils again when he swung her to the ground as if she were weightless.

Upon entering the restaurant, Cassie saw several of the diners wave to Colt. He returned the gesture.

Candlelight and the soothing sound of a string quartet contributed to the small establishment's relaxed atmosphere. It was a pleasant change from the raucous sound that often carried into the hotel's dining room from the bar.

Colt led her to a velvet-covered booth in the corner of the room.

The waiter, Harry Standish, greeted Colt like an old friend. Cassie got a casual "Hi," even though she and Harry had been schoolmates.

"How's your dad doing, Harry?" Cassie asked.

"Getting around slower these days since Bess kicked him. Tonight's specialty is chicken pot pie. So what's it gonna be, folks?"

"Sounds good," Cassie said.

"What about you, Deputy?" Harry asked.

"The sheriff told me this restaurant serves the best steak in town. I like mine rare. And, Harry, will you ask the chef to hustle it? The lady's as hungry as I am."

"Will do." Harry winked at him and sauntered away.

Clearly inquisitive, Colt asked, "Is Bess his wife or his mother?"

"Bess is their mule."

"And where did Bess kick him?"

Cassie blushed. "It would be indelicate of me to say."

Colt grinned. "I think I understand."

"And I hope you understand it would not be prudent to allow you to buy me dinner, so I'm paying for my own meal."

"Just because you're running around in men's clothing doesn't mean you can't be treated like a lady," he said, amused.

"Darn!" she said, snapping a finger. "Here I was hoping it meant that I'm capable of paying for my own dinner."

"Well, bravo to you, Miss Braden. There's nothing I admire as much as a good sport. To show you I'm the same, I'll even let you pay for my dinner if you want to."

She gulped in surprise. "Are you serious?"

"Certainly. I'm very comfortable in my own skin; I've got nothing to prove. That's why firecracker females dressed in men's clothing, bucking stallions, obnoxious children, and immature practical jokers don't scare me."

She couldn't help matching his grin. He was the good sport he claimed to be. "Welcome to Arena Roja, Mr. Fraser. I'm glad we understand each other."

His grin widened. "That we do."

"I don't think the town's ever met anyone like you before."

The room suddenly shrunk into an intimate corner booth that seemed to get even smaller when he leaned toward her and the full potency of his gaze focused on her.

"Does that bother you, Teach?"

She had backed herself into this corner, and she'd make the best of it.

"I'd have to say Arena Roja is impressed. You appear to be a welcome fixture around here, Colt."

It worked. He leaned back. "This is a small, friendly community."

"But you've only been here for a day. You've hardly had a chance to get to know us."

"Since I'm going to be the deputy for a week, I spent most of it meeting the local residents. I've always wanted to be a lawman, and this opportunity will give me some experience in upholding the peace in a quiet little town."

"The town's not so quiet when the hands come in Saturday night."

"That's even better. The experience will do me good."

He raised his hand to attract Harry's attention. "What would you like to drink? Wine? Perhaps a cordial?"

"Nothing for me, thank you. But don't let that stop you from having whatever you want."

He ordered a glass of beer, then studied her like a cat eyeing a bowl of cream.

She was certain he hadn't invited her to dinner just out of the goodness of his heart. If he was looking for a "good time" girl, he was in for a big disappointment.

"Deputy, I hope you understand there are no strings attached to this dinner."

"Doggone it! I was hoping you had an ulterior motive."

"Very funny, Deputy Fraser."

Colt picked up her left hand in a warm grasp, and her pulse leaped to the touch. "I'm glad to see that there's no ring on this hand, though."

"I am engaged." She quickly withdrew her hand from his.

"Really? Where's the lucky man hiding?"

"He hasn't returned from the war yet."

With an amicable grin, he leaned back again. "His loss is my gain, because engaged or not, I'm enjoying the company."

She soon discovered he was a delightful conversationalist, and she listened to his amusing descriptions of the pitfalls to avoid when you're too young to know what you're doing, most of which he had committed.

She found herself returning his entertaining chatter and disturbing grin with an amused chuckle or smile of her own.

By the time coffee was served, a relaxed companionship had blossomed between them. Colt leaned closer.

Cassie became very aware of huskiness in his voice, of his head bent attentively above hers as they talked quietly, and the warm pressure of his thigh against her own.

A long time had elapsed since she'd spent an evening with a man as attractive as Colt Fraser, and she felt a desire for him that she'd never felt for Ted. Yet she had only met this man the previous day!

Alarmed by her secret thoughts, when he slipped his

hand to her thigh, she snapped, "I'm an old-fashioned girl, Mr. Fraser."

"What does that mean?"

"It means I am not promiscuous." Cassie lifted his hand off her leg.

Weighing her through shuttered lids, he took a sip of coffee. "I'm impressed."

She gave him a skeptical glance. "I just bet you are."

"Why would you doubt it?"

"Do you have any idea how many times some passing cowboy has tried to get me to climb into the hayloft with him? Why do you think I prefer to dress in men's clothing?"

Colt burst into laughter. "Are you saying that beneath that men's shirt and pants lurks the heart of a frightened female?"

The amusement in his eyes was as compelling as his contagious laughter.

"Hardly *frightened*," she countered good-naturedly. "Merely bored with men who think I can't tell what their intentions are. For instance, yours."

"Mine are clear, Miss Braden. I only have a week to get you into that hayloft before I leave town."

"Then you're squandering valuable time on me, Deputy. It would be better spent with one of the girls at the Alhambra." She stood up. "The dinner was delicious, but I must get back home."

"Of course." He got to his feet and picked up the check.

"We had an agreement. I'll buy the dinner."

"Next time."

"What makes you think there'll be a next time?" she asked.

"You know as well as I do that there will be, Cassie."

"Is that a challenge?"

"Honey, it's been a challenge from the moment we looked at each other."

He's right about that, she thought as he took her arm and they departed.

Once again the intimate confines of the carriage's front seat made her disturbingly aware of him as he drove to her home. There, he jumped off, lifted her down, and walked her to the porch.

"I'll pick you up at eight o'clock for breakfast."

Cassie didn't want any further contact with Colt Fraser; he was too dangerous. "That isn't necessary. I'll be eating here with my sister."

"She's welcome to join us. Will you extend the invitation to her?"

"Colt, I just told you I don't intend to have breakfast with you."

His deep brown eyes locked with hers. "Do you really prefer that I don't attempt to see you again? Why are you afraid, Cassie? Nothing's going to happen between us unless you let it happen."

The challenge again. "And you can be certain nothing *will* happen. I enjoy your company, Colt, but it would be wiser not to see you again."

"Why?" he asked softly, "Is it me or yourself that you don't trust?"

He was too intuitive for his own good, but she

refused to be intimidated by that dark-eyed gaze of his.

"As I told you earlier, Colt, I'm engaged to another man."

"So you are. You're also a very lovely and fascinating woman, Cassie Braden. I want very much to see you again."

Mesmerized, she watched the slow, inexorable descent of his lips. He kissed her forehead—gently, tenderly and exquisitely excitingly, and then trailed light kisses down her cheek and claimed her lips.

The kiss sent shivers of excitement to the pit of her stomach. All evening, with his head so close to hers, she'd wondered what his kiss would be like. Now she gave herself freely to the delicious sensation.

"You really don't want to say goodnight now, do you?" he whispered when it ended, his warm breath a tantalizing temptation at her ear.

She was assailed with mixed feelings—anger toward him for being so aggressive and disgust with herself for allowing him to awaken desires that she had kept dormant for years.

"I . . . ah . . . most definitely do. Thank you again for dinner. I hope the kiss was worth the cost of it."

"I'll pick you up at eight o'clock on the dot."

Maybe that cocky confidence of his worked with other women, but he was dead wrong if he thought his will was stronger than hers.

"Goodnight, Colt."

Cassie opened the door and went inside.

Cathy was already asleep, so Cassie went to her own room. By rote, she got ready for bed. Every instinct she possessed warned her against Colt Fraser. Since Ted's departure, she had found it easy to shun involvement with any other man—until now. She touched her lips, which still tingled from his kiss.

Her attraction to Colt Fraser was a betrayal of her love for Ted.

"And if I *were* ever to fall in love with someone else, it wouldn't be a footloose womanizer like Colt Fraser."

With that determination, Cassie closed her eyes.

Chapter 5

The knock on the door promptly at eight o'clock the following morning came as no surprise to Cassie. She opened the front door with a firm intent to rid herself of the persistent Colt Fraser.

He stood there looking handsome and virile in clean jeans, a white shirt, and a silver star pinned to his buckskin vest. There must have been better sights to view in the morning, but at the moment, she couldn't think of one.

His gaze swept over her, from her long braid to the toes of her boots.

"Good morning, Cinderella. Eight o'clock and your pumpkin awaits to carry you to breakfast," he greeted cheerfully.

"My pumpkin? Now, Deputy Fraser, is that any way to talk about yourself?"

"Feisty in the morning, aren't you? Are you ready for breakfast?"

Cassie kept her expression as impassive as she could. "I believe I made myself quite clear last night that I do not intend to go to breakfast with you." She had no intention of peeking around corners to avoid him, so she had to make her position clear. "I told you I'm in love and engaged to another man, so there's no purpose in continuing to see one another."

The corners of his dark eyes crinkled with amusement as he broke into a warm chuckle.

"We're only talking breakfast here, Miss Cassie, and that sounds like a pretty heavy decision to arrive at on an empty stomach. Are you saying you've given up eating breakfast? Have a cup of coffee while I eat."

"I've already eaten."

"I believe I extended the invitation to Cathy as well."

"Cathy was asleep when I came back last night, and I was sleeping when she left this morning. I'm sorry."

She closed the door. The man would have to be totally devoid of pride to ignore her rejection of him.

Colt couldn't help grinning as he returned to the hotel. Her attitude only made him more determined than ever to win her over and get her into bed. She was afraid of him—or was she afraid of her own reaction to him?

As for her being engaged, this McBride fellow must either be dead, or he had decided not to come back, so it was every man for himself.

Entering the dining room of the hotel, he was delighted to see Cathy Braden. Unfortunately, her brother was seated with her. Nevertheless, he went over to the table.

"Good morning, Miss Braden." He nodded to Jeff.

"Mr. Fraser, what a pleasure," she said. "Do sit down and join us."

Her personality was such a contrast to Cassie's that

it was hard to believe they were sisters, much less twins.

Jeff, on the other hand, *could* be Cassie's twin; his mouth was twisted in displeasure. "So Dad talked you into it."

Colt knew Jeff was referring to the badge pinned on his vest. "Only until the Santa Fe stage comes through next week."

Braden shoved back his chair and stood up. "See you later."

"I hope he didn't leave on my account," Colt said.

"Jeff's probably upset that Dad didn't ask him to become the deputy."

"Why is that?" When Colt saw that Cathy was uncomfortable with the question, he patted her hand. "I apologize, Miss Braden. It's none of my business."

Just then, Samantha Starr delivered a big plate of pancakes and bacon to him.

"Morning, Belle," he said.

"Told you my name ain't Belle," she grumbled.

"Good morning, Sam," Cathy said pleasantly. "I didn't realize you were working in the dining room now."

"Morning, Cathy. Just helping out today 'cause Billy Campbell has an attack of ague again that he picked up during the war. Where's Cassie?"

"She was asleep when I left."

"She's awake now," Colt said. "I saw her just before I came in. I asked her to join me for breakfast."

"Oh!" Cathy said. "Is she coming?"

"She said no."

"Probably didn't want to spoil her breakfast," Sam said. She walked away.

Cathy's brows arched in amusement. "Did I detect some hostility there, Mr. Fraser?"

"It's Colt, please. And yes you did, Miz Cathy."

"Why? And it's Cathy, please." Her warm smile made him want to reach across the table and hug her.

"Well, Cathy, it seems that in the short time I've been in town, I've made three serious enemies—your brother, sister, and Sam."

"You have to cut Sam some slack, Colt. The poor girl's had a lot to overcome. She was only six years old when her father and her five siblings died from cholera. Her mother is the cook here at the hotel. Sarah Starr is a remarkable woman to have endured the grief she's gone through. Have you met her?"

Colt nodded. "Dan James introduced me to her yesterday. I'm sorry to hear about their tragedy, but that doesn't explain Sam's hostility toward me."

"That's just her facade. Cassie and the James brothers are the only people she shows any affection toward. I think she thinks of Cassie as one of the older sisters she's lost and the James boys as the brothers. So since you and Cassie clashed when you came to town—"

"Hey, don't blame me for that. Your sister was the one who declared war on me."

"Well, Sam worships Cassie and will always champion her, no matter what the cause. As for Jeff, he still has some growing up to do. Cassie and I have probably been overly protective of him. He's four years younger than we are, and our mother died giving birth to him. I think that weighs on him heavily. Cassie's afraid that Jeff will push you into harming him."

"I understand your motives, Cathy, but you and your sister have to let him fight his own battles—especially when he's the one who starts them." He reached over and squeezed her hand. "But I promise you, I won't let him goad me into any fight."

She sighed in relief. "Oh, thank you, Colt."

Cathy was a tender reminder of home. Of his mother, who had died during the war. Of Emmaline, his brother Will's wife, and of his sister Lissy, who had eloped with a Yankee. Cathy Braden had that same gracious manner, the same gentleness and sweet nature. It made him realize how much he missed all of them.

And how much Cassie differed from all of them, riding about dressed in men's clothing, snapping out orders and threats, with a gun strapped on her hip.

"Cathy, I'm surprised a woman as lovely as you hasn't been snatched up and married by now. I'm sure you've been asked. Haven't you ever been in love?"

"Only once," she said, "but he didn't love me."

"Then he's a fool. And what about this man Cassie's engaged to? Do you believe, as she does, that Ted McBride will come home?"

Tears misted Cathy's eyes. "I want to believe so . . . for Cassie's sake. But I can't deny that I sometimes harbor the belief he's dead, or he would have come home by now."

"Was Ted as wild as Cassie?"

"Cassie isn't wild, Colt." Her mouth curved into a loving smile. "She's always had a streak of tomboy-ishness, but underneath all that swagger she's no less a woman than I am. I think dressing up in men's clothing and wearing a gun is her attempt to hide how vulnerable she really is."

"And does Ted McBride love the vulnerable woman or the hoyden?"

"Ted is quiet and self-effacing. Very intelligent." She suddenly stopped and stared, horrified, at his plate.

"What?" he asked, and glanced down at it. A large bug had just crawled out from under the remaining pancake on the plate.

No wonder Sam had played waitress. First the frog in the bathtub, and now this.

"And which one of our hoyden's three buddies has a pet cockroach?" He shoved aside the plate as they broke into laughter.

Shortly after, they left the restaurant, and Colt walked Cathy to her house, which sat on a quiet street with trees, occasional lawns, and backyard gardens.

After saying good-bye to her, he cut back to the main road and found himself at the schoolhouse again. The door was open, so he went inside.

Cassie was on a ladder painting the ceiling.

"Looks like you've got your work cut out for you."

She turned her head in surprise. The quick move-ment set the ladder to wobbling, and white paint splashed over the side of the bucket. Cassie dropped the brush and grabbed for the bucket when it threatened to topple.

Colt rushed over and steadied the ladder, then reached up for her. "Get off that damn thing before it collapses." He grasped her around the waist and swung her to the floor. "What are you trying to do?"

"Until you arrived, I *was* painting the ceiling—very successfully, I might add."

"Cassie, that rickety ladder is on the verge of collapsing."

"I had no problem with it until you snuck up and startled me. Now, if you'll release me, I'll scrub the paint off the floor before it dries."

Until then Colt hadn't realized he was still holding her. For a long moment his gaze clung hungrily to the blue depths of hers. Her sweet fragrance teased his senses. "You smell tantalizing, Cassie—lavender and paint." He slipped his hands off her waist and stepped back.

And you smell just plain tantalizing. She grabbed an empty pail from the corner.

Colt followed her out to the well.

"Let me do that," he said as he drew a bucket of water and filled the pail.

Returning to the classroom, Cassie got down on her knees and began to scrub the smeared paint, while Colt climbed up the ladder and continued the task she had begun.

"Couldn't you have asked your brother to do this for you?" he asked.

"I'm perfectly capable of painting. I'm not asking for your help, so you can climb down from that ladder."

"I'll wait until it collapses. It'll be a quicker way of getting down."

She tried not to laugh but couldn't help it. "You're so exasperating, Colt."

"And you thought we have nothing in common."

As soon as Cassie finished cleaning the floor, she picked up another brush and began to paint one of the walls. She sang softly as she worked, and he soon joined her in the song. When Colt finished the ceiling, he did the top of the walls and she did the lower part. Working as a team, they finished the room in two hours.

Satisfied with their work, Cassie followed Colt to the well, where he drew a bucket of clean water. He ladled her a drink and then drank one himself. The two sat down against the shady wall outside, since the paint smell in the small room was overpowering.

"If we were at Fraser Keep right now, we could go down to the creek for a refreshing swim," he said, "then stretch out on the lawn and dry off. Here the yards are more scrub and weeds than green grass. Lord, I miss those rolling green hills of Virginia."

"Is Fraser Keep the name of the town you're from?"

"No, it's my home. My family has lived there since Virginia was colonized. Have you ever been east, Cassie? Do you object when I call you Cassie? Everyone seems to."

"Cassie's my name," she said lightly. "And no, I've

never been east—or south." She hugged her knees to her chest, her soft smile wistful and appealing. "I've read about the great cities of the North and the majestic plantations of the South, but I've never seen them. Maybe someday."

"A great many of those Southern plantations are destroyed now. Century-old homes burned or tragic shells of their former splendor. But it was spring when I left Fraser Keep. The scent of magnolias and jasmine, apple and orange blossoms was in the air. Here, the smell of dust stings the nostrils and chokes your throat."

"Since you love Virginia so much, why would you ever leave it? I can tell how much you miss your home."

"Virginia will always have a deep hold on my heart, but for now I've had my fill of war, devastation, and the damn Restoration."

"I'm sorry, Colt. Though many of us here in the West lost loved ones on both sides of that war, our homes and lives remained relatively undisturbed."

"That can't be said for the South. Everyone there paid a costly price for that war. My family alone lost five members. Both of our parents and Will's two-year-old son died of cholera. His eldest son died at Sharpsburg; Jimmy was only sixteen. My youngest brother, Andy, perished with Pickett's charge at Gettysburg.

"As if that wasn't enough, in the past year Yankee carpetbaggers converged upon the South like a plague of locusts in the name of Reconstruction, promising riches to the former slaves who were homeless but free. Those who are fortunate enough to find employment have ended up working from sunup to sundown for a pittance that doesn't even keep their families fed."

"I'm sorry to hear that." Compassion replaced the wistfulness in her eyes.

"For four years, my brothers and I fought that damn war," Colt continued. "Fortunately Will scraped and struggled to hold our home together, and we had something to come back to when the war ended. So many others didn't. The South's filled with maimed and broken men still wearing their ragged gray uniforms like badges of honor."

The grim line of his mouth slowly softened into a smile. "Between Clay and Lissy, I've got a couple of nephews I've never seen, as well as a Yankee brother-in-law and sister-in-law. They each have a baby now—part Yankee and part Reb." For a long moment he stared pensively into space, then looked at her and grinned. "I guess that's the start of the healing this country needs now."

"And what happened to your other brothers?" Cassie asked.

His grin widened. "Garth's off pursuing his dream of finding a gold mine, and has no intention of tying himself down to a wife and family. Looks like it'll be up to brother Jed to increase the family's ranks back home, because those are exactly my sentiments, too. Four years of fighting a war and another year of Reconstruction is enough hard times for any man. It's time to cut loose and sow some wild oats."

"So you're going to join Garth and become a gold miner?"

"No, ma'am. For as long as I can remember, I've always wanted to be a lawman. Growing up, I practiced drawing and shooting until I gained the reputation of being the quickest draw and best shot in the county."

Cassie laughed. "You won't get an argument from me. That was a pretty fast shot you got off during the holdup. So why didn't you become a lawman back home?"

"Unfortunately, there's no demand for a Southern lawman; the Yankee carpetbaggers were given those positions. But I've always heard that west of the Mississippi there's an untamed wilderness crying for law and order."

"So that's why you were so willing to accept my dad's offer to become his deputy."

"Yep. Between the stage holdup and dealing with those three outlaws of yours, I'm getting good experience."

"Dad would love to have you remain as his deputy."

"I'm bound for California, where it's greener. My brothers and sister there have written of wildflowers, tall trees, flowing streams, and, according to Lissy, who's more poetic than Clay and Garth, 'the blue waters of the Pacific Ocean caressing the rugged coastline.'"

He chuckled. It was a warm and pleasant sound. "Clay's even planted a vineyard in the hopes of building a winery. He wrote that California's a place where a man can achieve whatever he dreams of."

Cassie smiled. "I'm sure you will, Deputy Fraser."

Colt stood up. "I guess I better get to work, or I'll lose my new job the very first day."

"Thanks for your help, Colt."

"I enjoyed it. By the way, you might wash off that paint on your nose." He tweaked the end of her nose. "Cute as it is, Miss Braden, someone might take you for an Indian on the warpath." He winked at her and departed.

Cassie watched him as he strolled away with that smooth stride of his. When he had talked about the devastation of the South and his family, it had been with a poignancy that had torn at her heartstrings.

Watch yourself, Cassie. The man's even more dangerous than you thought.

As Colt finished making the rounds of the town, his thoughts were on those pleasant hours he'd spent with Cassie. It was hard to believe that during that time, sex hadn't entered his mind. It sure as hell was on his mind now. There was a lot more to that woman than the way she filled out a pair of pants.

Nearing the livery, he saw the three sprouts stretched out on their stomachs. Sam's and Bowie's noses were practically touching the ground as they studied two objects in the dirt. As he drew nearer, he saw that they were penny coins.

"What's going on?"

Sam looked up long enough to give him an irritated glance. "We're deliberating."

Amused, Colt shoved his hat to the top of his forehead. "Just what are you *deliberating?*"

"Which penny looks closer to the wall, Deputy Fraser?" Bowie asked.

Colt gave the coins a long look. "The one on the right."

"Told ya," Bowie said.

"Well, you're both wrong," Sam said. "It's the left one."

Colt hunched down and studied the pennies from another angle. "On second thought, I think they're even." He stood up. "What's this all about?"

"We're tossing pennies to see who can get their penny closest to the wall."

"And then what?"

"The one closest is the winner," Bowie said, "and gets to keep the other penny."

"Sounds like gambling to me."

"So what?" Sam declared.

"You kids are too young to gamble."

Bowie looked contrite. "Shucks, Deputy Fraser, we've only got two pennies between us."

"That's beside the point. You're setting a bad example for Petey."

Sam was not going down without a fight. "You can't stop us. There ain't no law against it."

"There is now. I just made one. No one under eighteen can gamble in the streets."

Sam was so mad that her eyes were spitting bullets at him. "You're only a deputy. You can't make up laws."

"I just did. If I see you gambling again on the street,

I'm going to fine you. And if you can't pay the fine, I'm going to lock you up." He tried to keep from laughing as he walked away.

"Yeah, but just for a week," Sam yelled after him, managing to get in the last word.

Chapter 6

Cassie fell asleep with Colt on her mind that night and awoke the next morning with him still there. Why? She had dealt with his type dozens of times. Leering strangers with the same intentions came and went all the time in Arena Roja, so what made Colt Fraser so different? Yesterday when he'd spoken of his home and family, she had seen a side she hadn't expected in the cocky deputy. But in truth, he'd been on her mind ever since he'd stepped into that stagecoach.

Thinking that her trouble came from the fact that she was too inactive, she decided to ride out to the ranch. Two weeks ago, she and Jeff had moved the cattle to lower ground, where there was better graze and water. It was time she checked on them, and the trip would help clear her muddled mind; she could always think better on the ranch.

Sam and the James brothers ran up to her as she was saddling Midnight.

"You going out to the ranch, Cassie?" Sam asked.

"Yeah. Thought I'd check the herd. Want to ride along?"

"We sure do, don't we, boys?"

Bowie and Petey nodded vigorously.

"Run home and ask your parents."

The three of them ran off squealing with joy, and Cassie unsaddled Midnight and started to hitch the horse to the buckboard.

She was certain that Sarah Starr and Nina James would give the children permission to go along, since the Apaches had been peaceful all winter and had moved in the early spring to their summer camping grounds. "Steady, boy," she cooed when Midnight shifted and began to fight the harness. She gently stroked the horse's neck. "I know you'd rather run free, but it's just for a short while, sweetheart. And you know how the children love to go to the ranch."

Within seconds the stallion had calmed, and she led the horse and buckboard outside just as Colt Fraser was passing the livery. Did he always have to show up to remind her of his existence?

He tipped his hat. "Morning, Cassie."

She nodded. "Good morning."

"Looks like you're going for a ride."

"Just out to the ranch to check the herd." She forced back a smile of amusement, seeing him wince as the children came racing back.

"We can go, Cassie!" The children clambered onto the wagon.

"They enjoy visiting the ranch," she told Colt. "The open space gives them a chance to run off some of their energy."

"Gotta say I appreciate your gesture. With them out of town, I can breathe easier."

"Yeah, well, so can we," Sam declared. "We won't have you sniffing at our heels all day like a sucklin' pig to a sow."

Colt turned to Cassie. "Where does she pick up that kind of language?"

"Not from me, I assure you. She reads a lot of Godey's Western dime novels," Cassie replied, barely able to keep from laughing.

Sam glared at Colt accusingly. "Quit talking about me as if I'm not here. You'd think we're the only ones in town who cause you trouble."

"To date you are, Belle."

"Yeah," Bowie complained. "You oughta find somebody else to pick on."

Petey seconded the motion with a pugnacious lift of his chin.

"So what assault on the human race are you three concocting, Belle?"

She put her hands on her hips and smirked. "You ain't so smart, Deputy. While you're working, we'll be having a picnic."

"A picnic, huh?"

"That's right." Sam held up the basket in her hand. "Mama packed us a picnic lunch so's Cassie wouldn't have to fuss feeding us. There's some for her, too."

"That was very thoughtful of her, Sam," Cassie said.

"Sounds like I'll just have to struggle through the day without you," Colt said. "With you three out of town, the crime rate should go down drastically."

"Are you calling us criminals?" Bowie asked.

"About as near as you can get," Colt replied, hiding a smile.

Petey's brows locked in a frown. "We ain't no crummy nails."

Sam slipped a protective arm around the boy's shoulders. "Don't pay him no mind, Petey. He's just mad 'cause he has to work while Cassie and us are having fun."

Chuckling, Colt tousled the boy's hair. "She's right, pal. She sure has me figured out. Enjoy your outing, sprouts. And you, too, Cassie. The town thanks you." He brought a finger to his hat and moved on.

"Boy, that deputy sure don't like us," Bowie said as they rode out of town.

"I can't understand why you children and Deputy Fraser can't get along. One has to think he either hates children"—which she doubted, remembering the way he spoke of his family—"or he believes you three are troublemakers." Which could be the case, considering their involvement in the incident when he tried to ride Midnight.

"Must be 'cause he's a spoilsport," Sam said.

"Really? He doesn't seem the spoilsport type." Cassie glanced up at the sky. "Well, let's forget about Deputy Fraser. It looks like we're in for another hot day. When I'm through with the herd, we'll go for a swim."

"Hooray!" the children shouted in unison.

She hoped she could practice what she preached

and put the deputy out of her mind, but Colt Fraser was a hard man to forget.

And he knows it. That's why he's deliberately playing a cat-and-mouse game with me. Well, she wasn't going to let the thought of Colt Fraser spoil her outing with the children.

Cassie started to sing "The Old Gray Mare," and the three children joined in. One song led to another, and the air rang with the voices of the enthusiastic chorus for the rest of the ride to the ranch.

When they reached their destination, she drove the buckboard down to the river and unhitched Midnight to let him graze. While she checked out the herd, the children played tag among the trees.

As soon as she finished, Cassie took the children to the best and warmest swimming hole on the ranch.

The area had many streams and springs, and the Santa Fe River ran right through the Lazy B, but this high in the mountains, the water always remained cool. Still, on a hot day, it felt good to jump into the water.

After drying off, they ate their picnic lunch, then hitched Midnight back up to the wagon and drove to the ranch house, to make sure the house and barn were undisturbed.

"How come nobody ever bothers this place, Cassie?" Bowie asked.

"Probably because they know it belongs to the sheriff," Sam said.

"Are you forgetting that rustlers stole our whole

herd? That's why we had to move into town," Cassie reminded her.

"What about Indians?" Bowie asked.

"The Indians never gave us many problems. Dad always gave them grain to get them through the winter,
and even some steers if they needed them."

"How come they didn't raid your ranch when they
were on the warpath?"

"It *was* kind of scary at times, but years ago, Dad
saved the chief's youngest son from drowning in the
Santa Fe. So they pretty much left us alone, except for
stealing a cow or horse occasionally."

"Why didn't they steal Midnight, Cassie?" Petey
asked. "Midnight's the bestest horse there is."

"We kept Midnight in town, sweetheart. I only
rode him out here when the Indians moved to their
summer camp."

"Ain't you ever gonna move back here to live?"
Bowie asked.

"After the herd was stolen, we couldn't afford to. We
had to let the crew go, and Dad took the job as sheriff."

"But you ain't poor now, Cassie," Sam said. "You
own the livery, too."

"Dad won't give up the sheriff's job. Besides, he's too
old now to go back to ranching."

"What about when you get married?" she asked.

"I guess that will depend on Ted. But I don't think he
knows too much about ranching."

Sam looked appalled. "But you love ranching,
Cassie. Wouldn't you want to marry a man who loves
it, too?"

"Of course I would. But a woman can't help who she falls in love with. I guess it might depend on who Cathy marries, because Jeff's never taken to ranching. But I'm sure when Dad retires he'd like to spend out his life here."

"What if Mr. McBride don't come back, Cassie?" Sam asked. "Will you live here or in town?"

"Then I'd live here for sure, Sam."

"Don't you ever want to get married?"

"Honey, there's no one in town I'd want to marry."

"Not even the deputy?"

"The deputy? You mean Colt Fraser? God forbid!"

"Mama said Colt Fraser would make a good husband for you."

The conversation had just become too absurd to continue. "Listen, it will soon be time to get back to town. How about you kids bring in some firewood while I finish dusting these rooms. And be careful, sometimes a snake crawls into the woodpile."

As she dusted, Cassie thought of the preposterous idea of marrying Colt Fraser. Where did people get such ideas?

"Cassie! Cassie!"

The shouts sounded desperate, and, fearing the worst, she rushed to the door. Sam and Bowie came running up to the house.

"What's wrong? Where's Petey?"

"At the woodpile," Sam said.

"And there's a skunk in it," Bowie cried out, breathlessly. "Petey's trying to catch it."

"Good Lord! Why didn't you stop him?"

"We did try," Sam said. "But he didn't listen to us. You know how he loves animals. He thinks it's a cat."

Cassie raced to the woodpile just as Petey caught up to the skunk.

"No, Petey," she yelled.

Petey giggled with delight. "Look, Cassie, a kitty cat."

"Petey, get away from it," she cried, but the warning came too late. The skunk stopped and lifted its tail.

"No!" Cassie ran up and pushed Petey away just as the skunk released its spray, and the stream hit her lower leg.

Sam and Bowie were jumping around, groaning and holding their noses. The stench made Cassie feel like gagging.

"I have to get out of these clothes. Bowie and Petey, get into the house, and stay there until I tell you to come out. Sam, I need your help. Start heating as many kettles of water as you can. I can't go inside, or the house will smell as bad as I do."

She ran into the barn, found a rain barrel, and poured several buckets of water from the well into it. Then she sat down and removed her boots and pants. The spray had soaked through the pants on the right leg and soiled the bloomer leg, too. Cassie pulled them off and climbed into the barrel. By this time, the air reeked with the smell of skunk. Unable to bear it another minute, she untied the kerchief from around her neck and plugged her nose with the loose ends of it, then removed her shirt and chemise.

Sam came running out, holding her nose. "The water'll soon be hot, Cassie."

"Don't get it too hot, Sam. I don't want you to burn yourself."

"It still stinks something fierce, Cassie."

"I know. I'm sorry, Sam, but you're going to have to bring me the bar of kitchen soap, and the box of baking soda and bottle of vinegar from the cupboard. Oh, and a washcloth and several towels."

Sam raced back to the house and returned within minutes with the items. "Cassie, the water is starting to bubble."

"That's good enough. Just be careful, dear. Do you think you can carry it out without burning yourself?"

"I'll have Bowie help me. We're used to carrying bath water at the hotel."

"Wonderful. Have him help you; I'll crouch down when he comes. Once a kettle is empty, fill it again and set it to boiling. I'll have to change this water several times before I get the smell off me."

Hoping to neutralize the skunk smell, she poured some of the baking soda and vinegar into the water. Then she worked up a good lather with the bar of soap and began to scrub her leg.

Sam and Bowie, looking like bandits with their kerchiefs tied across their noses, toted out the hot kettle. Cassie sank down shoulder deep into the water as the two children poured the hot water into the barrel. Then they ran back to the house for another kettle.

Over the next hour, Cassie dumped out the polluted water and refilled the barrel two more times to make certain she had rinsed the odor off her body, but it was difficult to determine if she'd succeeded, because the air was still heavy with the smell.

Sam had brought the washtub out of the house and was soaking Cassie's boots and clothing in a mixture of hot water, soap, vinegar, and baking soda.

"The well's gonna dry up if we keep hauling water," Bowie grumbled as he and Sam made their twelfth trip to the barn with a hot kettle.

"You just shut up, Bowie James. If it weren't for your brother, Cassie wouldn't be in this fix."

"Well, this is worse than hauling bath water the first Saturday of the month, when the cowboys come to town and take their monthly bath."

They were leaving the house with yet another kettle when Colt rode up and dismounted. "What's going on?" he asked when he saw them toting the heavy kettle. "You kids set the barn on fire?"

"We ain't got time to talk, Deputy," Bowie replied.

Colt watched them rush into the barn and looked up to see Petey standing at the front door, looking woeful.

"Hi, pal. Where's Cassie?"

Petey pointed to the barn. "I have to stay inside."

"Why? What did you do?"

The boy's chin began to quiver. "It was my fault the kitty cat hurt her."

"Kitty cat?" Had a rabid cat bitten her? Colt ran to the barn and drew up sharply when he smelled the pungent odor of skunk. A quick glance at Cassie's clothes and boots soaking in a nearby tub told him all he had to know. He tied his kerchief over his nose and continued on. Sam and Bowie rushed past him and ran back to the house.

Colt peeked cautiously inside. Cassie was sitting in a rain barrel, scrubbing her leg, which was hanging over the rim.

At the sight of him, she quickly pulled back her leg and slouched down in the water until only her head was visible.

"Get out of here!"

"Do you have a problem, Miss Braden?"

"What does it smell like?"

He couldn't help chuckling. "I would have thought you'd have known better. Good Lord, Cassie, anyone can smell a skunk before they see it."

"Tell that to a four-year-old."

"Petey? He looks none the worse. What—" He suddenly stopped as the pieces fell into place. "You took the bullet for him." He snapped to attention and saluted. "I've seen less courage on a battlefield receive a medal."

"I'm glad this amuses you, Deputy Fraser."

"Permission to approach and pin your medal on you, madam."

"Don't you dare come any closer, Colt Fraser," she warned when he took a step.

"Can I be of service? Wash your back? Assist you out of the barrel? Dry you off? I'm willing to suffer the odor to come to your aid, Miss Braden."

"No thank you, Mr. Fraser. One skunk a day is all I can tolerate, so please take yourself out of here. Your humor is *stinking* up the barn."

"What have you been using to kill the odor?"

"Soap, vinegar, and baking soda."

"I think I know something else that might help."

"If you're going to suggest tomatoes, you can save your breath. We don't have any."

"Our mother used to soak us in vanilla. Do you have some?"

"I would think we do; Cathy is always baking something."

"I'll take a look. And I recommend you change the vinegar water. Maybe the vanilla will help sweeten you up a bit."

The bar of soap bounced off his back as he left the barn.

The addition of vanilla seemed to work the magic Colt had indicated, but after Cassie pulled on dry underclothes and the fleecy robe Sam had brought her, she headed for the river.

"What are you going to do?" Sam asked as the children followed Cassie.

"Make sure all the skunk smell is off of me, now that we're in clear air. You children turn your heads."

She removed the robe and waded into the water in her underclothes, where she relaxed and stretched out with relief. It was considerably more comfortable than a rain barrel.

The three children remained, watching her intently.

"Be careful," Sam warned. "That river's got a strong current."

"Yeah, you washed off enough," Bowie added. "Now you should come out."

"Yeah, come out," Petey agreed.

Treading water, Cassie glanced at their concerned faces. "It wouldn't hurt for you children to do the same. You've probably picked up some of that skunk odor on your clothes. Just take off your shoes and come in."

"We already went swimming," Sam said. "How long are you staying in there?"

"Just a few more minutes."

Sam frowned. "Well, don't be too long." The children returned to the house.

Smiling, Cassie closed her eyes and lazed back in the water. She loved those three as if they were hers, and hoped that one day she and Ted would have children of their own.

After several more minutes she started to shiver, so she got out of the water, dried herself off hurriedly, and put on the warm robe.

"Oh-h-h I'm freezing," she murmured as she wrapped up her dripping hair in the towel.

Suddenly, a pair of arms wrapped around her waist and pulled her back against a very warm, solid body.

"Does this help?" Colt asked, enclosing her in his arms.

It helped, all right! The heat of his body was a delicious warmth and excitement. But propriety demanded she offer a protest. "Colt! You scared me. Let me go."

To her relief, he ignored her protestations. Instead, his breath brushed her cheek with a tantalizing warmth as he whispered, "If you keep jumping into cold water, that gorgeous body of yours is going to shrivel up like a prune. But have no fear. Though shriveled in limb and face, it's a body I yearn to embrace."

She groaned aloud. "That's such bad poetry."

"What do you expect on such short notice? I'm quite adept at other skills, though. Would you like a demonstration?"

To her regret, he released her, but then he began to dry her hair vigorously. "Now the arms and legs, please. The friction will warm you," he said, with a devilish glint in those dark eyes.

If she got any warmer, she'd burst into flames. "Not on your life, Fraser. How did you know where to find me?"

"The sprouts told me." Tossing aside the towel, he sat down and started to pull off his boots. "Actually, I intended to take a swim myself. I thought I'd try to work out some of the stiffness in my shoulder."

"How badly does it pain you?"

"More than usual."

"Be careful, Colt, or you'll get that wound bleeding again."

"The cold water will prevent that."

"Well, I'll leave you to your healing."

"Don't leave, Cassie. I enjoy your company. Stay. Please."

Her common sense told her it would be a mistake, but, confused by an overpowering desire to be with him, she ignored the warning and sat down, hugging her knees to her chin.

She had seen the strength and power of his tall, muscular body previously, and prepared herself for the sight of his beautifully proportioned physique when he removed his shirt. He was stunningly virile, the width and brawn of his shoulders and chest tapering down to a slim waist and narrow hips. Silky dark hair coated his powerfully muscular arms.

Shifting her eyes to the patch of dark hair on his chest, she felt her heartbeat quicken as she followed the narrow trail down the flat plane of his stomach to where it disappeared into his jeans.

Mesmerized, she watched his every move as he settled down in the water and closed his eyes.

"Cold, isn't it?"

"It makes that bathtub at the hotel very appealing, but my arm needs a workout."

In a short time, he left the water and quickly donned his shirt. "Arm feels better already," he said, settling beside her and drying his hair with the wet towel.

"Sitting here in wet pants isn't going to help your arm."

"I'm used to it; crossed more than my share of waist-high rivers during the war. You'd have been wiser to pull off those wet underclothes you have on."

She looked askance at him. "How long were you watching while I was in the river?"

He chuckled. "Long enough—but not long enough."

"You're a scoundrel, Colt Fraser."

With an amused grin, he began to recite,

"There once was a girl named Cassie,
As beautiful as she was sassy.
When approached by Colt, she'd tend to bolt,
With a comment as brittle as brassy."

"Colt, you have many capabilities, but trust me, poetry isn't one of them."

"It's not meant to be poetry, Miz Braden, just a simple little rhyme."

"More like simple*minded*," she quipped. "Tell me, Captain Fraser, is that something you learned at the military academy?"

"No, my lieutenant, Whythe Henry, and I used to make them up during the war during the lulls in battle. It helped to preserve our sanity. Do you have any idea how many words you can rhyme with 'damn Yankee'?"

"I don't think it succeeded, because you're insane."

"You're right about Whythe; he went into politics after the war."

"Thank goodness it wasn't pursuing a career as a poet."

They sat enjoying the sunshine, more comfortable together than she could have imagined.

"Okay, I'll try again," he said. "How's this one?"

"There once was a knight named Fraser,
Who yearned for the fair maiden Cass.
Despite his noble try, Casandra played shy—"

Cassie raised a hand and interjected, "Because the Fraser . . . didn't even faze her."

"I ought to throw you back in that water," he declared indignantly. "I was about to say, So he gave up on the coldhearted lass."

"That's the best news I've heard all day." Giggling, she scrambled to her feet and grabbed the towel.

Colt gathered up his stockings and boots and hurried after her. " 'The lady doth protest too much, methinks.' "

"And *methinks*, the man spends too much time thinking about something that will never happen."

She didn't like the confident gleam in his eyes.

When they reached the house, Cassie insisted upon taking a final hot bath in the privacy of the bathroom.

Colt took over the water duties from the exhausted children, who had fallen asleep in front of the fireplace. He heated water, then filled the tub for her.

After washing her hair with shampoo and more vanilla, Cassie leaned back and rested her head on the brim of the tub, lazing in the luxury of the warm, lavender-scented water until it cooled.

As she drained the tub, she thought of how sturdily Sam and Bowie had come to her aid earlier, and of how she would show her gratitude. In a way, she was also beholden to Colt, who'd been a big help at the end.

Drying herself and dressing in clean clothing, Cassie pulled on an old pair of boots she had dug out of the closet. When she entered the room, the children were still asleep on the rug in front of the fireplace. Colt was in the kitchen and had just finished putting away the kettles.

"I thought you could use this," he said, entering and handing her a cup of coffee.

"Thank you. The poor children are exhausted. I don't know what I'd have done if they hadn't been here."

"Most likely have avoided the encounter with the skunk."

"Do I still smell of it?"

He came over and leaned closer, and she felt a sudden surge of excitement. For a long moment his gaze held, then he lowered his head. His warm breath caressed her neck as he drew a deep breath. When he finally raised his head, she sighed with relief.

"You smell of lavender and vanilla, Miz Braden. Good enough to eat."

"Thank you for everything, Colt. You've been such a help."

She went over to a cabinet and took out a roll of bandage.

"Let me change that dressing on your shoulder. A soiled bandage isn't going to do it any good."

His nearness was seductive, and she deliberately avoided looking at him. Aching to run a hand across his bronzed, brawny chest, she tried to keep her fingers from trembling as she pressed the gauze to the wound.

"There, that should do it. Looks like it's healing well," Cassie said when she finished.

"Thank you."

Once again she felt his steady stare on her as she tended to his shoulder. She looked up into his hungry gaze.

"What?" she asked.

"Whenever I was hurt as a child, my mother always kissed it to make it well."

"I'd try, but I'd hate to infect you with my germs."

He grasped her arm and pulled her closer. "It's the gesture that counts. A kiss to the lips will do just as well."

At the touch of his lips, she felt heady, spiraling passion, and forced herself to break the kiss and step away.

"I wish you wouldn't do that," she said.

"Didn't you like it?"

"I didn't say that."

Still avoiding eye contact, Cassie put away the supplies and hurried from the room. The man was too, too dangerous.

Retiring behind the closed door of her room, she sat down on her bed and suddenly felt drained. Laying back, she stretched out and closed her eyes. As much as she feared the secret thoughts he aroused in her, he made her feel feminine and desirable. She liked that feeling.

A short time later, Colt tapped lightly on her bedroom door. When there was no answer, he opened it and peeked in. Cassie was sound asleep, so he closed the door quietly behind him and went outside.

The skunk smell still hung heavily in the air and would probably remain for a couple of days. Colt washed Cassie's soiled clothing and cleaned her boots, then placed the boots in the barn and hung the clothes on hooks.

When the sun began to set, he hitched her horse to

the buckboard, tied Bullet to the back, then went inside and awakened the others.

Colt drove the buckboard back to town. His drowsy passengers had little to say. He dropped the children off at the hotel, Cassie at her house, and returned the horses and buckboard to the livery.

As he made his rounds of the town later that evening, he wondered why he had ridden out to that ranch. He couldn't come up with an answer, but he was damn glad that he had.

Chapter 7

On Sunday morning Colt sat in front of the jailhouse, watching the many wagons roll in. Saturday had kept him busy with all the cowboys who'd come to town, so he hadn't seen Cassie until this morning.

But he'd surely thought of her. He'd done nothing but think of her. When he caught sight of her and Cathy with several other women preparing to set up the social that would be held following the siesta hour, he remembered the feel of her soft, curvy body pressed against his at the river, and his groin started aching.

Forcing his thoughts away from her, Colt decided to make a final sweep of the town. When he reached the residential area, he saw the three sprouts clustered at the base of a tall oak tree. All three stared worriedly up into the branches.

What were they up to now? Common sense told him to keep going, but it was his duty to assist the townsfolk.

Colt went over to them. "What's going on?" He looked up into the branches and immediately recognized Cassie's long legs and trim rear end. His breath caught in his throat. She must have been fifty feet above them.

"Cassie, what in hell are you doing up there?"

She turned her head and looked down at him. "Enjoying the view."

The view he was looking at made him feel horny as hell.

"She's trying to get Purr," Sam said.

"Let me guess. Purr's a cat."

Petey looked like he was about to cry.

"Cassie, get down here before you fall and break your neck," Colt ordered. The damn fool woman was determined to kill herself somehow.

"Is Cassie gonna get killed?" Petey whimpered and burst into tears.

Sam got down on her knees and hugged him. She gave Colt a scathing glare. "Now look what you did. You made him cry!"

"I've got him!" Cassie shouted from above. She tried to turn around to climb down, but her hand slid off the branch and she lost her footing. She managed to grab a branch and hang there with one hand holding the branch and the other, the kitten.

"Hold on, Cassie, don't try to move."

Colt leaped up and grabbed one of the lower limbs, then swung himself up. He worked his way from limb to limb up the tree as she dangled, her feet unable to make contact with a limb strong enough to hold her.

He finally reached her and braced his feet firmly on a branch below her, his back propped against the trunk. Satisfied the limb would take Cassie's weight too, he reached up and grasped her around the waist with both hands.

"All right now, let go of the branch."

"I'll fall."

"No, you won't. I've got a secure hold on you. Let go of the branch, Cassie," he repeated firmly.

Reluctantly she released her one-handed grasp on the limb, and he lowered her to the branch he was on. "Now, lock your arms around my neck and hold on."

"How can I? I'm holding the kitten."

"Tuck the kitten into the front of your shirt. My brothers and I did that all the time when we snuck cats into the house."

"I hope you know what you're doing."

"Like you did when you climbed up here?"

"I didn't ask you to climb up to get me. I can get down myself."

"Yeah, head first. Tuck the damn cat in your shirt."

She opened a couple of buttons on her shirt and put the kitten inside, then closed one of the buttons to hold it in place.

At the thought of the kitten snuggled against her breasts, his frustration escalated. Even a damn cat got a shot at that forbidden hunting ground!

"Now put your arms around my neck."

"I can make it down myself, now that both of my hands are free."

"Cassie," he said through clenched teeth, "put your arms around my neck." She did as told. "Now hold on."

With her hanging off his back like a knapsack, Colt worked his way down from limb to limb until he reached a sturdy one ten feet above the ground.

"Now lower yourself and straddle it."

Once in place, they both inched their way along the branch until there was no obstruction between the end of the limb and the ground.

"You can release your stranglehold from around my neck," he said.

Cassie dropped her arms and clamped her hands around the tree limb between her legs.

"I'm sorry. I didn't realize I was holding on so tightly."

"Give me the kitten. Or would you prefer I get it?"

His mouth went dry when she dug into the front of her shirt and pulled out the curled-up bundle, then handed it to him. He could swear the damn cat was smiling.

Colt put the kitten inside his own shirt. "Now just hold on for a minute." He clasped the limb and lowered his legs, dangled there for several seconds, then let go and dropped to the ground.

The three children rushed over and took the cat from him. Then Colt raised his arms to her. "Let go."

"You're in my way."

"I intend to catch you."

"How can you? You've got a sore shoulder."

"Trust me, Cassie. Just let go."

She closed her eyes and let go. The strength of his arms enfolded her before she hit the ground.

Colt put her down, and the three children hopped around her joyously. He slumped down on the ground to catch a second wind.

He'd survived four years of war and another year of Restoration, but between Cassie and the three sprouts, he'd never last the week.

"Colt, your wound's bleeding!" Cassie said, seeing a red stain spreading across the front of his white shirt. "Let's get you to the doctor's office. Are you strong enough to walk?"

Colt rose to his feet. His shoulder ached like hell, and he didn't have the strength to even raise his arm. His groin felt tied in a knot, from having her body pressed against his on the way down, but if it took his last breath, he *would* walk away on his own.

And he was angry. His physical frustration had been channeled into anger.

"Miss Braden, I'm sure that someday I'll be able to look back on my experiences here and manage to laugh. But not today."

With shoulders squared and head held high, Colt left them standing there, all speechless.

Cassie felt a painful tug at her heart as she watched him walk away. She had grown to like him and enjoy his company. He'd been honest with her from the start, about his intentions toward her and the fact that he would be leaving Arena Roja soon.

Under other circumstances she'd find the situation amusing, but she resented it, because deep down, his attention excited her. And she shouldn't allow it to; it was being unfaithful to Ted.

"Sam, what have you kids been up to that has made Deputy Fraser so angry?"

"Bowie put Leaper in his bathwater," she said.

"I see," she said with a stern frown at the boy.

"You're the one who put the cockroach on his pancakes," Bowie declared.

"A cockroach!"

"It was just a little one," Sam said, and glared at Bowie. "Must you blab everything?"

Bowie's eyes looked larger than ever behind his spectacles. "Well, you did. Right on his plate."

"Yeah, on his plate," Petey said.

Cassie shook her head, frowning. "I'm very disappointed in you children. First the trick pulled on him with Midnight—"

"That wasn't our fault. We even tried to stop him," Sam quickly said in their defense.

"And then you called for his hanging as a horse thief. What else do you have in mind for Mr. Fraser?"

"We ain't thought of anything yet," Sam said.

"Oh, yes, we have," Petey said.

Bowie looked contrite. "We won't do nothing else if you don't want us to, Cassie."

"You had no cause to do anything to him at all, children, and I would hope you don't *want* to anymore."

"Are you mad, Cassie?" Petey asked, his little chin quivering with the threat of tears.

"No, sweetheart. I just hope you're through playing these pranks."

She would have to apologize to Colt for everything. "You children stay out of trouble, and keep Purr away from trees."

Her face scrunched into a frown, Sam sat beneath the tree, crossed her legs under her, propped her elbows on her knees, and rested her chin in her hands. Bowie and Petey sat on each side of her and assumed the same position.

"What do you think we should do, Sam?" Bowie asked.

The frown deepened on Sam's freckled face. "I don't know. We've got some serious thinking to do."

"Yeah, ser'ous thinkin'," Petey agreed. He looked at his brother. "Whatta we got to think ser'ous 'bout, Bowie?"

"We could tell Mr. Fraser we're sorry," Bowie said, shoving back the spectacles that had slid down his nose.

"I don't think he'd believe us," Sam reflected.

"I suppose so."

"Yeah, s'pose so," Petey agreed, mirroring the others' frowns.

After a long moment, Sam jumped to her feet. "I've got it! First, we won't put Slinky in the deputy's bed tonight like we planned to do. That will make Cassie happy."

"I'm glad," Bowie said. "He might have killed Slinky when he saw him."

Sam snorted. "Why would he kill a grass snake?"

"'Cause the snake was in his bed and not in the grass."

"Well, maybe you're right," Sam conceded.

"And then what are we gonna do?" Bowie asked.

"Hmmm." Sam began to pace. "We gotta do something nice to him."

"We could show him Slinky and tell him that we changed our minds about putting it in his bed.

That would show him how nice we are," Bowie offered.

"I've got it!" Sam exclaimed. "We'll give him Slinky as a gift."

"Slinky's *our* pet," Petey said.

Bowie put an arm around his little brother's shoulders. "We've got lots of pets, Petey. Poor Mr. Fraser ain't got none."

"Can't we catch a different snake and give it to him?" Petey asked, pouting.

Sam sat down beside him and clasped his hand. "That wouldn't be the same as giving him something we care about."

"Okay," Petey said with a heavy sigh.

"Good. Let's go and find a box. We'll wrap it up real nice with paper and a bow," Sam said.

The three children raced back to the hotel.

Cassie returned home to freshen up for the church meeting before the annual social. She put on a plain white blouse and black skirt, but wore her usual hat and boots.

Once outside, she scanned the street for a glimpse of Colt. She wanted to apologize to him before the meeting began.

Seeing no sign of him, she hurried to the doctor's office. Dr. Williams said he'd changed the dressing on Colt's shoulder and Colt had left. He had appeared to be fine.

Next she headed for the jail. Her father told her

Colt had been there a short time ago. When she left the jail, she hailed Jeff, who was coming out of the Alhambra with Bob and Glen Callum, his best friends.

"Jeff, is Colt Fraser inside?"

"No. What do you want that deputy for?" Jeff asked contemptuously.

"I have something to tell him," she replied as she walked away.

"Well, tell him something for me, too," Jeff called, producing a laugh from his companions.

"Be sure and save me a dance tonight, Cassie," Bob Callum called out to her as she hurried away.

"Yeah, when Hell freezes over," she mumbled under her breath.

As a last resort, she went to the hotel, peeked into the dining room, then approached the desk.

"Haven't seen him, Cassie," Dan James said. "And his key is still in the pigeonhole."

Where could he have disappeared to? After another ten minutes of searching unsuccessfully she heard the church bell ring, so she had to give up. She'd apologize to him later.

What was she doing? Watching Cassie hurry from one spot to another, Colt leaned back against the wall as he sat on the floor of the hotel balcony outside his window. He almost hadn't recognized her in a skirt and blouse. If it hadn't been for her hat and long auburn braid, he probably wouldn't have even noticed her among the people who had crowded into the town.

Why had he gotten so angry over the tree incident? It wasn't like him to lose his temper. And why should he care if she wanted to break her neck? He'd be gone in less than a week and never see her again.

But for some damn fool reason, it mattered. From the time he'd met her, the woman had fascinated him—and for some reason other than just the challenge to get her into bed.

How many women did he know who'd risk their lives climbing up a tree to save a kitten? Back home, women just didn't climb trees. As a kid, his sister Lissy used to, to keep up with him and his brothers, until the day their mom had found out. The stern talk that had followed had convinced Lissy that it was improper and unladylike.

Everything about Cassie Braden was improper and unladylike: her masculine dress, her feisty attitude.

Even the way she'd candidly discussed his intentions toward her the other night. A proper lady would never discuss such a topic openly with a gentleman. She might giggle behind a fan, or appear indignant, but no proper lady would ever come right out and call a spade a spade.

Colt couldn't help smiling. Of course, Cassie would tell him that a proper gentleman wouldn't have such intentions to begin with.

She might not be a proper lady, but she was one fascinating female.

The smartest thing would be to figure out how in hell he was to keep away from her until he rode out of there.

But he knew damn well that she was a glowing flame and he was a moth dead set on becoming incinerated.

Chapter 8

After entering his room by the window to freshen up and change his shirt, Colt went downstairs to retrieve the key to lock his door.

"Cassie Braden was here a short time ago looking for you," Dan James said, handing Colt his room key.

"Looking for me, or gunning for me?" Colt asked.

James laughed but said, "She appeared worried, Colt."

"Did she say what she wanted me for?"

"No, but she kept her gun in its holster."

Dan James and his wife, Nina, seemed to be good people; Colt couldn't understand how they could raise such unholy terrors for children.

"Thanks, I'll look for her."

"You'll most likely find her at church now," Dan said.

Colt returned to his room, locked the window so those dratted kids couldn't sneak in his room for more tricks, locked the door, then headed down to the jail.

The door was unlocked, and Colt sat down to study the Wanted posters piled up on the desk.

A short time later the sheriff returned. The two men talked for a short time, then Jethro decided to go home to take a nap.

"You'd be wise to take one, too, Colt," he said. "In a couple hours the social will start, and it'll be a long day. Come nightfall, we'll be haulin' some of them boys in here to sleep it off."

"I thought the town had an ordinance against selling beer or alcohol on Sundays."

"It has," Jethro said. "That's why the beer's free for the social. See you later, son."

It was high noon and hotter than Hades when Colt stepped outside again. Since it was siesta time, the street had emptied and businesses had closed up for the next two hours. Most of the merchants would remain closed so that all could enjoy the social.

Colt was surprised to see Cassie and the three sprouts reading a notice announcing a cooking contest during the social.

"So, Miss Braden, as competitive as you are, I'm sure you'll be entering the dessert contest," Colt said. "What will you be making?"

Jeff Braden, who was lounging nearby, overheard him and broke into laughter. "Miss I-Can't-Boil-Water enters a cooking contest! That's funny, Fraser."

Cassie glared at her brother. Couldn't he keep his big mouth shut for once? It was none of Colt Fraser's business whether she could cook or not.

"I don't see you entering any shooting contests," she retorted. "For your information, Mr. I-Can't-Hit-the-Broad-Side-of-a-Barn, I've already entered the contest. Let's go, children."

"Did you really enter the cooking contest, Cassie?" Sam asked when they were out of earshot.

"Of course not."

"Then why'd you say you did?" Bowie asked. "Jeff and the deputy will only laugh again when they find out you were lying."

"I guess I'll just have to enter the contest. It says partners can enter. I'll get Cathy to help me."

"What are you gonna make, Cassie?" Bowie asked.

"Whatever Cathy thinks best."

Her sister was in the kitchen when they rushed into the house. "Cathy, I need your help."

"What's wrong?"

"Our big-mouth brother goaded me into saying I'm entering the cooking contest."

"Oh, Cassie, why did you let him?"

"Because he did it in front of Colt Fraser, and I wasn't about to back down with those two laughing at me. Anyway, the rules say that two people can work together, so I thought you and I could be partners."

"I've already agreed to make a chocolate cake with Rosalie Murphy. I'm sorry, Cassie."

"What are you gonna do now, Cassie?" Sam asked.

Desperation called for desperate action. She stared at the young girl. "You and I will be partners, Sam. Your mom's the best cook in town; go get her recipe for that tea cake with the caramel icing. That can win any contest. Meanwhile, I'll go and register us."

Bowie shook his head. "Something tells me this is gonna be disastrous."

With a shake of his blond-thatched head, Petey mimicked his brother. "Yeah, 'sasterus."

At two o'clock the streets began to fill again. As he passed through the streets, Colt thought to himself that he hadn't shaken so many hands since the day he'd said good-bye to his comrades-in-arms in the war.

The social was being held behind the church. Sides of beef, legs of mutton, racks of ribs, and wild turkeys were roasting on a dozen spits. Beans and potatoes bubbled in cast-iron pots on fires, and he inhaled the tantalizing smell of baking bread.

Platters of steaming tortillas filled with ground meat and cheese, bowls of tasty corn and pickle relishes, potato salads, plates of deviled eggs, and jars of spicy tomato sauces with onions and peppers were set out on tables. Many of the men were clustered around the beer kegs and the women, the lemonade, while the children chased each other around.

Spectators sat on blankets spread out around a roped-off area, where two dozen teams of women stood behind small, brick-enclosed cooking fires erected in a square. A metal grate was set atop each fire, with a small reflector oven on each grate.

In the middle of the square stood a table containing crocks of butter, syrup, molasses, baskets of eggs and assorted fruits, and pitchers of milk and water. In addition, there were baking staples such as flour, sugar, and salt, as well as flavorings such as chocolate, vanilla, and coconut.

With the heat from the fires coming at them from all four directions, Cassie figured it had to be over a hundred degrees within that square. As she glanced around at the spectators shouting and clapping, she felt like a Christian about to be fed to the lions.

To her chagrin, she spied Colt lolling against a shady tree. His amused grin was infuriating. To her further aggravation, Jeff and the Callum brothers stood nearby, applauding like bloodthirsty Romans, there to enjoy the slaughter. She picked up a wooden spoon and shook it at Jeff, which only produced more hoots from the trio.

Well, her impulsiveness had landed her in worse pickles before, and she'd show them all! She glanced at her three partners. Undaunted by the heat, the teasing, or their lack of experience, Sam looked the crowd over like a general surveying an inferior enemy's army. It helped restore some of Cassie's faltering confidence.

With a theatrical flair, Sam pulled the recipe her mother had given her out of her pocket. As she handed it to Cassie, the paper slipped through her fingers and fell on the hot grate. They watched in horror as the edges of the paper curled up, then burst into flames. The ashes dropped into the fire below.

"What do we do now?" Cassie said, feeling the rise of panic.

"We mix the cake and get it baking," the general replied calmly.

"But what ingredients do we use?"

"I remember Mama said we use three eggs and three cups of sugar."

"Do you mean three cups of eggs and sugar together, or three cups of each of them separately?" Bowie asked.

"Three cups of sugar and three separate eggs. And we need one cup of butter and four cups of flour. As soon as we get the signal, Cassie," the general ordered, "you get the sugar. Bowie, you get the flour, and, Petey, you get the eggs. I'll get the butter."

Cassie was so impressed with Sam's memory that she felt more confident with every moment.

A pistol blast officially announced the start of the contest, and the race was on.

"Stampede!" Jeff called out at the top of his voice. He and the Callum brothers began to bawl like cattle when the women rushed in a thundering horde to the center table.

Bowie and Petey squeezed between the women and were the first to get back. As soon as Cassie and Sam returned, they cracked the eggs and dumped all the other ingredients together in a bowl.

Cassie frowned. "Seems to me that when Cathy bakes a cake she mixes the butter and sugar together first, and then adds the eggs and flour."

"We ain't got time to do all that separately. Oh, I just remembered—we need a cup of milk, too."

With all this flour, don't we need more than just a cup?"

"No, I'm sure Mama said one cup." Sam began to stir the ingredients together. "This is really hard to stir," she complained.

Cassie came hurrying back with the milk, only to hear Sam say, "I forgot to tell you to bring some vanilla for flavoring." Cassie handed her the milk, which she dumped into the batter.

"How much vanilla do you need, Sam?"

"I don't remember. Maybe you better bring a cupful, same as the milk. Oh, yeah, we need baking powder, too. That should be the end of it."

Cassie hurried back with the vanilla. "There's no more baking powder."

"Then go back and get some sour milk and molasses."

"Sour milk and molasses!" Cassie exclaimed. "Are you sure?"

"Yeah, Mama said that lightens the batter."

"I don't see how sour milk and molasses can lighten the batter," Cassie said. "They're both heavy ingredients."

"Well, I remember for sure that's what my mama uses when she's out of baking powder."

"How much?"

"I guess a cup of each of them should be enough. And hurry up. My arm's getting tireder and tireder."

"I'm not going back for another item," Cassie declared upon returning. "You don't see any of the other women doing it, do you? People are laughing at me running back and forth."

As if reading her mind, Jeff called out, "Hey, Cassie, why don't you get a horse? You must've run five miles by now."

Cassie gritted her teeth.

"Okay, this is mixed up good," Sam said. "Let's pour it into the pan and set it to baking."

Cassie heaved a sigh of relief when they finally slid the cake tin into the oven. She threw her arms around the girl and hugged her. "We did it, Sam! We did it!"

Cassie's elation was short-lived when Sam's freckled face puckered and the girl began to tap her chin with a finger, deep in thought.

"What's wrong?" Cassie asked. "Did you forget to put something in the cake?"

"I don't think so. I can't remember exactly what goes into the frosting. I know Mama said to cook it until it caramelizes."

"What does that mean?" Bowie asked.

"'Til we can spread it, I guess. If I remember right, we need syrup, butter, and salt. I think that's all."

"How much?"

"I think it was four cups of butter and a cup each of syrup and salt. Or maybe it was four cups of syrup and one cup of butter and salt?"

"Usually the first thought is the right one," Cassie advised.

"Well, since I don't remember exactly, let's be safe and use the same amount for all the ingredients."

After collecting the syrup, butter, and salt, they poured the ingredients into a cast-iron kettle on the hot grate. In a short time the mixture was bubbling, and Cassie began to stir it.

"This is getting very thick and harder to stir. It's sticking to the bottom of the pan."

"Hmmm," Sam said. "Maybe we need some more liquid. What have we got in there so far?"

"Four cups of syrup, butter, and salt."

"Now I remember—Mama said a pinch of salt."

Cassie groaned. "We used four cups."

"Must be the salt that's making it stick. Too late now to change it; just keep stirring."

"Maybe if we put in some more syrup, that will help."

"Okay, but just a couple more cupfuls. We don't want it too sweet."

Sam glanced over at the station next to them in time to see them drop a spoonful of their mixture into a glass of water.

"Bowie," Sam said, "go over and find out what Emily is doing with that water."

Bowie scampered away and returned within minutes. "They're making fudge, and she said that if it forms a ball when they drop it into the water, the fudge is done."

"Maybe we ought to try that," Cassie said. "Quick, get a glass of water."

They dropped a spoonful of the bubbling mixture into the water. It formed a rock-hard ball.

"It must be done," Sam said.

Suddenly a burning odor permeated the air. "Oh, look," Cassie cried, "the frosting's boiling over." The hot, syrupy mixture was rolling over the top and down the sides of the kettle.

The odor stung their nostrils as the girls grabbed spoons and tried to catch the liquid and scrape it back into the kettle. It continued to roll down the sides onto the grate and the fire below.

"We have to get the kettle off the fire!" Cassie cried through the smoke that was rising from the grate.

"The handle's too hot to lift," Sam yelled, drawing back a burned finger.

Cassie bunched up the bottom of her apron and used it to lower the kettle to the ground, where it continued to gurgle and spit random bubbles.

"Everyone get back," Jeff shouted. "The volcano's about to erupt!"

The nearby crowd broke into laughter.

"I'm going to kill him when this is over," Cassie murmured.

"What do we do now?" Sam asked desolately.

"I guess we're supposed to spread it on the cake."

Cassie reached for one of the wooden spoons that were sticking out of the mixture like flagpoles. It would not budge. Sam tried to pull out the other one. It, too, was stuck solid.

They each grabbed the end of a spoon and yanked. When that didn't work, they raised the kettle by the spoon handles and tried to shake them loose. In desperation, they finally pounded the side of the kettle against the ground. Neither spoon nor mixture budged.

Now hysterical with laughter, Jeff shouted, "Try using a hammer, girls. If that don't work, you can always saw through it."

"If you don't shut up, Jeff Braden, I'll throw this kettle at you," Cassie shouted.

In their struggle with the kettle, they'd forgotten about the cake. Black smoke began to billow from the reflector oven.

The girls rushed over to the oven and extracted the cake tin, then stared down forlornly at the charred remains.

"I guess we're not going to win," Sam said woefully.

Seeing Sam's misery, Cassie's heart ached for the girl. Her own embarrassment forgotten, she slipped an arm around Sam's sagging shoulders.

"That's all right, honey. At least now we don't have to worry about frosting it."

Sitting side by side, the James brothers looked as woeful as their beloved leader.

"Told ya it was going to be disastrous," Bowie said sorrowfully.

"Yeah," Petey replied. " 'Sasterus."

Cassie cast a disgruntled glance at Jeff and his friends. "Look at them, grinning at us like baboons." Colt's expression was inscrutable, but he was probably thinking the same as her loudmouth brother. "Well, I'm not giving up," she declared with a determined lift of her chin. "We'll just start over."

"But we don't have time. The contest ends in twenty minutes," Sam said.

"That doesn't mean we've lost. We'll just make a little cake and spread it with icing."

"It takes longer than twenty minutes to bake a cake."

"Then we'll make a thin one . . . a flat one."

"You mean like a pancake?

"Yes!" Cassie cried excitedly. "Exactly! You make the cake, while I make the icing. This time we won't use as many ingredients. Hurry."

They rushed to the table, which had been pretty much picked clean by now. They got the remaining four eggs and a couple cups of milk, a cup of flour and sugar each, water, and a smidgen of molasses and vanilla.

A bottle of brandy caught Cassie's attention, and she poured a little bit of that into a cup, then scooped up the few remaining raisins and cherries that were left into bowls. Maybe those would add to the taste of the dessert.

Sam took the four eggs and half the sugar, flour, and milk, then mixed them into a nice, smooth batter. With time running out, she rolled the batter into a thin sheet no thicker than a pancake and put it in the oven to bake, while Cassie mixed the butter, sugar, molasses, milk, and vanilla together in a pan and set it on the grate to cook. When she added the half cup of brandy she'd salvaged, the mixture became more saucelike than thick.

The clock was down to three minutes to go when Sam removed the cake-flavored pancake from the oven. Her face dropped in dejection when she saw the sauce. "Now what do we do with it? That icing's too thin to spread."

Cassie glanced around in desperation. Only the raisins and cherries remained; there were no other ingredients to thicken it with. She dabbed a spoon into the intended icing and gingerly tasted it. To her surprise it was very tasty. And suddenly, she thought of the solution.

"Sam, hurry and cut that pancake into six pieces," she said. Sam quickly obeyed. With only a minute remaining, Cassie sprinkled the raisins and cherries onto the pieces and folded them over. Sam pinched the pieces closed, and Cassie scooped spoonfuls of the brandy-flavored caramel mixture over the top of the last one just as the gunshot sounded, ending the contest.

Colt was one among the six judges who came to sample their offering.

"These are delicious, ladies," Don Peterson, the head judge, exclaimed. "What are they called?"

"Ah . . . Samanthas," Cassie replied with a glance at Colt.

He grinned and winked at her.

"Delicious," Peterson said, marking the score sheet. "I must tell Mrs. Peterson to get the recipe from you," he added, moving on.

A short time later, Cassie and Sam held hands—and their breath—when Peterson announced the winners.

"Congratulations to our gold ribbon winners, Miss Cathy Braden and Miss Rosalie Murphy, for their most delectable chocolate cake."

"That's to be expected," Cassie whispered to Sam. "No one can bake a better chocolate cake than Cathy."

"In second place and winner of the blue ribbon is Mrs. Sarah Starr for her banana and cherry torte."

"It ain't looking too good, Cassie," Sam whispered.

"Keep the faith, sweetheart. At least we finished."

"And in third place, keeping it all in the families, the winners of the red ribbon are the Misses Cassie Braden and Samantha Starr for their raisin and cherry Samanthas."

Hugging and squealing, Cassie and Sam jumped up and down with joy.

"Let's have a round of applause for all the contestants, whose efforts we're about to enjoy. *Bon appétit,* my friends," Peterson shouted above the whistles and applause of the crowd.

"I never figured they had a prayer of winning," Bowie said to Petey. "It's a miracle."

"Yeah, miragal," Petey replied, with a grin from ear to ear.

"Well, what have you got to say now, little brother?" Cassie said when Jeff joined them.

"Samanthas!" Jeff snorted. "You didn't actually name a dessert after that hoyden."

"We named the first one Jeffrey," Sam said, "'cause it turned out to be such a disaster."

Cassie grinned. "I'd offer you a piece of the red-ribbon-winning dessert, Jeffrey, except that you probably won't be hungry after all that crow you have to eat."

Bestowing a smug smile on him, she and Sam walked away with Bowie and Petey at their heels.

Colt wanted to congratulate Cassie on snatching victory out of disaster, but she was always in the midst of a crowd or helping to serve food.

After a couple of hours, he sat down under the shade of a tree to enjoy a tortilla and beer.

Cassie and her three buddies approached him. "Colt, the children are sorry for how they've been acting, and they have a gift for you," Cassie said.

Beware of Greeks bearing gifts, Colt thought to himself, but he was sorry for his skepticism when little Petey stepped forward and handed him a small square box tied with a bright red ribbon.

"We couldn't find any paper to wrap it with," Bowie said.

"But we used one of my hair ribbons to tie it shut," Sam added with a smile.

Funny, he hadn't realized how sweet she looked when she smiled. Maybe it was because she was always scowling at him. Today she wore a blue dress embroidered with tiny pink-and-white flowers at the neck and hem, and her red hair was brushed out and tied back with a blue ribbon.

"You look very pretty today, B— . . . ah, Sam."

In lieu of her usual sharp retorts, she blushed and murmured, "Thank you."

"Well, thank you, children. This is quite a surprise," Colt said, eyeing the ribboned box.

"Go ahead. Open it," Sam said.

Colt winked at Petey as he untied the ribbon. The youngster's face was glowing with expectancy.

Cassie and the three children wore broad smiles as he removed the lid.

He stared down at the coiled contents in the box in shock, then threw it to the ground. The snake crawled out of the box, and Colt raised his foot to trample it.

"No!" Petey screamed in horror. The snake slithered away, and the youngster chased after it.

That did it! Colt stared coldly. "I have had enough of your practical jokes. I suggest you remain out of my sight until I leave this town."

"Colt," Cassie said, "I don't think you understand. They wanted to give you—"

"The same goes for you, Miss Braden," he said, cutting her off. "You're too old to be a party to these pranks, so keep a wide berth from me. If there's a God in Heaven, I'll never have to see you, your brother, or these three brats ever again." He spun on his heel and returned to the jail.

Colt fumed nonstop for the next hour before his anger cooled. He had never been one to sustain anger for very long, and he couldn't understand why he'd reacted so angrily to the antics of Cassie and the sprouts; it was out of character for him.

By late afternoon he had cooled down, and he returned to the social to quiet down a couple of cowboys who had indulged in too much free beer.

Through the rest of the day he caught glimpses of Cassie, who was always busy cutting pies and cakes.

When the sun went down, the piano from the Alhambra was lifted onto a wagon and driven to the site. A fiddler and a banjo player climbed up on the wagon as well, and the dancing began.

Time and time again one of the women grabbed Colt's hand and pulled him in. He danced a couple of times with Cathy, but not Cassie. He wanted to apologize first and preferred they were alone when he did.

As the evening wore on, the crowd gradually thinned. Many of the cowboys wandered back to the Alhambra in pursuit of the services of the ladies, or to wait out the clock until midnight, when they could buy some hard liquor.

Some of the folks packed up to return to their ranches that night. Others bedded their families down in their wagons.

Soon the makeshift tables were taken down, the piano hauled back to the Alhambra, and the cooking fires extinguished until just a few remained for light.

Only then did Colt go over to where Cassie and Cathy were packing up the back of a buckboard.

"Here, let me do that," he said, grabbing one of the baskets.

"We can do it," Cathy said. "You should take it easy with that shoulder. Dr. Williams said you opened the stitches again."

Cassie remained silent and continued what she was doing.

"It's fine," he said. "Cassie, I heard you were looking for me earlier."

"It was nothing important."

Cathy climbed up on the wagon and took the reins. "I'll go on home so you two can talk."

"I'm coming with you," Cassie said quickly as she

followed her sister onto the wagon. "I have nothing more to discuss with Deputy Fraser."

"Please, Cassie. I'd like to talk to you," he said.

"You said enough earlier. I'm not interested in anything further you have to say."

"Give the man a chance, Cassie," Cathy said.

"Let's go," Cassie said, with an impatient glance at her sister.

Cathy looked at Colt sympathetically. "Goodnight, Colt." She flicked the reins, and the wagon began to roll away.

"Goodnight, Cathy," Colt called back.

He liked that woman. It was a shame her sister wasn't as even tempered. Well, he would have to try again tomorrow.

Chapter 9

Early the following morning, Sam and the James brothers were crawling around looking for Slinky when they saw the deputy approach Cassie's house. Sam crouched down behind a nearby privy and pulled the others down.

"Why are we hiding, Sam?" Petey asked.

"I don't want Deputy Fraser to see us," she said. "He might be mad enough to put us in jail."

"I don't want to go to jail, Bowie," Petey said.

Bowie slipped his arm around his little brother's shoulders. "Don't worry, Petey. Uncle Jethro won't let him do that to us."

Sam shook her head. "Uncle Jethro ain't in town. I saw him ride out early this morning."

"Maybe we better go back to the hotel," Bowie worried.

"What makes you think the deputy won't find us there? I bet that's why he went to Cassie's house."

"You mean he came to put Cassie in jail?" Petey asked.

"What should we do, Sam?" Bowie asked, hugging his brother tighter to comfort him.

Sam frowned. "You keep watch to see if he hauls her off to jail while I think about this."

After several long moments she said, "We best get out of town."

"Cassie would hide us," Petey said.

"How can she if he locks her up, too?"

"Where will we go?" Bowie asked. "The Lazy B?"

"No, he could find us there. We gotta go farther than that. Maybe all the way to Gila Rock."

Bowie snorted. "We'd have to take a stagecoach to go that far."

"And the stage bound for Gila Rock will be arriving in an hour," Sam said triumphantly.

"Won't do us no good. It cost two dollars each for a ticket, and we ain't got no money."

"Yeah, no money," Petey said.

Bowie peered around the corner of the privy, then dodged back when he saw Colt knock on Cassie's door. His hand touched something metallic, half-buried against the side of the wall of the outhouse, and he pulled it up.

"Hey, look. It's an old gun."

"You be careful with that, Bowie James. You know your daddy said it's dangerous to play with firearms."

"This ain't dangerous. It's all rusty, and the trigger's broken off," Bowie said. He grinned at Petey and pointed the gun at him. "I'm Deputy Colt Fraser, and you're under arrest," he said in a deep voice. "Get them arms up, partner, or I'll plug you full of holes."

Giggling, Petey raised his arms in the air.

"We've got a serious problem and this ain't no time to be playing games," Sam declared. "Where can we get six dollars?" She looked at Bowie, who was trying to twirl the gun like he'd seen some of the cowboys doing. "Hey, give me that gun."

Sam studied the gun and checked out the chamber to be sure it was empty. "I've got an idea. Right before the stage is due, we could use this gun and hold up the bank."

"I don't think that's a good idea," Bowie said. "They'd know it was us."

"Not if we put bandannas over our faces. We'll hold up the bank, get out of town until Deputy Fraser leaves Thursday, and then come back. Come on, let's get our bandannas."

"Can we take our pets along?" Petey asked as the three hurried off.

Cassie pulled the cake out of the oven, dropped the pan on the stovetop, and stared grimly at the cake's sunken middle. Though she'd followed Cathy's recipe closely, the cake had collapsed. And the cookies she'd tried baking had ended up so hard and tasteless she'd almost broken a tooth trying to bite through one. Every other female over twelve in this town could mix flour, sugar, and eggs together and end up with a tasty confection! She was a total failure as a woman and knew it. Winning that red ribbon yesterday had been pure dumb luck. And Colt Fraser knew it, too.

Their dinner conversation last Thursday had been preying on her mind. She had known from the beginning that his attention to her was just a game, a temporary challenge before he moved on. Yet despite knowing that, she liked him and enjoyed being with him. What was wrong with her?

He'd said he wanted to have sex with her—all men thought alike in that respect—and what frightened her was how much she was tempted by him. If only Ted were here. He was the only man who really understood her, who recognized her feelings of womanly ineptitude.

In frustration, she swept the cookbook off the table, then kicked it across the floor, when a knock sounded on the front door.

When she opened it, Colt Fraser, looking bigger than life, stood braced against the threshold. His tall frame filled the door, and the sight of his abominable, smug grin incensed her.

She slammed the door in his face.

His incessant knock forced her to return to open the door. This time his grin was contrite.

"Did that help?" he asked, with an intuitiveness she found frustrating.

"Immensely!" She spun on her heel, leaving him standing in the doorway.

Stepping inside, Colt closed the door behind him and crossed the room to her.

"Why did you come here, Colt?"

"What are you mad about?"

She stopped and pivoted, infuriated by his feigned innocence. "Yesterday, I foolishly wanted to apologize for the tree incident. I appreciated your help, and I was sorry that it aggravated your wound," she said.

"No real harm done," he replied.

His blasé acceptance only fueled the fire more. "And the fuss you made over Slinky—"

"The snake?"

She nodded. "I hadn't known about the tricks they'd been pulling on you, but I know they meant well with Slinky. The snake is one of their favorite pets, and they were giving it to you as a gift to say they're sorry. You broke their hearts when you blasted them and me in front of the whole town."

"I guess I got carried away. Those three are always up to something, and one of these days somebody is going to get seriously hurt as the result of their pranks."

"They can be mischievous, but they really aren't bad children."

"Yeah, I know. They aren't any worse than my brothers and I were at that age. I don't know why I got so angry."

"It was just a harmless grass snake."

"I have to admit something, Cassie: I've always hated snakes. I can't bear to touch them. I literally freeze up when I see one. So, I'm sorry about how I reacted; they had no way of knowing how I feel about snakes. I thought it was just another mean trick. I should have realized their good intentions from the look on Petey's face when he gave it to me."

Colt grasped her lightly by the shoulders. "So now that the apologies are out of the way, Miz Cassie, shall we kiss and make up?"

She wasn't about to give in to his charm. "I accept your apology, and I hope you accept mine," she retorted. "If you'll excuse me now, I must get back to the kitchen. I have something in the oven."

"Will you have dinner with me tonight, Cassie?"

"I'm sorry, I've already made other plans," she lied.

"Okay, I'll go," he replied, before cupping her face between his palms and claiming her lips in a kiss that was excruciatingly sweet in its tenderness, yet set her legs to trembling. "Have a good day, Cassie," he said and turned on his heels.

As he walked away, Cassie felt a tightness in her heart. After only a few days, Colt Fraser had aroused confusing feelings that threatened her love for Ted. It didn't make sense—and it scared her.

First thing in the morning, she would go back to the ranch until he left town. That was the safest thing to do.

The clock had just struck high noon when three masked bandits entered the bank. They had chosen their moment wisely, knowing it was siesta time and the streets would be deserted. The tallest of the trio held a rusty pistol in hand.

"This is a holdup. Hands up," the weapon-toting leader said in a deep, funny-sounding voice.

"Don't shoot," Don Peterson said, then glanced at his teller. "Get your arms up, Joseph," he said as he raised his own in the air.

The bandit leader threw a pouch on the counter. "Okay, put six dollars in the bag, and don't try anything smart or I'll have to gun you down. I might be little, but this gun makes me as tall as anyone."

"I would say so," Peterson said. "Maybe we should talk about this. I might be willing to lend you the money, stranger."

"Mama said it's not proper to borrow money from friends."

"What did she say about stealing it?" Peterson asked, amused.

"That stealing's a sin, but we promise to pay it all back as soon as we can save up the money."

"What do you need six dollars for, Sam?" the banker asked as he placed the six gold pieces in the bag.

"I don't know any Sam," the bandit growled. "My name's Belle."

"Yeah, her name's Belle," one of her cohorts said. "And mine's Frank."

"And I'm Jesse," the smallest of the three said.

"Frank! Jesse! Oh my, Joseph, it's the James Gang!" Peterson said, feigning fright.

"We're sorry, Mr. Peterson, but we gotta get out of town quick. The deputy's mad at us. No telling what he might do to us."

"Hmmm, Deputy Fraser struck me as being a reasonable man. What did you do to him now?"

Suddenly three men entered the bank and drew their guns. "Hands up. This is a holdup," one said. "Get that safe opened and make it quick."

"Hey, we're holding up this bank," Sam protested.

The man snorted. "With that, kid?" Snatching the rusty gun out of her hand, he held it up for the others to see. "This gun's empty and ain't even got a trigger."

"Now you went and blabbed," Sam said angrily, then kicked him in the shin.

"You little brat," he snarled, and backhanded her across the cheek. "I oughta kill you." He raised a hand to hit her again, and Petey began to cry.

"Pike, we ain't here to watch you beat up kids," one of the men said, impatiently.

Pike lowered his hand and shoved Sam away. "Go sit against that wall, and shut up that wailing kid." He turned a wrathful glare on the two boys. "You two'll get the same as her if you don't listen to me."

Leaning against the livery, Jeff Braden grinned when he saw Sam and the James brothers enter the bank with red bandannas over their faces. What were they up to now? He couldn't blame them for being bored. He'd lived in Arena Roja for almost nineteen years, and it was the most boring spot on earth. Maybe he should move on to some place like California, like Colt Fraser was doing. He knew his sisters would be sorry to see him go, but his dad sure didn't have any use for him.

He was turning to go inside the livery when four riders rode up to the bank and dismounted. They looked vaguely familiar; did they work for one of the local spreads? The men tied their horses to the bank's hitching post, and three of them went inside.

Jeff's instinct kicked in. The whole thing was suspicious. To avoid attracting the outside man's attention, he went inside the livery, then climbed out of the back window and raced down the road to the jail.

"Where's my dad?" he asked breathlessly.

Colt glanced up from the pile of Wanted posters he was going through. "Rode out this morning and said he won't be back until afternoon. What's the problem?"

"Four strangers just rode into town and three of them went into the bank."

"You didn't recognize any of them?"

"I don't think so. One of them rode a bald-face sorrel that looked familiar, but I don't remember where I saw it before."

Colt jumped to his feet. "Was another one a dappled gray or a black-and-white calico?"

"Yeah, you know them?"

Colt pulled out the gun on his hip and checked the chamber. "Those are the same men who held up the stage." He unlocked the rifle case and grabbed a weapon. "You say three went inside. What about the fourth?"

"He stayed with the horses."

"How long ago?"

"Just a couple minutes. I ran down here as soon as I saw them go in."

"How many employees are inside the bank?"

"Peterson, the owner, and Joe Adams, the teller. But Sam Starr and the James brothers are inside, too."

"We can't try to rush them, then; one of those children could get hurt. Is there a back door to the bank?"

"Yeah, it opens into Peterson's office."

Colt thought for several seconds, then said, "Okay, here's the plan. I'll go in and hit them from the rear, but I need you to take out that sentry in the front."

"You mean shoot him?"

"Hell, no! That would alert the others in the bank. Create a diversion to distract him. Don't try to pull any fool stunt like you did when that stage was held up; remove that damn holster and conceal your gun. Pretend you're drunk or something. Just get close enough to either knock him out or disarm him."

Colt opened the desk drawer and pulled out a pair of handcuffs. "Try to get these on him. Do you think you can do that?"

"I can try."

"All right, let's go. Remember, no shooting unless you absolutely have to."

"All right," Jeff said. "But to be honest with you, I miss anything I aim at."

"You'll do fine. Let's go!"

The two of them ran back to the livery and saw that the robber was still with the horses.

"All right, Jeff, let's do it," Colt said. "Good luck." He moved on to the rear of the bank.

Jeff took a deep breath and stepped outside the door of the livery. The outlaw saw him and was watching; Jeff knew he had to cross the street without the man becoming more suspicious.

"Sam," he shouted loudly. "Bowie, Petey." He started to cross the road. "Where in hell are those kids?" he grumbled loudly enough to be overheard.

"Hey, Charley," he yelled to a man who had come out of the merchandise store to shake out a rug. "Have you seen Sam or the James boys? They were supposed to muck out the horse stalls and they ain't done it yet."

"See one, you see all three," Charley said. "But I ain't seen them, Jeff." He went back inside.

The man at the hitching post watched and listened to every word.

"Howdy," Jeff said, approaching him. "You seen three kids around here?"

"No," the man said and leaned back against the hitching post.

"Thanks, stranger."

As Jeff started to pass, he whipped out his gun, pressed it against the man's stomach, and cocked the trigger.

"One move and I shoot," he warned. "Put both hands on that hitching post."

"What are you doing? I ain't done nothin'," the man protested, but he did as told. Jeff pulled the man's gun out of its holster, then reached for the handcuffs.

"Now turn around slowly and put your hands behind your back. My finger's on this trigger, so no foolish moves."

"Okay, okay, just be careful."

Jeff cuffed him. "Now let's you and me take a stroll over to that livery."

Once they were inside, Jeff found a rope and tied the man to a post.

Cassie came in. "What's going on here?" she asked, startled at seeing the bound man.

"Fraser and I are foiling a bank robbery. He's gone in to stop the others."

"He went in alone?"

"Yeah. He told me to create a diversion and take out this guy."

"We've got to help him. Get some of the other men in town," Cassie cried as she rushed to the door.

"Wait, Cassie!" Jeff yelled. "Sam Starr and the James brothers are inside. Fraser doesn't want us to rush the bank. He's afraid the children will get hurt."

"The children! Oh, dear God!"

She fought back her panic and tried to think. Somehow she had to help Colt. If they couldn't rush the bank, maybe creating a diversion inside would be just as helpful.

Cassie raced across the street.

Chapter 10

Rifle in hand, Colt eased the back door open and crossed the office, then paused to listen at the door that opened into the bank.

A loud voice declared, "You better move faster gettin' that safe open, or start prayin', mister, 'cause I ain't plannin' on spendin' the day here."

Colt recognized the speaker's voice at once—it was the same gang that had held up the stage.

"I'm going as fast as I can," Peterson said.

"Benson, watch the street to see if we've been spotted," the gang leader ordered.

"Ain't nobody out there, Pike. You know this town closes down at noon. Hey, I don't see Colby and the horses," Benson said.

"It's taking so damn long, he probably got out of the sun," Pike grumbled. "Mister, either you get that safe open now or I'm blowin' a hole in you and that clerk."

"For God's sake, man, you've got him tied up. He can't do you any harm," Peterson said.

"It'll be your fault if you don't move faster."

"There, the safe's open," Peterson said.

"You don't know how close you came to dyin', mis-

ter. Get over against that wall with those kids. Keeler,
start stuffin' that money into a bag."

Colt heard Peterson cross the room and now had a
good idea where the children were. One man was at
the window and one was at the safe. Question was,
where was Pike standing? With one of the men at the
safe stuffing money into a bag, that meant there
were only two men with drawn guns. Now was the
best time to make his move. He reached for the handle of the door but paused when one of them said,
"Boss, there's a woman running across the street
headed this way."

"*Dammit!*" Colt muttered when he heard the front
door open.

"You children come with me at once," Cassie's voice
demanded.

Colt froze. Lord, she had placed herself squarely in
danger.

"They ain't goin' nowhere, lady, and neither are
you," Pike said. "Get over there against that wall
with them."

"I'm doing no such thing. I'm taking them out of
here right now. Come on, children, we're leaving."

Colt's heart pounded. It had to be now, before Cassie
got herself shot. He threw open the door. "Drop those
weapons and get your arms up!"

Benson and Keeler did as told and raised their
arms in the air, but Pike grabbed Cassie to use her as
a shield.

"Don't you hurt her," Sam yelled, charging to
Cassie's aid.

With all her might, Cassie poked her elbow into Pike's midsection. Grunting, he doubled over, and Sam clamped her teeth on the hand that was holding the gun, biting him hard.

Yelping, Pike dropped the gun and tried to shake her loose, but Sam held on like a bull terrier. Cassie struggled to free herself from Pike's one-armed grasp as Bowie and Petey ran over. She raked her nails across Pike's face, and he let go of her.

Sam released her mouthhold on Pike's hand when Bowie shoved the man backward over Petey, who had hunched down behind him. The outlaw landed sprawled on his backside on the floor.

Seizing the opportunity, Keeler and Benson tried to break for the door. Don Peterson caught up with Keeler and landed a right punch on the outlaw's jaw, and Keeler went down. A crack on the head from Colt's rifle took care of Benson just as Jeff and several armed townsfolk burst through the door.

Colt kept the rifle trained on the outlaws while Jeff tied their hands behind their backs. Then he searched them for any concealed weapons. By the time he finished, he found four guns and four knives. While Cassie gathered up the weapons, Colt and Jeff marched the men to the jail.

Colt opened one of the two cell doors, then untied Pike's hands.

"You fellows are going to have to double up. You first, Mr. Pike. Take off your boots."

"My boots! What for?" Pike snarled.

"Just in case you've got something hidden in them.

Besides, a man can't run too far in his stocking feet. A little trick I learned during the war."

"Got it all figured out, ain't you, Deputy?" Pike hissed as his glare swept over Colt with loathing. "I recognize you now. You was on that stage last week. You the one who shot my brother?" Colt nodded. "Where is he?"

"In the cemetery, Pike. Robbing stagecoaches isn't good for a man's health," Colt said.

"Yeah, I recognize you now." He turned his wrathful glare on Cassie. "You and that pants-wearin' bitch." He tossed his boots at Colt's feet. The outlaw's eyes gleamed with malevolence. "Reckon I've got a score to settle with the both of you."

"Get in there," Colt ordered with a nod toward the open cell. He turned to the next outlaw. "Off with those boots, Keeler."

All four men were soon behind bars, and Colt listened to Don Peterson's account of what had transpired prior to their capture. Now that the incident had passed without anyone getting hurt, tears of laughter streaked the banker's cheeks as he described the children's attempt to hold up the bank.

"We sure were lucky you were around, Colt," Peterson said as he was leaving. "Hate to see you go. With Jethro wanting to retire, you sure would make a good replacement."

"I'm sure someone will come along to fill his boots, Mr. Peterson." Colt glanced over to where Jeff Braden was standing with Cassie and the children. "Jeff Braden has the makings to become a good lawman. He showed a good head and a lot of courage today."

Peterson snorted. "Jeff's got a lot of growing up to do before he could be trusted to be a lawman. And I'm told he's a poor shot." He shook Colt's hand. "Thanks again. This is the second time the bank and this town are beholden to you."

Colt walked over to where Jeff, Cassie, and the three children were clustered together.

"Jeff," he said, offering his hand, "thanks for your help. That was quick thinking on your part."

Jeff blushed. "I didn't do that much. You took all the risk, going into that bank."

Colt turned to Cassie with a frown. "Speaking of risks, Cassie, you not only could have gotten yourself shot, but the children, too. Do you *ever* think before you act? I had the situation in hand and you almost fouled up the whole thing."

"I—" Cassie began.

"Don't yell at her," Sam declared. "She—"

"You stay out of this, young lady. You and your two cohorts have done enough damage for one day. If I had another cell, I'd lock you all up just to keep you out of trouble. Have any of the four of you thought of what might have happened in there? You might have been killed! Those outlaws aren't playing silly games; they'd just as soon shoot you as look at you."

Sarah Starr and Dan and Nina James came running down the street, and Bowie ran into his father's arms as Nina scooped up a crying Petey in hers. The two parents hugged their crying children as they fought back their own tears of relief. Sam ran to her mother, and Sarah knelt and hugged and kissed her daughter.

Colt had to admit that Sam was pretty remarkable. How many twelve-year-old girls would take a slap in the face and not shed a tear, face drawn pistols in the hands of ruthless outlaws, and still have the grit to go to the aid of a friend by attacking the outlaw.

Sarah looked at her daughter's face. She gently caressed the bruise where Pike had struck her, then tenderly kissed the spot.

The three parents picked up their children. Thanking Colt, they left to carry their precious bundles home.

When Colt turned around, he discovered that Cassie and Jeff had left, too. It was just as well. He didn't feel like arguing anymore with Cassie; all the fight had gone out of him. He was going to go back inside, lean back with his feet on the desk, and enjoy the peace and quiet of this so-called sleepy little town.

Jethro returned a short time later, and Colt filled him in.

"I'll send for the marshal: I'm sure these hombres are wanted for worse crimes, and this bank holdup will only get them a prison sentence. I'd like to see them hung," Jethro replied after listening to the entire story.

"What about the stagecoach robbery, and shooting Buck? He almost died."

"They're cold-blooded killers all right, and I'll put that all in the record. I don't want the hangin', here. Did you ever see a hangin', son?"

"No, sir."

"It's not a pleasant sight, and not one you ever forget. I'll turn 'em over to the marshal and let Santa Fe deal with 'em."

Jethro slapped Colt on the back. "You best go back to the hotel and get some sleep. With these prisoners locked up here, one of us is gonna have to stay here all the time. We'll take eight-hour shifts. It's two o'clock now. Come back at ten."

Colt felt drained emotionally. All he could think of was how close the people in that bank had come to getting killed. He soaked in a hot bath, then tried to nap, but he couldn't relax.

When he went downstairs for dinner, the diners applauded him when he entered the room, and the Jameses treated him like a hero. Sarah Starr insisted on personally serving him his dinner.

He felt undeserving of the recognition. What would the outcome have been if Jeff Braden hadn't taken out one of those men, or Cassie hadn't charged into that bank? Or if Samantha hadn't aided Cassie at the risk of her own life?

He'd acted out of a sense of duty; their actions had been done out of love and loyalty. Those instincts were the truly heroic ones.

At ten o'clock he went back to the jail and relieved Jethro. He lay down on the cot the sheriff had brought in, but it wasn't until midnight that he finally closed his eyes.

After an uncomfortable night on the small cot, further aggravated by a thunderous downpour, Colt was just getting up when the sprouts arrived with breakfast trays for the prisoners. The children said nothing to him but plopped the trays down on the desk. As they prepared to leave, Colt met up with Sam's usual glare.

"What?" he asked.

"I hope you're satisfied," she declared.

The three started to walk away. "Hey, get back here," Colt ordered. "What's the matter?"

"You drove Cassie away! She went back to the ranch this morning and said she ain't coming back for a while. It's all your fault!"

They stomped off.

So Cassie had skipped town to avoid him. Since he'd be leaving Arena Roja the day after tomorrow, it was probably the right move on her part.

You can't win them all, Fraser, he admonished himself and settled down for a dull day without Cassie to argue with.

Jethro came in a short time later with a breakfast tray for Colt. "Mornin', son. Prisoners give you any trouble durin' the night?"

"No, they were peaceful as lambs. They're probably afraid we'll set those two she-wolves on them again."

Jethro chuckled. "Eat your breakfast while it's hot."

Having learned his lesson, Colt checked his tray for any uninvited visitors before taking the first bite. The bacon and eggs were done to perfection, and the coffee was strong and hot. He finished off all of it.

"You and Cassie still arguin', son?" Jethro asked.

Colt put aside the tray. "What makes you think so?"

"Cassie had no cause to leave town so fast." Jethro's eyes narrowed in a reflective gleam. "'Less she was runnin' away from somethin'—or someone."

"I can't envision Cassie running away from anything or anyone. I'm disappointed she left without even saying good-bye."

"Seems a pity, considerin' the ranch is only five miles straight north from here. Person couldn't miss it if they tried."

"You know, Sheriff, if you don't mind, maybe I'll ride out and beard the lion in her den."

"You do that, son. Get one of the Lazy B horses. No charge," he added with a grin. "Ain't no cause to hurry back, I can handle the prisoners."

Colt decided to take the man at his word. Returning to the hotel, he shaved and changed clothes, then headed to the livery.

The three sprouts came running up to him.

"Where are you going?" Sam asked suspiciously.

"That's for me to know and you to wonder about."

They followed him into the livery, where Colt chose a horse, saddled it, then mounted.

As he rode off, he glanced and saw the three of them still standing where he'd left them. They looked rather pathetic.

Those three kids had actually begun to grow on him. Sam was a younger version of her idol, spunky and spirited. And he'd bet that ten years from now, those two boys would be just as devoted to her as they were now.

Hard as it was to believe, he was going to miss the sprouts when he left Arena Roja.

Jeff had spent the night with Lucy Cain. He liked her better than any of the other gals at the Alhambra. Besides being good in bed, she always made him feel like he was somebody, not just tolerated because he was the sheriff's son.

When he saw the livery door was open, he realized he'd forgotten to lock it the night before when he'd met up with Lucy. She'd taken his mind off the task.

A sinking feeling hit the pit of his stomach when he saw that Bullet was missing. Either the horse had wandered off, or, with all the strangers that had been in town yesterday, someone might have stolen him. He checked the saddles and discovered one of them was also missing, along with a bridle.

Other than Midnight, the gray gelding was the best horse in the stable, and he could just hear what his dad would say when he found out.

He might just as well get it over with; he only hoped that Fraser wasn't around to hear his father chew his ass off.

On his way to the jail, Jeff saw Sam and the James brothers shooting marbles. Mmm, those kids never missed a thing.

"You kids see who rode off on Bullet?"

Sam had her nose practically touching the ground, lining up her shot. "Yep." She took the shot, and the marble rolled into the circle they had traced in the dirt.

"So who was it?"

"The deputy," Bowie said.

"He's got a lot of nerve, taking a horse without asking."

"How's he s'posed to ask if you ain't there?" Sam said. "If you'd spend less time at the Alhambra with Lucy Long-Lashes, maybe you wouldn't have a problem."

"And if you'd keep your big nose out of my business, maybe I wouldn't have that problem, either."

"I ain't got a big nose," Sam yelled.

"How can you tell under all those freckles?"

Jeff strode away. Smart-mouthed brat. It was no wonder Cassie was her idol.

Sam stole a look at Jeff as he walked away. She'd seen him coming out of the Alhambra and knew he'd been with that Lucy Cain again, drinking and sidling up to her like a lovesick cow. There was no accounting for men's tastes. Couldn't he see she was turning him into a drunk? No. All he saw was her big bosom and curly blond hair. Men sure were dumb.

"What are you waiting for, Sam? It's your turn," Bowie said.

"Hold your horses," she grumbled and lined up her shot.

"Mornin'," Jethro said when Jeff entered. "Missed you at breakfast."

"Dad, Fraser rode out of here on Bullet. He's got no right to take one of our horses without paying."

"I said he could. Didn't he tell you that?"

Jeff lowered his eyes. He couldn't look his father in the eyes and lie to him.

"Or weren't you there?" Jethro asked.

"Not exactly."

"Left the livery open again, didn't you?"

"I'm sorry. I got occupied with something and forgot to lock it up."

Jethro snorted. "One of the whores at the Alhambra, no doubt. I can't even depend on you to do the simple task of lockin' up the livery at night. It's no wonder I lose my patience with you."

"I'm sorry, Dad," Jeff said.

"Not as much as I am."

"Hey, Sheriff," Pike yelled from the lockup. "I could use a drink of water."

"I'll get it for him," Jeff said.

"Just be careful," Jethro warned. "You can't trust any of them."

Grabbing the water bucket and ladle, Jeff went into the lockup. Pike and Keeler were waiting at the bars of their cell.

"I want a drink, too," Keeler said.

"Get back 'til I'm through with your friend here."

Grumbling, Keeler moved away, and Jeff scooped out a ladle of water. As he started to hand it through the bars to Pike, the outlaw grabbed his wrist and yanked him forward, slamming Jeff's forehead into the metal bars. Jeff dropped the bucket and tried to reach for his gun, but Pike wrapped his other arm around Jeff's neck and flattened him against the cell door. Keeler hurried over, reached through the bars, and pulled Jeff's pistol out of the holster.

Still keeping a firm hold around Jeff's neck, Pike

took the pistol from Keeler and pressed it into Jeff's stomach.

"Now, you call your daddy in here with the key to this cell, boy, 'cause it takes a long time dyin' when you're gut shot."

"What's goin' on here?" Jethro said as he appeared in the doorway.

"Drop the gunbelt and unlock this door, or your boy's gonna be suckin' air through a hole in his gut."

"No call to harm the boy, Pike," Jethro said. He loosened the belt, and it dropped to the floor.

"Kick it over to the other cell," Pike ordered. Jethro did as told, and Colby reached the gun through the bars.

"You boys know you can't get far before a posse or the army catches up with you," Jethro said.

Pike snorted, then his face twisted into a snarl. "No more stallin', Sheriff. Get these cells open."

Jethro complied; once freed, the outlaws cuffed Jethro's hands behind his back and locked him in a cell. After locating their boots and gunbelts, Pike looked out the window.

"There's a couple horses hitched to the post across the street. We need two more. Keeler, you go to the livery with the kid here and saddle up a couple horses. Benson, you and Colby load them rifles and bring all the ammo you can find," he ordered as he started to go through the desk drawers. He found the moneybox and stuffed the cash into his pocket. "Remember," he snarled at Jeff, "we've got your daddy here. Any wrong move from you will get him shot. You got it?"

"I understand," Jeff said.

The few people going about their business paid little attention to Jeff and Keeler as they walked to the livery. However, Sam and the two boys were still shooting marbles when they passed by.

Sam looked up suspiciously. "Hey, Jeff," she called out. "Ain't—"

"Don't bother me, Samantha, I'm busy," Jeff said sharply, cutting off her question. He never called her by her proper name and could only hope she had noticed. The kid had a quick mind.

"You can move faster than that," Keeler ordered when Jeff tried stalling as he saddled the horses. By the time he and Keeler left the livery a few minutes later, the three kids had disappeared.

They returned to the jail. "Lock him up," Pike ordered, indicating Jeff with a wave of the hand. "Too bad he ain't that deputy. I've still got a score to settle with him for killing my brother."

"This'll get you hung for sure," Jethro warned as they cuffed Jeff and shoved him into the other cell.

"Reckon I've got nothin' to lose then, old man." With a malevolent smirk, he pulled the trigger.

"Dad!" Jeff cried out in horror when his father pitched forward and fell to the floor.

"Pike, there's some armed men heading this way. Let's get the hell out of here," Keeler snarled.

As Pike ran out he fired a couple of quick shots at Jeff but missed. The trigger clicked on an empty chamber and he tossed the empty gun away in disgust.

Chapter 11

When Colt rode up to the Lazy B ranch house, he saw Cassie on top of the barn, repairing the roof. She wasn't overjoyed to see him.

"Cassie, what are you doing up there?"

She gave the nail she'd been pounding several additional whacks. "It rained last night, Deputy, and the roof leaked."

"I meant why are you doing it? Don't you have a ranch hand to do that kind of work?"

"Jeff, Cathy, and I are the ranch hands. We let the crew go and moved into town when outlaws ran off our herd. We've been slowly rounding up strays and collecting a herd again. What do you want, Colt?"

"I understand you won't be returning to town for awhile. Did you really want me to leave without saying good-bye?"

"Good-bye. It has been a pleasure to know you, and if you ever come through again on your way back to Virginia, I hope you'll drop in and say hello. Now, I'm sorry, but I have work to do." She returned to pounding nails.

"You're not fooling me," he yelled. "You ran away because you were afraid to trust yourself."

Cassie halted. "You know, Colt, your swelled head is unbelievable. I'm not running away from anything or anyone, especially you. I know what you want from me, and I've been telling you as politely as I can that you're wasting your time. *It's not going to happen, Deputy Fraser.* So give it up!"

She tossed down the hammer and pouch of nails, then began to walk over to the ladder. The boot heel on her right foot slipped out from under her, and she slid down the sloped roof with a shriek. A protruding nail at the roof edge snagged the back of her belt, and she dangled from the tenuous snare.

"Stay still and don't move or that nail might pull out," Colt called.

"Well, what should I do? Even if I could reach behind me and unhook myself, I'd fall."

He moved the ladder directly under her and climbed up.

"I'll get your feet on the top rung, then you can scoot yourself back a little to dislodge yourself. I'll be right here holding your legs."

"The ladder won't hold both of us."

"Sure it will. Okay, here's the top rung. Now scoot back!"

With Colt supporting her, Cassie tried to free herself from the nail. As she moved up and down to unsnag herself, her lower body rubbed repeatedly against his, and Colt felt himself grow hard.

He gritted his teeth. "Tell me, Miss Braden, do you always have these mishaps, or are you doing it to attract my attention?"

"You flatter yourself, Deputy Fraser."

Cassie slid free into his arms, and there was a horrific crack as the rung splintered from their full weights. They dropped into the pile of hay below, Cassie on her back, with Colt on top of her. Her cheeks reddened under the intensity of his stare.

"Well, here we are, smack dab on the middle of a haystack. Do you believe in fate, Miz Braden?" He ran a finger gently down her cheek, then kissed her.

Gentle at first, his mouth quickly became demanding. Cassie's pulse leaped, and as his hand ran up her side to cup her breast, she arched beneath him, yearning for more. His thumb brushed her nipple and she whimpered, wanting flesh to flesh. She wanted to rip her clothes off, to rip his clothes off, to . . . In panic, she shoved him off her.

They lay there silently for a moment.

"Whew. That was a close call," she said.

"I wish it had been even closer," Colt said with a sexy grin.

His dark-eyed gaze was riveted on the parted moistness of her mouth, and he began to trace her lips with his thumb. "You know I want you, Cassie. I've wanted you from the first moment I saw you on that stagecoach." Pulling her closer, he murmured in her ear, "And I know you want me, too."

"I admit I find you attractive and you're fun to be with, Colt, but it's just not going to happen."

"Why not? Why are you fighting it?"

"Because I'm not ready for what you want—even if I *weren't* engaged."

He slid his hands slowly down the slim lines of her back, and she knew he could feel her quivering response.

"Cassie, you're ready," he whispered. "Every inch of you is ready."

She had to keep a firm grip on herself.

"Are you so shallow, Colt, that the only thing you want from a woman is her body? You may win the skirmish, but you'll lose the war because it's a temporary victory. You'll move on to fight the same battle again and again with other women. If anyone's running, it's you. You're afraid to fall in love and settle down."

When his hands slipped away and he drew back, Cassie knew she had won. But there was no satisfaction in the victory.

"I admit I'm not ready to settle down right now, but it's just human nature to want to mate."

"That may be your philosophy, Colt, but not mine. I could never 'mate,' as you put it, without being in love. It would be against the moral concepts I've lived by my whole life."

"Sounds more like romantic concepts, Cassie. Believe me, one of these days you'll find out you can't keep denying these urges. They're normal and healthy."

The feelings he stirred in her might be healthy, but they were anything but normal for her.

She turned away from him, though it was hard to deny the urge to feel his hands on her again. She and Ted had never gone beyond kissing and caressing.

Maybe because he'd never stirred the physical excitement in her that Colt did.

Cassie stiffened when he grasped her by the shoulders. She leaned away in an effort to escape him, but he slid his hands down her arms and trapped them at her sides. Shuddering when he pulled her against him, with a remorseful sigh she allowed herself to lean back against his warm and muscular strength. It felt so good. His mouth became a husky seduction at her ear.

"Cassie, just moments ago your body responded to my touch. I felt it and so did you. There's nothing moral about denying a God-given gratification when no one will be hurt by it."

"Ted would be hurt by it."

He turned her to face him. "He may never come back. After all this time, it's unlikely that he will. Could you be using him as a shield to avoid facing these feelings, Cassie?"

She stared at him, wide-eyed, and he lowered his head. "One last kiss."

Her lips parted beneath the warm pressure of his, and a delicious sensation swirled in the pit of her stomach.

Shocked by the thrill of her reaction, she fought to retain hold of her senses when the kiss deepened. As passion swelled through her, she realized how much she wanted Colt. Perhaps the need to be loved *was* an overpowering urge in everyone.

For the past five years she had yearned for such a moment, and now that it was here, the right or wrong of it was no longer a consideration. The need for it was.

Slipping her arms around his neck, she moved closer into his embrace. The sensuous slide of his tongue past her lips elicited a throaty moan, sweeping away any remaining resistance.

She had no conscious awareness of when he opened her shirt and pushed the straps of her camisole off her shoulders, or when he lowered her to the floor. Awareness was the exciting feel of his body stretched out on hers. The exquisite ecstacy of his tongue laving her nipples to hardened peaks, the heated moisture of his mouth enclosing them, his palms caressing them—and the core of her womanhood throbbing for the same attention.

She was shocked out of the rapture when he stopped abruptly and pulled her to her feet.

"Someone's riding in fast." Seeing she was too stunned to react, Colt went outside to intercept the arrival.

The rider was Harry Shannon, the waiter from the restaurant. "What's wrong, Harry?"

"Glad I found you, Deputy," he cried, his eyes wild with near panic. "Sheriff's been shot. Where's Cassie?"

Having swiftly rebuttoned her shirt, Cassie appeared at the door. "Harry! What are you doing out here?"

"Them bank robbers broke out of jail and shot your pa, Cassie. He's in bad shape. You best hurry."

"Oh, dear God!" she cried.

Colt had already headed for the barn. "I'll saddle your horse!"

* * *

Cathy was sitting at her father's bedside when Cassie and Colt reached the house. She shot to her feet, and the two sisters rushed to embrace each other.

"Is Dad—"

"He's still alive," Cathy said. "The next few hours are critical. Dr. Williams said if he makes it through the night, it'll be a good sign he might pull through."

"Where is he wounded?" Colt asked.

"He was shot in the back. The bullet's lodged in the lung. Dr. Williams said we'll need a more skillful surgeon than he is to remove it and he wired an associate in Santa Fe. Needless to say, Dad's lost a lot of blood."

Cassie walked over to the bed and stared down at her father. "He looks so peaceful." She leaned down and pressed a kiss to his cheek. "One would never know he's fighting to—" She swallowed hard, unable to continue.

Her heartache was so visible that Colt moved to take her in his arms to comfort her. He halted when Cathy slipped an arm around Cassie's shoulder instead. Hand in hand, the two sisters gazed down at their father.

"Do you think he's in pain?" Cassie asked.

"He shouldn't be. He's been drugged pretty heavily to keep him still. Dr. Williams gave him an antipyretic along with some laudanum to fight the fever and pain."

"Cathy, do you have any idea how they escaped?" Colt asked.

"A little. Jeff was at the jail when it happened. He

said one of them asked for water, and the other man in the cell was able to grab his gun." She glanced at him sorrowfully. "Colt, he was shot in cold blood. Dad's hands were cuffed behind his back when Pike shot him."

Ridden with guilt, Colt left the room. He was the deputy. As long as dangerous outlaws had been incarcerated, he should have remained in town to back up Jethro. Instead, he'd been trying to seduce the sheriff's daughter while the poor man had been shot down.

A short time later, Cathy left the bedroom and came over to him. "I'm about to have a cup of coffee. Would you care for one?"

Colt shook his head. "No, thank you."

She put a hand on his arm. "Colt," she said gently, "you mustn't blame yourself."

Her eyes were red from weeping. Despite her own grief, she still was sensitive to his feelings.

"I should have stayed in town, Cathy."

"It wouldn't have changed what happened. I know you were on duty all night. Had you stayed in town, you most likely would have been asleep in your room when it happened."

"I can't just stand here and do nothing. Who's the best tracker in town?"

"Bob Callum. Jeff and a few other men have already ridden out with him to try and pick up the trail."

"Dammit! I should be with them."

"There's nothing you can do now until the men get

back. Nothing any of us can do except pray. Are you sure you don't want a cup of coffee? I think we could all use one."

There was a serenity about Cathy that generated a sense of hope and belief in the Almighty. Colt squeezed her hand. "I think you're right, Miz Cathy. I will have that cup of coffee, after all."

Chapter 12

The exhausted posse returned late that night. They had found no sign of the outlaws. Cathy insisted that Jeff sit down and put some food in his stomach; as soon as the women went back to their father's bedside, Colt sat down at the table. He couldn't help feeling sorry for Jeff, who was stricken with guilt.

"Think you're ready to tell me what happened, Jeff?"

"It was all my fault. Dad warned me to be careful, but I wasn't careful enough. Pike asked for a drink, so I took it in to him. When I was handing it to him, he grabbed my hand, slammed my head against the bars, and got a chokehold around my neck. Keeler was able to reach my gun." He buried his head in his hands. "Pike stuck it in my stomach and threatened to shoot me when Dad came in to help out. Dad did what they asked and gave up." Jeff cried out in anguish, "He should have shot the bastard then. I'm not worth dying for."

"Jeff, any father would have done what he did to save his son. And don't count him out yet. Your dad's tougher than you think."

"I've been a disappointment to him my whole life," Jeff said bitterly. "A stranger like you can ride into town and he can see you as the son he wished he had. Even my own sister is more of a son to him than I am. Cassie can ride and rope better and shoot straighter than I do. The gun I wore on my hip was a big show—the same gun that was used to put a bullet in my own dad."

"Why did they shoot him, Jeff?"

"Because they're vicious, rotten killers, that's why. Dad was helpless. His hands were cuffed behind him and he was locked in a cell. And the bastard still shot him."

"Which one of them did it?"

"Pike. He took a shot at me, too. Some day, some way, I'll get even for what he did to Dad."

"How did they get away?"

"Stole a couple horses from in front of the grain store and two more from the livery. Sam and the James boys apparently guessed what was happening and ran for help."

"Those kids don't miss a thing."

"Yeah, but it was too late to do Dad any good."

"How old are you, Jeff?"

"Come December, I'll be nineteen." He shoved back his chair and went into the bedroom and joined his sisters.

So Jeff was only an eighteen-year-old kid strutting around with a pistol strapped on his hip. Colt had seen boys as young or younger die during the war. His own nephew was only sixteen when he was killed in battle.

But looking back at his own life, Colt realized he

hadn't been much more mature at eighteen than Jeff was. He'd been obsessed with becoming a straight shot and quick draw. His dedication to becoming a lawman—and the influence of parents and older brothers—had probably kept him from becoming reckless with that ability. The ravages of war also matured a young man quickly.

Cassie came into the kitchen and sat down. "Any change?" Colt asked.

"No. At least his fever's not getting any worse. That's a good sign, isn't it?"

He reached over and squeezed her hand. "That's a real good sign, honey."

She offered a weak smile. "You and Dad are the only two men who have ever called me honey," she said. For a moment the sadness in her eyes deepened into tenderness. "Dad always said he couldn't tell Cathy or me apart when we were babies, so he called us both honey to keep from hurting our feelings. He still does."

She looked up. "You should be trying to get some sleep. You'll have to ride out early with a posse in the morning," she said, then got up and walked away.

Colt gathered the cups, washed them out, and put a fresh pot of coffee on the stove to brew. It was going to be a long night, and that coffeepot would see a lot of action.

Colt woke up with a start. He'd dozed off after the doctor had left at midnight, and he had no idea how long he'd been asleep. A dimly lit oil lamp showed Cathy asleep in a nearby chair and Jeff stretched out on the couch; all three of Jethro's children had maintained a vigil throughout the night near or in their father's room.

Colt went over to the doorway of Jethro's room. Cassie was kneeling at her father's bedside, holding his hand and speaking to the unconscious man. He knew he should leave during this private moment, but he remained transfixed as he listened.

"You can't leave us now, Dad," she whispered. "We would be lost without you. We still have so much growing up to do. Especially Jeff and me.

"We don't tell you often enough how much we love you, and we should. But you know we do, don't you? The three of us are all so different, but the one thing we have in common is our love for you. I know you don't believe this, but I think Jeff loves you even more than Cathy and I do, if that's humanly possible. And I know, despite all your scolding, you feel the same towards him. Oh, you both are so stubborn—if only you would admit what's in your hearts."

She pressed a kiss to his hand. "It's been so long that it's hard to remember everything about Mom, but I do remember her gentleness and kind eyes. Cathy has that same gentleness and kindness. And I remember the love in your eyes when you looked at Mom. I see it often now when you look at Cathy. The love and pride you feel for her because she's so like Mom. I know you miss Mom, Dad. I know how much you want to be with her again, but we need you.

"I know I'm as much of a disappointment to you as Jeff is—I'm headstrong and reckless. But deep down, I wish I could be more like Mom and Cathy. I wish I could have their gentle ways, and be the sweet reminder of Mom to you that Cathy is. But I most likely never will be, and I'm sorry. Not only because I've disappointed you, but because my actions have unintentionally harmed Jeff."

Her eyes glistened with tears. "Do you see, Dad? You've got to let Jeff and me make it up to you. You can't diminish Cathy's hope and faith. We all still need you so much and can't let you go."

Tears streaked the cheek she pressed against his still hand. "We can't let you go," she repeated in anguish.

Colt turned away and went outside, feeling like an interloper. He didn't want to know their secrets; he had no right to invade their privacy in their crisis. Cassie and Jeff weren't the only ones wrestling with guilt. Not only had he failed Jethro but he had also tried to seduce Cassie. He sure was one hell of a deputy.

He had felt so good about heading west; now he was beginning to have doubts. He'd never thought about the emotional entanglements of being a lawman, with people he cared about being killed or wounded.

He knew he had the courage to face down an outlaw, but maybe this job took a lot more than a quick draw and steady aim. Maybe he needed the courage to face the good people affected by his actions, too.

Maybe he just wasn't cut out to be a lawman.

The tears dried on Cassie's cheeks as she rested her head on her father's hand, fighting a losing bat-

tle against the drowsiness that threatened to overcome her.

Her eyelids flickered several times when she felt a
slight twitching against her cheek. In a haze of
lethargy she closed her eyes, then felt it again.

Thinking it was an insect, she raised her head and
stared transfixed at the hand on the counterpane.
When several of the fingers twitched, she quickly
swung her gaze to her father's face. His eyes were open,
and he was watching her.

"Dad!" she cried as tears of joy slid down her cheeks.

"Why the tears, honey?" Jethro asked. "Last time I
saw you cry wuz when we buried your mom. Hope you
ain't thinkin' I'm dyin' or some such nonsense."

Unable to contain her excitement, she called out at the
top of her voice, "Cathy, Jeff, come here! Hurry, it's Dad."

Cathy and Jeff raced into the room, and she greeted
them with laughter and tears.

"Dad's conscious. He's made it through the night."

Joyously the three hugged and kissed each other, unable to sustain their joy.

Seeing Colt in the doorway, Cassie went over and
hugged him. "Isn't it wonderful news, Colt?"

"You bet, honey," he said.

"Dr. Williams said if Dad survived the first twelve
hours and regained consciousness, he'd make it." She
trembled with excitement. "He will, won't he, Colt?"

Colt pulled her close in another hug. "Sure he will."

Sighing, Cassie remained in his arms and leaned her
head against his chest. "This has to be the happiest day
of my life."

He kissed the top of her head and tightened his arms around her. She stood in the circle of his arms, basking in the contentment of the moment.

Cathy came over to them. "Dad fell back to sleep."

Cassic's breath caught in her throat. "Are you sure he's just sleeping?"

"Yes. So let's all get out of here and let him sleep. Come on, Jeff, you, too." She herded them out like a mother duck with her ducklings.

"Since I can't do any good around here, I'm going to my room and freshen up," Colt said. "Jeff, I'll be taking a posse out at six o'clock. Will you be riding with us?"

Jeff nodded. "Of course."

Colt went outside, paused on the porch, and took a deep breath. Glancing up at the sky, he saw that the stars had begun to fade and the first streaks of a rising sun had begun to creep across the horizon. He thought of how his mother had often told them that the sunrise was God's symbolic covenant with the world He had created—the promise of a new day, of new hope.

He'd always been told that everything happens for a reason, so why had fate brought him to Arena Roja? What was the purpose for his path to cross this family's?

"Well, one thing's for sure, Coltran Hunter Fraser," he murmured to himself. "Considering Jethro's condition, you've got about as much chance of climbing on that stagecoach this week as a snowball has in Hell."

Chapter 13

After shaving and changing his clothing, Colt went down to the jailhouse. A posse of a dozen men was waiting, and a small crowd had assembled. Of course the three sprouts were among them. Jeff handed Colt a rifle and the reins of a saddled horse.

"Men, I appreciate your volunteering," Colt said. "Callum, I understand you're the best tracker among us, so we'll follow you."

He was about to mount up and wasn't pleased when Cassie joined them astride her black stallion, Midnight.

"Cassie, may I speak to you for a moment?" he said quietly. She dismounted, and he led her a short distance away from the others, where they would not be overheard.

"Cassie, I know you're anxious to help find the gang that shot your father, but I prefer you stay here."

"I want to help, Colt."

"These outlaws are cold-blooded killers who wouldn't hesitate to shoot a woman. If we meet up with them, none of us will have time to take care of you."

"I can take care of myself. And many of these men

have wives and children. You aren't asking them to stay behind because of the danger; why is it different because I'm a woman? I can ride and shoot as well as any among them. If you don't believe me, ask any one of them."

"I don't doubt that, Cassie, but I still think it would be wiser if you stay here. Your father's still not out of danger, and the doctor who's going to operate on him should be arriving on the incoming stage. Even though the good ladies of the town will be a comfort to Cathy, don't you think she could use your moral support more than we need your help in running down those outlaws?"

Cassie paled. "You're right. How could I have been so thoughtless?" She glanced up at him with a game smile. "Be careful, Colt."

He wanted to hug her, but there were too many eyes fixed on them. "You and Cathy hang in there, honey. Jethro's going to pull through this."

As he went back to his horse, he stopped to give the sprouts a warning. "You three stay out of trouble today. There's enough problems as it is."

"Why are you picking on us?" Sam said. "We ain't done nothing."

"Make sure you continue doing just that," Colt replied.

Bowie looked perplexed. "Don't make sense. How can we continue doing what we ain't doing to begin with?"

Colt shook his head and swung into the saddle. "Time to mount up. We're wasting daylight."

As the posse rode away, the crowd began to disperse until only Cassie and the children remained.

Sam came over to her. "The deputy had no call to make you stay behind, Cassie. You're the best shot among them."

"No, he's right, Sam. My dad's still in danger and I can be of more use here." Cassie smiled tenderly. "He kind of grows on a person, doesn't he?"

Sam glanced askance at her. "So do warts."

"Sam, what did Cassie mean?" Bowie asked as Cassie left them. "Is she mad at the deputy, or ain't she?"

"Trouble with you, Bowie James, is that you just don't understand women," Sam declared imperiously. She pivoted and headed back to the hotel.

"Come on, Petey. Let's go," Bowie said, taking his brother's hand.

"Bowie, is Cassie mad at us?"

"No."

"Is Sam?"

"No. You just don't understand women, Petey," Bowie said. "They're very complicated."

By midday they'd still had no luck in finding any trace of the outlaws. Pike and his gang were probably long gone by now. Colt spied the dust of the approaching stagecoach from Santa Fe—the same coach he had planned to climb on tomorrow on its return trip to Santa Fe.

The posse rested their horses as they waited for the stage to approach, then stopped it. Colt recognized the driver from a week ago.

"Gus, have you seen any sign of four riders? They're the same ones who robbed the stage last week."

Gus shook his head. "They the ones who shot Jethro Braden?"

"Yeah."

"They're probably in Santa Fe by now. How's the sheriff doing?"

"He was still alive when we left this morning."

"Doc Hubbard's one of my passengers. Said he was heading to Arena Roja to take a bullet out of ole Jethro. Hope he can cut through that old bird's tough skin." The fondness in the driver's voice belied the light remark.

"Well, we won't keep you any longer. See you in town."

By sunset, the posse decided that the outlaws were long gone, and the search was called off.

Returning to town, Colt wired the sheriff in Santa Fe the names of the four men and warned him to be on the lookout for them, then he went over to the Bradens' home.

Cathy opened the door when Colt knocked. Her broad smile told him all he had to know.

"The operation was successful," Colt said, grinning.

"Oh, yes. Isn't it wonderful, Colt?"

"How's he doing?"

"He's sleeping. Dr. Hubbard removed the bullet, and although Dad's weak, his body signs are encouraging, and the doctor said barring infection or any other setback, Dad should pull through with flying colors."

"Well, he's got a couple of good nurses. As long as the sheriff's sleeping, I'm going back to my room and get rid of this trail dust. I'll stop by later this evening."

After washing up and changing his shirt, Colt ate dinner at the hotel, then returned to the Braden house. Cathy informed him that her father was resting comfortably but still sleeping.

"I'll stop by in the morning and see how he's doing," Colt replied. "Where's Cassie?"

"Now that the worst is over, she went to the livery to work off some of her tension. Currying Midnight soothes her."

"Cassie's the only woman I know who would find working around a high-strung stallion relaxing. How do you choose to relax, Cathy?"

"I like to sit quietly and embroider or read."

"I rest my case. See you in the morning."

Since the livery was on the way to the hotel, Colt stopped and peeked in the door. Midnight was tied to a post, and Cassie was bent over, shoeing one of the horse's hind legs.

For a couple of seconds he thought she was talking to him, then realized she was speaking to the horse.

"So that's the whole story, Midnight. It looks like Dad's going to pull through this, and should be up and around in no time. But you know how stubborn he is. What are we going to do with him? The old darling just won't admit he's getting too old for the job. And one of these days . . ." She sighed deeply. "He might not be as lucky."

Putting aside the hammer, she picked up a rasp and began to file the shoe. "I'm almost through, boy. Just need to smooth down a rough spot on this edge."

Colt remained quiet as he watched, fascinated. Her movements were competent and steady, with the loving tenderness of a mother bathing or feeding a beloved child. There were so many facets to Cassie Braden.

He'd never met a woman like her before, and the danger of remaining in Arena Roja now had nothing to do with the Pike gang: She'd begun to mean too much to him. Soon it would be difficult to ride away from her. What had begun as simple physical desire was developing into deeper feelings, and dammit, he wasn't ready for it! It plain didn't fit into his plans.

"There. All through." She stood up and pressed her cheek against the big stallion's neck. "You were an angel as always, sweetheart."

That's when she saw Colt standing in the doorway. "Oh, it's you."

"Don't you have a blacksmith in town?"

"Of course."

"Why don't you have him shoe the horse for you?"

Cassie wondered how long he'd been standing there. Suddenly feeling self-conscious, she brushed back some hair that clung to her cheek and wondered how she must look.

Funny how that had never mattered to her before. Why should it now?

"I've been shoeing Midnight since he was a colt."

She untied the stallion and led him back to his stall. "Jeff was here a short time ago. He said you didn't have any luck today."

"No. It was good to hear your dad's operation went well."

"It certainly was."

She felt uncomfortable under his steady stare. She felt messy, and she didn't know what to do with her hands. And she didn't want to look him in the eyes.

"What's wrong, Cassie?" He came over to her, and his nearness encompassed her as if he were touching her. She quickly turned away and began to pitch hay into Midnight's stall.

"Are you still angry about this morning?"

This morning? What was he talking about?

"I was concerned about your welfare, Cassie, that's why I didn't want you to come with us."

"Oh, that!" She'd already forgotten about the posse. "No, it's just as well I didn't go with you. I'm just tired, Colt. The last couple days have been hard and I've barely had any sleep."

"I understand."

He came over and she drew a deep breath when he put his arms around her. His touch was so comforting.

Sometimes there was little satisfaction in being a strong-willed, independent female. Sometimes it would feel so nice just to lean back into the strength of a man's arms, the comfort of his touch. Someone to take care of her, to watch over her.

And why did she wish that man would always be Colt Fraser? Why had he begun to fill her thoughts more than Ted? Could her growing desire for him diminish the memory of the man she once believed she loved?

Once believed she loved! Cassie was shocked by her traitorous thoughts.

The growing attraction she'd felt for Colt had forced her to weigh her true feelings. It wasn't love that kept her faithful to Ted—it was loyalty. And if everyone was right about his continued absence, how long could she remain loyal to a dead man?

Common sense told her that even if she succumbed to Colt's seduction, it wouldn't keep him from riding away as soon as he could. He made no attempt to pretend otherwise. Was she willing to settle for just that?

It would be so wrong. But, dear God, it would feel so right.

She felt bereft when his hands slipped from her shoulders and turned her to face him. "Lock up here and go home, honey. Take a hot bath, and get some sleep." He leaned over and kissed her lightly, his lips warm and gentle, and she drank in the comforting sweetness of the kiss.

The brief contact was tantalizing, and she was disappointed that he'd pulled away. *Foolish girl!*

Cassie forced a game smile. "I'll lock up here as soon as I water the horses."

"I'll help you."

Together they filled the horse buckets and tossed

some straw into the stalls. When they finished, Cassie locked up the livery.

"Thanks for your help," she said.

"I'll walk you home."

Nightfall and a cooling breeze had transformed the hot day into a a pleasant evening. They strolled along in silence, enjoying the change. Too soon, they reached the house.

Cassie turned to him. "Well, I guess this is good-bye again."

"It's not so final, Cassie. It's just good night."

"I thought you were leaving tomorrow."

"I can hardly leave with Jethro flat on his back and no deputy to take over."

"It's not your problem, Colt. You fulfilled your promise to Dad."

"What do you think I am? I couldn't walk out on him now."

As pleased as she was to hear he was remaining, she felt an acute sense of wounded pride. "But you could have walked out on me."

"I don't understand what you mean."

"Yesterday morning at the ranch, we almost . . . that is, if Harry hadn't ridden up when he did, we would have . . ." She drew a deep breath that pained her chest. "You would have climbed on that stage tomorrow morning with no regrets."

"You're wrong, Cass. It would have been one of the biggest regrets in my life. But we've made very different plans for our futures, and I don't think either of us is ready to abandon them. So I would have had plenty of regrets climbing on that stage tomorrow, the greatest being that most likely I'd never see you again."

He gently caressed her cheek. "I'd never again look into those beautiful blue eyes of yours, bright with humor or darkened with emotion; never hear the laughter in your voice when you're happy or see your infectious smile. I'd regret never tasting again the sweetness of your lips, knowing the warmth of your arms.

"In this past week, you've touched an emotion in me I didn't think was vulnerable, and I believe the same is true about you. I'd also regret that we *didn't* make love, Cass. And you should, too."

He cupped her cheeks between his hands. "Ah, Cass," he said tenderly, "making love is never cause for shame or guilt. Had we made love, I would never have looked back on it with regret. It would have been a very precious memory.

"Think with your heart, Cass. If Ted McBride never returns, won't you regret that he hadn't made love to you before he left you?"

He lowered his head and pressed a kiss to her forehead. "Now get some sleep. Good night."

Long into the night Cassie lay awake, confused and struggling with Colt's words, and the mixed emotions she felt for him.

Chapter 14

Early the following morning, Colt watched the Santa Fe–bound stagecoach pull out of Arena Roja.

When only dust clouds remained to mark its passage, he turned with a resigned sigh to walk away and saw that the three sprouts were watching him.

"Thought you were leaving today," Sam said.

"And you came to say good-bye? I'm overwhelmed with emotion."

"Somebody had to," Sam said quickly. "Figure we owed you that much."

"Well, Belle, you can't be more sorry than I am. Unfortunately, right now your town needs a lawman."

"Ain't that what you've always wanted to be? Now you've got the chance."

He cocked his head reflectively. "Maybe you're right."

That was the reason he had accepted the job. Without the sheriff to lean on, this would be the true test of whether or not he had the right stuff to stick it out.

"Looks like I'll be around for a while. I can't very well leave with the sheriff flat on his back."

"Why not?" Bowie asked.

"Yeah, why not?" Petey echoed.

"It would be running out on a responsibility."

"Town's not your responsibility," Sam said.

"Well then, let's just call it conscience, Belle. You kids do me a favor and stay out of trouble today."

"Sam, what does conscience mean?" Bowie asked when Colt left and headed for the Braden house.

"Ain't sure. Let's go to the schoolroom and look it up in the dictionary."

"How can we look it up if we don't know how to spell it?" Bowie asked.

Sam frowned with annoyance. "I'll figure out something."

The three children raced down the street. Cassie was at her desk and glanced up when they entered.

"Good morning, darlings. School doesn't begin for another two hours."

"We know that, Cassie," Sam said. "We came to look up a word in the dictionary."

"That's wonderful that you're eager to improve your minds. No wonder this little guy's so smart." She tousled Petey's hair and he giggled in response.

Always the pessimist, Bowie said, "Yeah, but how can we look up a word 'til we know how to spell it?"

Cassie couldn't help smiling. "That can be a problem. Maybe I can help. What's the word?"

"Conscience," Sam replied.

That took her by surprise, since she'd been struggling with her own conscience over her feelings for Colt.

"Conscience? My goodness, what brought that on?"

"What does it mean?" Sam asked.

"Well, conscience is the moral goodness of one's character." At the sight of their perplexed looks she added, "You could say that a conscience is what gives a person a feeling of obligation to do what is fair or right."

Sam frowned in deep reflection. "Do you think Colt Fraser has a conscience?"

"Why do you ask, Sam?"

"Colt told us his conscience would bother him if he left while the sheriff was flat on his back."

"But it ain't his fault the sheriff is wounded," Bowie said. "Colt only promised to be a deputy for a week."

"Yes, he did. But as a man of conscience, he feels he would be deserting the town when it needed him the most."

Petey grinned up at her. "Hooray! I'm glad he's a man of consheks."

The boy's grin was too adorable to resist. She pulled him into her arms and hugged him. Leaning her cheek against his wheat-colored hair, Cassie murmured, "We all are, sweetheart. We all are."

She had to admit that Colt was a good example for the children to look up to. That was why she struggled so much with her confusing thoughts of him. Integrity was as intrinsic to his nature as his warm chuckle or sense of humor—yet even though he knew she was engaged, Colt wouldn't hesitate to satisfy his sexual desires if she allowed him to do so. The man was an enigma!

As soon as the children departed, Cassie opened the book she'd been reading—or trying to read. Since Colt Fraser had come to town, it was hard to concentrate on anything except him and her sinful lusting for him.

After another five minutes she succeeded in reading only a few more paragraphs and couldn't remember what she had read on the previous page. She slammed the book down. How long was she going to moon over Colt Fraser like a lovesick schoolgirl?

Her trouble was that she'd been too idle. She needed to do something physical to take her mind off her troubles—which meant Colt. If only he'd left town this morning as he'd planned, she would have forgotten him in a couple of weeks.

She shook her head in derision. *Do you really believe that, Cassie Braden?*

She walked over and gazed out the window. Maybe when her dad was well again, she'd talk Cathy into taking the stage to Santa Fe and doing some shopping. Shopping! What was she thinking? She hated to shop!

There was plenty to do on the ranch; that's what she should be doing instead of lolling around town. The trouble with that idea was her bedridden father. She should remain in town to help out at home.

Deciding to go back to the house, she paused in the doorway, when she saw Colt walking up the street. He turned into her house. He always walked tall, darn the man! As annoying as he was, he was about the handsomest man she'd ever seen.

So what now, Cassie? With Colt there, the house is the last place you'd go.

With a desolate sigh, she went out to the well and drew a bucket of water. She'd wash the schoolroom window. *Idle hands make idle thoughts—or something like that.*

"It's good to see you're feeling well enough to sit up in bed, Jethro," Colt said when Cathy left the room and returned to the kitchen.

"I'm beholden to you for stayin' until I'm well enough to get on my feet," Jethro said.

"Another week more or less doesn't make much difference to me. The important thing is that you take it easy and don't worry. I'm not about to walk out on you, Jethro."

"Hell, I figured as much," the sheriff said. "That backbone of yours is used for more than holdin' your head up." He cast a disparaging look at Jeff, who sat slouched in a chair in the corner.

"Is there anything special that has to be done right now?" Colt asked.

"Naw," Jethro said. "Just keep your eyes open, son. I figure Pike's gonna show up again. He said he's got a score to settle with you for killin' his brother, and twice now he's tried to hold up the stage and our bank. He ain't leavin' this territory 'til he gets what he wants."

"Or dies trying," Colt said as he rose to his feet. "Well, I'll get to my duties and you get to resting." On the way out, Colt motioned to Jeff to follow him.

"What do you want?" Jeff asked when they were outside. His eyes flashed with belligerence.

So the boy's hostility had returned. With the events of the past few days Colt had hoped Jeff had put aside his bad feelings toward him.

"Let's saddle up a couple of horses. We're going for a ride."

"It's a waste of time to try and pick up that trail again."

"We're riding out to the Lazy B."

"What for?"

"We've got some business to take care of."

"If it's about the ranch, you best talk to Cassie. She's the rancher in the family."

"I know what I'm doing," Colt said.

The three sprouts were outside the livery when the men led the horses out and mounted up.

"Where are you two going?" Sam asked.

"None of your business, squirt," Jeff snapped.

"You going away and leaving us unprotected?"

"We won't be gone much more than an hour. Take care of the town until we get back, Belle."

"What if them outlaws come back?"

"They'll know better than to tangle with you three again."

The two men galloped away, leaving the children with puzzled looks on their faces.

"What in hell are we going out to the ranch for?" Jeff demanded.

Colt grinned secretly. "There's a nice big barn there."

"Damn you, Colt, you're worse than my dad. Quit treating me like a kid."

"You're right. I'm sorry. You once told me you couldn't hit the broad side of a barn."

"You fixing on shooting up the side of the barn?"

"Could be." Colt goaded his horse and galloped ahead.

Jeff took off his hat and scratched his head. Holy Jumping Jerusalem! Cassie would fill them both full of lead if they put one hole in the side of the barn. He grinned, then whipped the reins of his horse and followed.

With Cassie in town, the Lazy B was deserted, and Jeff watched with curiosity as Colt studied the trees until he found one to his satisfaction.

"All right, that one's perfect," he said, pointing to a dying oak with leafless limbs. He paced off a distance away from it and drew a line in the dirt. "This is where you'll begin."

"Begin what?" Jeff asked.

"Target practice."

"This is a waste of time. Don't you think I've tried doing that?" Jeff said. "I've told you, I can't hit what I aim for."

"Then it's time you learn. Now get on over here and step up to this line."

Grumbling about the waste of time, Jeff did what Colt ordered. "This isn't even fifty feet away from the target."

"And in most cases when you have to use a gun, you're closer than fifty feet, whether it's a bank robbery or shooting a snake. Just be sure that if you point a gun at someone, you're prepared to fire it. It's a mistake to think that person won't try to kill you. It takes three elements to be a successful shot: a good eye, a steady hand, and a decent weapon. Now let's see what you can do. Hit the trunk of that dead oak."

Jeff drew the gun on his hip and fired. The shot whizzed past the oak. He turned to Colt in disgust. "What did I tell you?"

"First off, you're not ready yet to draw and fire. Draw and aim, then fire."

"That's what I did."

"No, you didn't. If you're going to attempt to draw and shoot, you have to cock the gun and adjust for the motion. For now, don't try to do both. Forget a fast draw, Cock the hammer and take careful aim at the tree. Then hold your arm steady. Don't jerk the trigger, just gently squeeze it."

Jeff tried three more shots and still missed the tree.

"Let's see that gun." Colt aimed carefully at the tree and fired. The shot missed its mark.

"Is this the only gun you've ever had?" Colt asked when his next shot hit the target.

"Yes," Jeff replied. "Dad wouldn't let me pack a gun until last year."

"I can tell you some of the problem. It shoots wide to the right. You need to make a slight adjustment when you shoot. Aim about two inches to the left of your target."

Jeff reloaded the pistol and fired off several more shots.

"You're jerking your hand. Hold that hand steady."

After thirty more minutes, an ecstatic Jeff succeeded in hitting the mark more times than missing it.

A short time later, Colt called a halt to the session. "We'll practice again tomorrow morning."

Colt glanced at the young man as they rode back into town. Jeff sat slumped in the saddle, and his previous jubilation had dissolved into silence.

"Something bothering you, Jeff?"

"Considering the bad blood between us since you came to town, I know I ain't got no right to ask a favor of you."

"What's chewing at your craw?"

"It's about today. I'm asking you not to tell anyone about . . . well, that you're teaching me how to shoot."

"I had no intention of telling anyone, Jeff."

Jeff grinned. It was Cassie's grin, and once again Colt was reminded of how much more Cassie resembled Jeff than her twin sister.

"You've got my word on it, pal. Now I want your word that you'll cut down on your drinking. Guns and alcohol are like oil and water—they don't mix."

"It's a deal," Jeff said.

"Are you particularly fond of that gun of yours, Jeff?"

"How could I be? It's the one Pike used to shoot my father."

"Then get yourself a new one, and test its accuracy before buying it."

When Colt appeared at the Braden door that evening to report the day's activities to Jethro, Cathy insisted he join them for dinner. Jeff was in good humor, Cathy was her usual pleasant self, but Cassie barely spoke. She wasn't hostile toward him, but rather seemed uncomfortable around him.

This disturbed Colt. She was clearly unhappy beyond her concern for her father. As soon as they finished dinner, Colt visited with Jethro, while the two women cleaned up the kitchen. By the time Colt left Jethro's room, Cassie had retired to her own for the night.

For the next several days, Colt saw little of Cassie. It was clear she was avoiding him so he respected her feelings and didn't seek her out. Yet in knowing that he was remaining in Arena Roja longer, his desire to make love to her was monopolizing his every thought.

He would have to convince her that their mutual desire for each other would only get greater. But how? Cassie Braden was a strong-willed and determined woman. If she'd only apply that will toward making love, instead of not making love, there'd be no—

"That's it!" he exclaimed. "What if she became the aggressor?"

He'd been trying to break down her resistance, but what if he used a different approach? An *indifferent* one? Would she go for the bait? He was desperate enough to try. The only question was, did he have enough self-control to carry it out?

The next morning, Colt and Jeff repeated what had become their daily routine. They rode out of town early in the morning, practiced for an hour, then returned. Jeff's improvement was remarkable. He was hitting a chosen target now at a distance of a hundred feet. The boy listened carefully and followed advice. Why hadn't Jethro taken more time and patience to instruct him?

A couple more shooting lessons, Colt figured, and he'd be able to tackle Jeff's problem with handling a horse.

Every day, the sprouts checked out their departure each morning and their return later. Whether or not they reported daily to Cassie, Colt didn't know.

And he wasn't about to ask.

Bowie glanced at Sam, as they sat on the steps of the jail. "Boy, this taking care of the town is sure boring," he complained.

"Yeah, boring," Petey agreed.

"What are you thinking about, Sam?" Bowie asked.

"The deputy. I'm thinking we ought to do something nice for him, 'cause he's a man of conscience and is doing something nice for the town."

"Ain't we doing something nice by watching the town for him these past days?"

"That ain't hard; nothing's happening."

"Well, let's give him a gift," Bowie suggested.

"The last time we did that, he didn't like it and got mad at us."

"He liked us giving him a gift; he just didn't like what we gave him," Bowie reasoned.

"Slinky," Petey said.

"How'd I know he didn't like snakes," Sam grumbled.

Bowie thought a moment, then his face lit up with a smile. "Let's buy him something nice."

"We ain't got no money, Bowie." Sam got up and began to pace back and forth.

After another long moment of concentration, Bowie jumped up next to her. "I know. Why don't we just stay out of trouble, like he asked us to?"

"Bowie, that don't make sense," Sam said. "We don't cause no trouble."

The two sat down again. "We gotta think of something nice to do for him," Sam said.

"Yeah, something nice," Petey agreed.

Chapter 15

"Any trouble while we were gone?" Colt asked the sprouts, dismounting when he and Jeff returned.

"No," Sam said.

"Any strangers ride in?"

Sam eyed him with a disgusted glare. "No. And if you expect us to keep doing your job, you can start paying us."

"And in money, not lollipops," Bowie said.

"I like lollipops," Petey spoke up.

"If you kids muck out the stalls I'll give you a quarter," Jeff said.

Arms akimbo, Sam declared, "Sure, and while we do all the dirty and stinky work, I suppose you're gonna head over to the Alhambra and start drinking and cottoning up to that Lucy Long-Lashes." She batted her eyelashes in imitation.

"Maybe so or maybe not. But since you're not my wife, Freckle Face, it's not your problem."

Sam's freckles melded into a solid red blush. "Your wife! When I get old enough to marry, it sure won't be to a toad-ugly, no-account like you, Jeff Braden."

Bowie clutched at his sides laughing. "Sam marry you!"

"Yeah, fat chance," Petey said and joined in his brother's laughter.

Colt couldn't help smiling.

"And another thing, Jeff Braden," Sam declared. "Your shiftless friend, Bob Callum, has been drinking all morning. You best go over and get him out of the Alhambra."

The arrival of the stage interrupted their conversation.

"What Bob Callum does is no concern of yours, Miss Nosey Rosey," Jeff said as he and Colt started to walk up to the stage office.

The driver jumped down from the box and opened the door of the stage. "Thirty minutes rest, folks."

At that moment, Bob Callum staggered out of the Alhambra. Seeing a friend who had been riding shotgun, Callum let out a welcoming yell and fired two shots in the air.

The startled team bolted, pulling the driverless stagecoach behind them with its door flapping and passengers crying for help. People scurried in all directions to get out of its path. Colt leaped on the back of Bullet and rode after it. As he drew even with it he jumped from his horse onto one of the lead horses, and managed to grab the reins and bring the runaways to a halt. The driver ran up to him as Colt climbed off the horse.

The spectators applauded and cheered.

As soon as the commotion died down, Colt headed for the jailhouse. The sprouts followed behind.

He drew back in surprise after he entered. "What the . . ." The floor was freshly scrubbed, Jethro's brass spittoon next to the desk was shiny bright, and the window glistened.

He checked out the cells and saw that they'd been swept clean and scrubbed, as well.

The sprouts were huddled together, giggling with pleasure.

"Do you like it?" Sam asked.

"It's great. Who cleaned it up, Cathy or Cassie?"

"We did," Sam said.

"I shined up the spis'toon," Petey said proudly.

"You did a great job, pal," Colt said, tousling the youngster's hair. "I can't thank you kids enough. I sure wasn't looking forward to having to do it. So what's the charge?"

"There ain't no charge," Sam said. "We did it 'cause we wanted to do something nice for you."

"And stay out of trouble like you asked us to," Bowie added.

Colt felt like a bastard. It was time he set the record straight. "Hey, boys, would you mind leaving Sam and me alone for a moment?"

Petey's mouth curled in a pout. "You gonna yell at her."

"Nothing like that, pal. I swear."

"Okay, but we'll be right outside, Sam, if you need us," Bowie said.

Colt walked over and sat down behind the desk. "Come over here, Sam."

"You gonna hit me?"

"Of course not."

Suspicion gleamed in her eyes when she came over

and stood beside him. He reached out and grasped her hand. Funny, how small it felt in his own.

"Sam, you understand what teasing means, don't you? It's often saying just the opposite of what you're really thinking. I've fallen into the habit of teasing you and the boys, just as I do with Cassie. But sometimes it sounds more serious than I meant it to be, especially when I tease the very people I like the most. Do you understand?"

"No."

"What I'm trying to say is that I don't really think you and the boys are trouble. I like you, so I tease you. The people I really dislike, I don't even talk to. Does that make sense?"

"Guess so." She hung her head. "I reckon I'm a worse teaser than you, 'cause I don't mean what I say to you, either. I don't know what makes me talk so mean."

"Maybe you're afraid to show your real feelings to people, so you act as if you don't like them."

"But why would I do that?"

"Maybe you're afraid of getting hurt again. I understand you suffered a big tragedy when you were only six years old. Honey, losing your father, your three older sisters, and two younger brothers is a lot for one so young to have to bear."

Tears glistened in her eyes. "I reckon God didn't want me."

The tough little hoyden began sobbing her heart out, wrenching Colt's heart, and he reached out and hugged her. Sam buried her head against his chest.

"Sam, where did you get an idea like that?"

"God took them all. Poppa, Jessie, Carrie, Essie, Matt, and Harry. But not me. He didn't want me."

"Sam honey, did you ever think He spared you because He knew your mother needed you to carry on?"

She stepped back, and her tear-filled eyes looked up at him. "Why didn't He just take Mama and me, too?"

"I don't know the answer to that. It's difficult to understand the Lord's motives sometimes, but I believe He's a loving God and has a reason for everything He does."

When her sobs reduced to sniffles, Colt said, "You've got Cassie now. She's like a sister to you, isn't she? And she loves you as much as she does Cathy."

Sam nodded. "And Bowie and Petey are like my brothers."

"So maybe that's why you were spared. He knew you could be a younger sister to Cassie and an older sister to Bowie and Petey. And maybe He knew you were the only one who could do it. Don't ever believe He spared you because He didn't want you, honey. He has a plan for all of us."

Sam managed a game smile. Looking deep into her eyes, Colt saw the little girl she tried so hard to conceal behind a gruff and sassy façade.

"And sooner than you think, honey, you'll grow up to be a beautiful young woman. And the man who loves you will adore every single freckle on that cute nose of yours."

"Not me. I'm gonna be just like Cassie."

"That's just what I said—a beautiful woman."

Her eyes brightened. "Do you think Cassie's beautiful?"

He lowered his head and whispered, "Can you keep a secret?"

Sam nodded. "Cross my heart and hope to die."

"I think she's the most beautiful woman I've ever seen."

"But other men don't think she is, 'cause she wears pants and rides a horse. And she don't act like some of those uppity church women, or as dumb as those women at the Alhambra with their fancy dresses."

"Wearing pants doesn't make her any less a woman."

Sam smiled. "So you really think she's beautiful."

"Everything about her, Sam."

"So when you argue with her—"

"I'm only teasing, because I like to see that fire in her eyes when she's angry."

"And when Jeff tells me I'm ugly—"

"He's only teasing because he likes to make you mad."

She straightened up and, with a final sniff, declared, "Okay, I gotta go to school now. It was nice talking to you, Deputy."

She ran out and joined the two boys, who'd been waiting anxiously for her. Under all that sass and bravado lay the strength and vulnerability that one day would develop into one hell of a woman.

And speaking of a hell of a woman, it was time he sought out Cassie and put his plan into operation.

* * *

As soon as school was over and the other students had left, Sam and the James brothers came up to Cassie's desk.

Leaning over it, Sam whispered, "Cassie, there's something suspicious going on and you ought to know about it."

Cassie figured she had all the trouble she could handle at the moment between Dad and Colt Fraser. She frowned.

"What is it, Sam?"

Sam related Jeff and Colt's early morning trips during the past few days.

"So what do you think?" Sam asked when she finished. "When Colt came to town, they didn't like each other. Now they're thicker than flies on a cow turd."

"Sam, it's not proper for a young lady to use that kind of language."

"My mom always says 'thicker than molasses in January,'" Bowie said proudly.

"Just the same, them two are up to no good."

Cassie was still skeptical. "I doubt that very much, Sam. Jeff is probably just familiarizing Colt with the territory."

"Then why do they head out in the same direction every morning?"

"I don't think it's worth fussing about. Besides, as soon as my father is on his feet, Colt will be leaving Arena Roja."

"Just the same, I think it's very suspicious," Sam declared.

"Yeah, 'speeis,'" Petey agreed.

Cassie smiled as she watched the three march off. She adored them and cherished their friendship, but sometimes they came up with some pretty wild ideas. Colt and Jeff friends! She turned away with a laugh.

However, throughout the day, the thought kept creeping back into her already muddled thoughts about Colt. So at supper that night, rather than come right out and ask Jeff and look like a fool, she decided to be more subtle.

"I've been so busy these past days with Dad, I've barely had time to stick my head out the door except for school. Anything important going on?" she asked.

"Nothing that I know of," he said.

"Is the deputy still searching for the outlaws that shot Dad?"

"Not to my knowledge."

"Is he still lamenting having to remain in Arena Roja until Dad's back on his feet?"

"I'd be complaining if I was in his boots, too." Jeff shoved back his chair and stood up. "Cathy, this was about the tastiest stew you've ever made."

Cathy raised her brows. "Well, thank you, Jeff."

He rarely, if ever, complimented her cooking.

Cassie picked up several plates and carried them to the sink. "They're right," she murmured when she heard Jeff go outside.

"What are you talking about?" Cathy asked, following her with her hands full of dishes.

In a low voice, Cassie replied, "Sam and the James

brothers think Jeff and Colt are acting suspicious. They appear to be friendly toward one another and ride out together every morning."

Cathy shrugged. "Don't you think that Dad getting shot might have altered their relationship?"

"I thought of that, but it wouldn't explain why they ride out and return together every day."

Grinning, Cathy shook her head. "I know just what you're thinking. You aren't really going to, are you?"

Cassie chuckled and winked at her. "You bet I am, sister dear. Tomorrow morning I'm following them."

Buoyed, Cassie began to sing softly as she washed the dishes. Cathy joined in the song as she dried them. Then, giggling like schoolgirls, the two left the kitchen arm in arm.

Bright and early the next morning, Cassie left the house. She waited until the men rode off, then quickly saddled Midnight and followed them, staying far enough behind to avoid being observed.

After a mile she guessed their destination was the Lazy B. What could they be up to there?

As she was concealing Midnight, she heard a gunshot. She rushed to a nearby copse of elm and halted in her tracks when she saw that both men were on their feet and neither appeared concerned. Then she saw Jeff take careful aim at a nearby tree. Colt walked over to him and spoke a few words, then Jeff took aim again. Much to her surprise, he blew off the end of a leafless limb.

Jeff was all smiles when Colt gave him a manly slap on the shoulder.

For several more minutes she continued to watch. Colt would pick a random target and Jeff would shoot at it. More times than not, he hit the mark.

So that was the big mystery. And the way they were joking and laughing with each other, it was clear there was no animosity between them any longer.

Cassie withdrew before they discovered her. For whatever reason, Jeff chose to keep this a secret, so she would respect his desires—although she'd have to tell Cathy.

Why was Colt taking the time to teach Jeff? Soon he'd be gone, so what did it matter to him?

The man and his mixture of good intentions and aggravation were driving her crazy.

Chapter 16

A thunderstorm arrived in the middle of the night. Jagged lightning speared the sky, accompanied by booming crashes of thunder that seemed to rock the buildings. A voracious wind bombarded the windows with a pelting rain and wrenched shutters from their fastenings.

Frightened children awakened by the fury of the storm ran crying into the security of their parents' beds; the Reverend and Mrs. MacKenzie knelt at their bedside in the parsonage and prayed that God would see any poor souls out in the storm safely through the night; Father James went into the chapel of the Catholic mission, lit a candle and prayed that Judgment Day hadn't arrived; and the more pragmatic Doc Williams got out of bed and dressed, for surely as God made green apples, he would be called out in the storm.

Cassie Braden stared out the window and worried about their cattle herd. The storm was sure to scatter them. As soon as it stopped raining, she would ride out to the Lazy B.

Colt Fraser, awakened by the storm, hoped the creaking hotel wouldn't collapse under the force of the gale winds and decided that he couldn't prevent it if it did. He rolled over and went back to sleep.

Water cascaded like waterfalls off the roofs and down the sides of the buildings, gouging deep ruts and potholes into the earth below.

Though the lightning and thunder finally passed over, the torrential rain continued to fall. It continued throughout the following day, and by day's end, many of the shallow streams had overflowed their banks.

When another day dawned and still the rain continued, Cassie was beside herself with worry. Donning a poncho, she went to the livery and saddled two horses. Jeff came in as she was on the verge of departing.

"Where are you going?"

"I'm riding out to the ranch."

"What for?"

"To drive the cattle to higher ground. If the Santa Fe overflows, the cattle will be right in its path."

"Cattle can swim, Cassie."

"Not if they're mired down in mud."

"Did you tell Dad what you're doing?"

"No, he was asleep. You can tell him when he wakes up." She mounted, goaded Midnight to a gallop, and rode off with the other horse tied to the saddle horn.

One more day of rain, and Colt would be ready to start walking to Santa Fe—rain or not. The streets were practically impassable. If you didn't stay on the boardwalk, you'd end up ankle deep in water or with your foot sunk into a muddy pothole. Why hadn't they put some kind of pavement on the roads by now?

When Cathy opened the Bradens' door in answer to his knock, her worried look made him ask what was wrong.

"Jeff just told us that Cassie's gone out to the ranch to drive the herd to higher ground."

"Why'd you let her go, Jeff?" he said.

Jeff snorted. "You know by now that there's no changing Cassie's mind once she's got it set. She already had Midnight saddled up, and she took Bullet along, too. She said Bullet's a better cutting horse when you're driving cattle."

"How long ago did she leave?" Colt asked.

"About three hours."

"And where's the herd?"

"At the north end of the ranch near the river," Jeff replied.

Colt headed for the door. "I'm going to need a horse."

"You figure on following her?"

"Dammit," Jethro grumbled, "that gal ain't got a mite of sense when it comes to mothering that herd."

"Shall I go with Colt?" Jeff asked.

"No," Colt said, "I'd appreciate it if you kept an eye on things in town until I get back."

Jeff stood up and grabbed a poncho. "I'll saddle you a mount, at least."

"If you have to hogtie that gal, son, bring her back here," Jethro said.

"That's probably what I'll have to do, sir."

"Be careful, Colt," Cathy cautioned when Jeff returned with a saddled horse.

"Careful's my middle name, Cathy. Don't worry. And don't let your father get excited. We don't want him to have a relapse."

The sooner Jethro got back on his feet, the sooner he could climb on that stagecoach out of this godforsaken, water-soaked spot.

Despite all the prodding Cassie was doing to keep the cattle moving, their progress was slow. Water had begun to spill over the riverbanks in some sections, and the hundreds of cattle hooves that had trampled the area had turned the ground into a guagmire. If the rain continued throughout the night, by morning the river would certainly reach flood stage.

Even worse, the booms and flashes in the distant sky brought the added fear of another thunderstorm moving in.

There were a couple hundred cattle in the herd, but Cassie had only been able to round up about half of them. The others either had scattered or were stuck in the mud. Until the wind and rain stopped, there wasn't time to round up the scattered ones, but once she got the bulk of the herd to higher ground, she hoped to go back and try to free some of the helpless ones mired in the mud.

The wind was so powerful that she sat hunched in the saddle, leaning her body into it to keep from being blown off her horse.

Between the howling wind, falling rain, and bawling

cattle, she failed to hear the approach of the rider who rode up to her.

"Cassie, what in hell do you think you're doing?"

Suddenly the wind's force didn't seem as mighty, the rain as chilling. She should have guessed he would come. Man of conscience, Southern chivalry, masculine pride, and the dozen other endearing qualities would make it impossible for Colt Fraser to stay away knowing she was out here in the storm.

"Yaw," she shouted at several cattle that had stopped moving. "What does it look like I'm doing, Deputy?"

"Can't this wait until it stops raining?"

"I didn't spend the last couple years rounding up these cattle to let them drown in this damn rainstorm. Yaw! Yaw," she shouted as she moved on, driving the cattle ahead of her.

"Where are you taking them?" Colt asked.

"About a quarter of a mile ahead, there's an opening with a trail wide enough to get them to higher ground."

"Don't you think they might find it themselves?"

"You haven't been around cattle very much, have you?"

"Not at all. Yaw, yaw," he shouted, imitating her motions to keep them moving.

"Well, cattle are the dumbest creatures you'll ever find. It just takes one to start a stampede. One runs and they all do, trampling the calves or anything else that gets in their path."

"At the rate they're moving now, you won't have to worry about any stampede."

"I still have to worry about the calves. I've passed several that are mired in mud. As soon as we get this herd to higher ground—"

"What do you mean, *we?* I don't know a damn thing about driving cattle; I just came out here to make sure you were okay."

"Just keep them moving, Deputy." She wheeled her horse and rode back to a mewling calf struggling in the mud.

"Talk about the blind leading the blind," Colt grumbled. "Keep moving, you stupid cows! Yaw. Yaw," he shouted, prodding them along. If driving cattle in a thunderstorm was typical of ranch life, a rancher had to be dumber than the cattle.

They worked throughout the day and night. The thunder and lightning passed over as they labored to free the cattle trapped in mud or entangled in mesquite thickets. Colt was awed by Cassie's relentless effort to save whatever she could. Time and time again she'd rope, tug, and pull free a calf from the mud, then stagger with the heavy load and lift it onto her saddle to take it to the higher ground. Then she would ride back and do it again with another one.

By daylight, they had succeeded in getting most of the herd onto the mesa above. The wind had subsided and the rain had changed to a hazy drizzle that was thicker than fog. With such bad visibility, it finally became impossible to continue.

"Cassie, aren't you about ready to call it quits? You must be exhausted. You should get out of your wet clothes and climb into bed, or you won't be any good to yourself or these cattle."

She nodded. "I guess it's pretty useless to go on. At least the river didn't flood. As soon as the sun comes up and starts drying the ground, I'll round up the rest of what's left of them later. Let's get back to town and out of these wet clothes."

By the time they reached the edge of town, Cassie was almost asleep in the saddle. "Go straight home, Cassie. I'll take care of the horses," Colt said.

"You're just as tired as I am," she said. "Five more minutes won't make that much difference."

"You've got a lot of stamina, Cass."

She smiled tiredly at him. "You don't do so bad yourself, Deputy. You've got the makings of a good rancher."

When they reached the livery, Colt glanced around in surprise. Small groups of people gathered in the street, and the air was rife with excitement. Many of the storeowners were nailing up bunting on their storefronts. "What the hell's going on?"

The three sprouts were standing in front of the livery with Jeff Braden, and they rushed up to Colt and Cassie as they dismounted.

"What's going on?" he asked.

"General Carson's coming to town for the next couple days," Sam said.

"Who is he?"

Mouth agape, Bowie exclaimed, "You ain't ever heard of Kit Carson!"

"Kit Carson! You mean the famous Indian fighter?"

"There ain't none famouser," Sam said.

"'More famous,' Sam," Cassie corrected.

"You're wasting your time trying to teach her anything, Cassie," Jeff said, taking the reins of the horses.

"You ain't my schoolmaster, Jeff Braden, so I don't need advice from somebody who ain't got nothing under his hat but an addled brain."

"So Kit Carson's a general," Colt said, ignoring their running battle. "I don't suppose he fought on the side of the Confederacy."

"No," Cassie said. "When the war broke out and so many of our men went East, the Indians started raiding the farms and ranches. General Carson organized a military infantry here in New Mexico and brought the Indians under control. He went back to being an Indian agent after the war."

The children followed them as they went inside to unsaddle the horses.

"So there really is a Kit Carson," Colt said. "Tales of his early exploits among the Indians and the Frémont expeditions made him sound more legendary than real."

"I reckon a few of his exploits were legendary," Cassie said, "but on the whole he's one heck of a man. Frontiersman, guide, trapper, Indian fighter, soldier. He lived among the Indians and can speak their languages like he was born to them, and there's no man more courageous."

"He sure is," Sam said proudly. "I read about him all the time in my Godey's books. And to think he's coming here tonight!"

"Well, right now, I'm going home to a hot bath and bed," Cassie said.

"You coming to the shindy tonight, Deputy?" Sam asked.

"Wouldn't miss it for the world, Belle."

"I told you to stop calling me Belle," she yelled as he and Cassie departed.

"Colt, why do you call Sam 'Belle'?"

Colt grinned. "Shortly before I met her and the two boys, I'd been reading about the James Brothers, and a female named Belle who rides with an outlaw gang led by Tom Starr."

Cassie shoved back her hat. "I know Sam can be a real pain in the rear at times, but that seems a little extreme."

Colt slipped his arm around her shoulders. "Just my peculiar sense of humor, honey. She's a great little gal." He yawned. "You know, you've got the right idea. I'm going to my room to take a hot bath and then hit the mattress for a couple hours. Tell your dad I'll drop by later."

Colt returned to the hotel, went upstairs, shucked his clothing, and dropped onto the bed. He was asleep before his head hit the pillow.

After a six-hour sleep followed by a hot bath, Colt headed over to the Bradens'. When he walked through the door, the kitchen smelled like a bakery, and the tantalizing aroma of a ham roasting on a spit on the hearth permeated the house. It reminded Colt of how the kitchen at Fraser Keep used to smell whenever a big party was being prepared.

Cathy was rolling out a piecrust, and Cassie, looking refreshed, was peeling apples.

"You don't look any the worse after the busy night you had," he said to Cassie.

"Thank you. I can say the same about you."

"You both deserve a pat on the back. It must have been horrible out in that storm all night," Cathy said. "Did you hear that General Carson's coming to town?"

"Yes, it's the topic on everyone's lips. How long will he be here?"

"A couple days, according to the telegram," Jeff said, joining them at the table.

Cassie put down her paring knife and said to Cathy, "That's the last of the apples in the barrel. Don't you think four apple pies and a baked ham will be enough of a contribution? I poked so many cloves into the ham that my fingertips will be scarred forever, and I peeled enough apples to feed every horse in the United States Cavalry." She tossed a curly apple peeling at Jeff, and he caught it and popped it into his mouth.

"You going to save me a dance tonight, Cassie?" Colt asked.

That produced a big snort from Jeff. "Cassie only dances with her horse."

"At least Midnight doesn't step on my toes like those horses' rear ends that you call friends, Jeff Braden."

"You gals should save something for some of the other ladies to bring," Jethro said from a nearby rocking chair. The pleasure he got from listening to his children's banter was evident by his big grin.

"Dad, what are you doing out of bed?" Jeff asked.

"Now don't start bellerin' like a rained-soaked rooster, boy. Doc Williams said I could."

"And I think you've sat up long enough," Cathy said. "Jeff, will you help him back to bed?"

"I'll give you a hand," Colt offered.

With every step, the older man grumbled about them treating him like an invalid.

"Like it or not, Dad, you are an invalid right now," Jeff said.

"Now don't you give me any sass, boy. It's bad enough I have to listen to your sisters'." Jethro turned a steely eye on Colt. "You got somethin' to say on the matter?"

"Not a word, Sheriff. I don't have any horse in this race."

Within the hour, wagons from the surrounding ranches started to roll into town. Due to the past days' rain, folks decided to hold the shindy in the hotel's dining room. While the women spread out their food, Colt helped several of the men carry out the tables and push the chairs back against the walls.

By the time they finished, General Carson had arrived with his entourage—three Navajo chiefs and several dozen of their tribesmen. The Indians wanted no part of the celebration or the town, and made camp behind the church.

After setting out their food, Cassie and Cathy returned home to change clothes. As she dressed for the affair, Cassie felt excited. It had been a long time since she'd worn a fancy gown. She had two party gowns, one yellow and the other green, and she chose the green one. Tonight was a special occasion. After all, how often did they get to see General Kit Carson?

General Carson my foot, Cassie Braden! You're getting all prettied up for Colt Fraser.

After brushing out her hair, she pulled it behind her ears and wove a green satin ribbon into its thickness. Then she stepped back and took a long look at her bare neck and shoulders, and the green gown that clung to her breasts.

What are you thinking? Why should you care how you look to Colt Fraser?

She pulled the ribbon out of her hair. She looked too coquettish, too flirtatious. It would be an invitation to him, and a temptation to her.

Cassie stepped out of the gown and reached for her black skirt and white blouse. She'd suddenly lost all her enthusiasm for the party.

"Why don't you wear your green dress tonight for a change?" Cathy asked a short time later as she braided Cassie's hair.

"I'm more comfortable in a blouse and skirt."

"Honey, why don't you dress up for him just once?" Cathy said with a sweet smile.

"Why would I dress up fancy for General Carson?"

"You know I'm not referring to the general," Cathy said. "What are you afraid of, Cassie?"

Cassie sighed deeply. There was no sense in trying to

fool Cathy. As twins, each often knew what the other was thinking without even speaking.

"Oh, Cathy, I'm so unhappy. I don't know what to do." Suddenly she found herself fighting back sobs. "I've tried to fight it, but I'm so attracted to him. And it's so wrong. So very wrong."

Cathy sat down beside her and hugged her. "Why is it wrong, honey?"

"Because I'm engaged to Ted. I love him and he loves me. I can't be unfaithful to him."

"Honey, what if Ted doesn't come back? Are you going to remain true to his memory forever?"

Cassie stared into the compassion in her sister's eyes. "But I believe Ted is still alive."

"That's your decision to make, Cassie," Cathy said, wiping the tears off Cassie's cheeks. "I'm only suggesting you trust what's in your heart, because none of us know what's in our future."

"Well, I know what's in Colt Fraser's future. He makes no secret of the fact that he's riding out of here as soon as he can."

"Then that makes your decision more urgent, doesn't it?" Cathy kissed her on the cheek, then pulled her to her feet. "Come on, honey. You don't want the party to start without us, do you?"

Chapter 17

Studying her image in the mirror, Sam ran a hand across her chest.

"Flat as pancakes," she muttered. When would she develop breasts like that Lucy Cain at the Alhambra?

She wondered if what the deputy said was true. Would she really grow up to be as beautiful as Cassie? If so, there was no sign of it now. But if the deputy was right, it would sure show up that Lucy Cain and serve that Jeff Braden right.

She took another look in the mirror at her flat chest, then turned away in disgust.

"What do I need breasts for, anyway?" she grumbled. "Ain't got no use except nursing babies, and I ain't gonna have any of them."

She pulled on her dress and went into the kitchen. Her mother was busy at the stove, as usual.

"Mama, ain't you coming to see General Carson?"

"No, darlin'. As soon as I'm done here, I'm goin' to bed. Let me brush your hair before you go."

Sarah sat down, and Sam stood between her legs as Sarah did her hair. When she finished, Sarah smiled with pride. "My, you look lovely, darlin'. That dress brings out the blue of your eyes."

"Are your feet still aching, Mama?" Sam asked, concerned.

Sarah sighed. "Just a little."

The young girl's face saddened. "You work so hard, Mama. When I grow up, I'm gonna buy us a ranch so you won't have to work so hard. You can sit all day with your feet on a pillow. Would you like me to rub them for you before I go?"

Sarah reached out a hand and caressed her daughter's cheek. "No, darlin'. Go and have a good time. And don't pester the deputy. He's a very nice man."

"I know. We're good friends now. He told me I'll grow up to be as beautiful as Cassie."

"And you will."

Sam hugged and kissed her. "I love you, Mama."

For the past thirty minutes, Colt had listened to General Carson speak. He had expected a boisterous, buckskin-clad giant with a beaver tail dangling from his hat. Instead, Carson was of slim stature, reserved, temperate, and extremely modest.

Bombarded with one question after another, Carson was an amusing raconteur as he described the Western wilderness, yet not once did he mention his own accomplishments in helping to tame that wilderness.

When he found out that Colt had fought on the side of the Confederacy, Carson took him aside and asked him how the Reconstruction was going in the South.

Carson listened intently as Colt described the problems in the South's struggle to regain some of its former splendor, knowing it could never return to the life it had once known.

"The same could be said about the Indian, Captain Fraser," Carson said. "Their way of life can never return. Not only did our government move them hundreds of miles from the land they once roamed as free men but it moved them onto reservations that restrict them from doing what is familiar to them. The Navajo Nation was an agrarian society, unlike many of the other Indian nations. They farmed the land and planted orchards. Our government rounded them up and moved them hundreds of miles to a reservation where the land is too poor to yield any crops, so now we have to dole out rations to them in order to keep them from starving."

"But it's my understanding, sir, that Indian tribes such as the Apaches and Comanches are warlike, are they not? They never lived peacefully with one another, much less the advent of white neighbors."

"That is true, Captain. I'm afraid most of the major Indian nations have raised their war clubs and arrows against us. It will take twenty or thirty years before we see the end to these Indian wars. Let us hope that will not be true between the North and the South."

Colt thanked the general for his time and excused himself. He hadn't seen any sign of Cassie for the past half hour, and he still wanted to dance with her. Seeing no sign of her, he went outside in case she'd gone out for some fresh air.

* * *

Cassie felt hot and uncomfortable. In addition, Bob Callum stepped on her toes for the third time, and she couldn't wait for the dance to end. Her gaze kept stealing to the open door. It was too inviting to resist. As soon as the dance ended, she thanked Bob and hurried outside before anyone could stop her.

Cathy's advice had sounded so right, but it was easier said than done. She still couldn't convince herself that she could put the memory of Ted behind her. She needed some proof, some sign that he was not coming back.

She was no longer certain she had ever been in love with Ted. She'd been so young, so girlish five years ago, with romantic fantasies. Was her resolve to wait for him just a way to resist the temptation of her attraction to Colt? All she was certain of was that she had to choose one or the other. The issue was tearing her apart.

Colt hadn't even approached her since the party had begun. He'd been so occupied talking to General Carson that he'd ignored her entirely. If she was looking for a sign, that alone would surely be an indication of *his* true feelings for her. But he'd made his intentions quite clear; she was the one who was moping around trying to justify her own feelings.

Well, she'd had enough of the party. Rather than go home, she walked down to the schoolhouse. She felt nearer to Ted there than any other place.

Moonlight cast a silver streak across the darkened room as she went to the chalkboard and stood before the message Ted had written when he'd gone away.

She closed her eyes. "I need a sign, Ted. I need something more than your promise to return. Something to release me from this struggle."

"Cassie, what are you doing standing alone in the dark?"

Her eyes popped open, and she spun around in surprise. "Colt! You startled me."

"I'm sorry. When I couldn't find you at the party, I figured you might be here."

"Why would you think that?"

"I don't know. It just came to me, that's all."

Could this be the sign she was asking for? "You mean like an epiphany?"

Colt chuckled. "My thoughts of you are rarely divinely driven. Weren't you enjoying the dance?"

"No. I don't particularly enjoy dancing."

"That's unusual, particularly for a woman as young and beautiful as you are."

"Save the seductive flattery for someone who wants to hear it, Colt."

"What is your problem, Cassie?" The edge in his tone made his anger clear. "I just came down here to see if you're okay."

"Bah!" she scoffed. "You came down here hoping I'd be interested in playing your games. Well, I'm not interested in playing the giggling coquette. I'm not interested in flirting with you, dancing with you, and most certainly not interested in making love to you."

"Me or any man, Cassie. You've convinced yourself that men are all lecherous predators. The real problem is that I've broken through that protective armor you wear like some damn Joan of Arc, and that now you feel guilty for feeling real passion."

"You think you've got me all figured out, but you're wrong, Colt. I have the same dreams, feelings, and desires as any other woman."

"Then start acting like one before it's too late. And you can begin by erasing this damn epitaph. It belongs on a tombstone, not the blackboard of a classroom."

Colt strode over to the chalked message and began to erase Ted's good-bye to them.

Horrified, Cassie rushed over and yanked at his arm. "Stop it! Stop it!" she cried. She burst into tears of fury. "You have no right. Stop it."

He tossed aside the eraser and grasped her by the shoulders, his eyes blackened by the anger he was trying to temper.

"My God, Cassie! You're a beautiful, passionate woman who's wasting her life. Face the truth, Cass. Only death would keep a man from returning to the woman he loved."

"That's not true. You're wrong," she sobbed.

He pulled her into his arms and held her as she wept, his cheek rubbing the silky auburn head buried against his chest. Her tears dampened his shirt as he breathed in her sweet scent, and he felt the warmth of her soft curves against the hard angles of his own body.

Cupping her cheeks between his hands, he tangled his fingers in her hair. "Ah, Cass," he murmured, "I don't want to hurt you, and it seems like I keep doing so."

He lowered his head and kissed her forehead, then trailed kisses along her tear-streaked cheek, the day-long stubble on his chin a tantalizing scrape against the soft skin of her jaw. He reached her mouth and covered it with his own.

The kiss was gentle, tender in intent. She could taste the salt of her tears on his lips. She parted her lips to choke back a sob, and the pressure of his mouth deepened as he slipped his tongue between her lips and began to stroke the chamber of her mouth.

Her body throbbed with sensation as their tongues met and tasted.

Ted had never kissed her with such fervency, had never aroused such overpowering desire. She moaned with sheer pleasure at the tingling sensations swirling through her body when his tongue traced the outline of her lips. Then he reclaimed her lips in a consuming kiss that made her want to believe there had never been any woman before her, any man before him. She closed her eyes and surrendered to passion as he lowered their bodies to the floor.

When nothing else happened, Cassie opened her eyes and discovered he was staring at her. Confused, she stared back. She tried to slide her arms around his neck to draw him closer, but he held them away. Then he sat up.

"I can't do this. I'm sorry, Cass." He stood up and reached out a hand and pulled her to her feet.

She felt more bewildered than ever, and embarrassment killed the hot passion that had been building within her.

"Is this another of your jokes, Colt? The cat playing with the mouse?"

He grasped her shoulders. "Cass, I've never wanted a woman as much as I want you. But not this way. Not on the floor of the schoolroom, knowing that when it's over, you'll be eaten up with guilt for betraying the man you love."

He was right. But still . . . "Why should my feelings make any difference to you? You'd have gotten what you vowed you'd get before you left Arena Roja."

"I know what I said—so call me a damn fool. Or maybe it's become a matter of personal pride—that I don't want to take, I want you to give."

He reached out and tenderly brushed back some errant strands of hair from her cheek. "I wish I understood it myself. Maybe I believe you deserve something better. I'm sorry, Cass."

He spun on his heel and left.

Cassie moved to the doorway and watched his tall figure as he disappeared into the darkness.

"Or maybe it's because you're a man of conscience, Colt Fraser," she murmured softly.

It was late when Carson retired and the party broke up. As usual, the Braden twins were among the women busy cleaning up.

After helping Dan James move the tables back into the dining room, Colt made his final round of the town. When he returned, Dan had retired. Colt retrieved his key and was about to go up to his room when he saw a light still burning in the dining room. He went in to turn it off, and Cassie stood up when he entered.

"Cassie, it's past midnight. What are you doing here alone?"

"Waiting for you," she said. "It seems all I do is apologize to you. I hate what happened between us tonight, Colt."

"I told you I was sorry. At least you didn't do something you'd regret tomorrow."

"I don't mean that. I'm referring to our argument. Why do we quarrel, Colt? I don't mean to, but it seems we always end up in an argument. And I wish we could be friends."

"We *are* friends. Trouble is, we're both strong-willed people. But I won't lie to you, Cass: I want you, and I can't pretend I don't when we're together."

"I'll be just as honest. I feel the same way about you, and I admit I'm running away from it, because—"

"I know. We've been through that enough times, and you know what I think of your arguments on that subject. So I guess we're at an impasse, Cass."

"I guess we are," she said sadly. "But I want you to know that regardless of what I say to you when I'm angry, I think you're one of the finest men I've ever known, and I care for you very much. I don't think I'll ever forget you."

"And I don't believe I'll ever erase the vision of you struggling to free a calf mired in the mud in that storm last night. You're an incredible woman, Cass.

"Come on, honey, it's late. I'll walk you home." He grinned mischievously "If you're sure that's what you want to do."

"Colt!" she chided.

"Cassie!" he countered.

Then he chuckled, took her hand, and walked her home; and Colt, true to form, kissed her goodnight at her front door.

Chapter 18

After a restless night of trying to convince himself that he wasn't the world's biggest fool for passing up the opportunity to make love to Cassie, Colt checked in with Jethro and then made his morning rounds.

The town was finishing cleaning up after the previous night's affair, but as usual, at siesta everything came to a stop. He took the opportunity to go back to the hotel to eat lunch.

When he entered the dining room, Colt was surprised to see the Braden siblings.

"Sit down and join us, Colt," Jeff said cordially.

Neither woman appeared surprised by their brother's sudden change of heart toward him, and Colt wondered if Jeff had told them about the shooting lessons. Regardless, it was a relief not to have the tension that had once existed whenever they'd been together.

He certainly had had his own change of heart toward Jeff Braden. Under Jeff's former surliness had been a young man whose lack of confidence was taking him down a road toward destruction. Colt held great expectations for him now.

"So what was your impression of General Carson, Colt?" Jeff asked.

"Quite a remarkable man."

"Indeed he is," Cassie said lightly.

Colt smiled at her. She looked very lovely today; apparently she had spent a better night than he had.

"You look none the worse after the ordeal you and Cassie went through," Cathy said.

With the cattle or each other last night, he wondered wryly.

"Ah do declare, my eyes must be deceivin' me. Is it really you, Coltran Fraser?"

The unexpected greeting caused them all to glance up at the frilly-groomed woman with a large peacock-feathered hat perched on her dark hair.

Colt's surprise was apparent as he jumped to his feet.

"Rose Lee Beckenridge! I don't believe it!"

The woman offered her hand to Colt, and he brought it to his lips in a quick kiss. Cassie and Cathy exchanged amazed looks when their brother followed Colt's example and rose to his feet.

"This is a surprise, Rose Lee," Colt said.

"A pleasant one, ah hope."

She appeared to Cassie to be one of those self-confident women who monopolized the attention of any crowd she was among. She certainly had done so with the two men at their table.

"We're about to order lunch, Rose Lee. Would you care to join us?" Colt asked.

"Ah'd be devastated if you didn't ask me, Captain Fraser."

The woman turned her attention to Jeff, who was

still standing, looking unsure of what his next move should be.

"And who might this handsome gentleman be?"

"Jeffrey Braden, Miss Rose Lee Beckenridge," Colt said.

"My pleasure, ma'am," Jeff replied, his face coloring in a deep blush.

"The pleasure is all mine, Mr. Jeffrey Braden." Her tongue curled around his first name as her long lashes battered her cheeks in a flirtatious fluttering.

Rose Lee offered her hand to Jeff, and he kissed it awkwardly, unlike Colt's smooth gesture.

"But ah do declare, ma'am sounds so matronly, Mr. Jeffrey. Y'all just address me by my given name."

"And these two lovely ladies," Colt said, "are the Misses Cassandra and Catherine Braden, Jeff's sisters."

"How do you do?" Rose Lee gave them cursory glances and sat down in Colt's chair. He pulled one over from the next table and squeezed it in between Rose Lee and Cassie. The waiter hurried over, and they ordered lunch.

Once settled again, Colt asked, "Perhaps I misspoke, Rose Lee. It is still Miss Beckenridge, isn't it?"

Her hand fluttered to her ample bosom, which appeared even more bodacious on her tiny frame.

"Ah do declare, Captain Fraser, Y'all are embarrasin' me." Her pink lips pursed in a pout. "Despite Bubba Danforth's and Billy Bob McCurty's offers of marriage, ah could never think of marryin' any man other than you or Garth." Frowning, she suddenly grasped his hand. "Garth did survive the war, didn't he?"

"He did, thank God. Last time I saw him he was very much alive and well."

She clutched at her chest, and once again her bosom became the center of everyone's focus.

"My heart would shatter into a thousand pieces if Garth had perished."

"What brings you to Arena Roja, Miss Beckenridge?" Cathy asked.

"The mornin' stagecoach, Miss Catherine." Rose Lee tittered in amusement at her own humor. "And please address me by my given name, too. You, too, Miss Cassandra."

"That's most kind of you, Miss Rose Lee," Cassie said. "Such a lovely name, isn't it, Miss Catherine?"

The corners of Cathy's mouth turned up as she tried to suppress a smile. "Indeed it is, Miss Cassandra."

Rose Lee preened with pleasure. "Thank you." She giggled in delight. "But my daddy always calls me Miss Sugarplum." Modestly lowering her eyes, she added, "He always tells me I'm as sweet as a piece of candy, doesn't he, Colt?"

Colt cleared his throat. "Yes, I remember he did quite often."

Cathy smiled. "Isn't that delightful, Miss Cassandra?"

"Delightful, Miss Catherine. And how long will we have the pleasure of your company here in Arena Roja, Miss Rose Lee?"

"Ah understand the stagecoach will be leavin' in the morning." She leaned over and placed her hand over Colt's, lying nearby on the table. He had to duck his head to keep from getting poked in the eye with the peacock feather that jutted from her bonnet.

"Though if this handsome rogue tried, he could persuade me to extend my visit, Miss Cassandra."

"Oh, do call me Miss Cassie. We don't stand on formality here." The woman's honeyed coquettishness was becoming as difficult for Cassie to swallow as a spoonful of castor oil.

"Other than the morning stagecoach, what did bring you to New Mexico, Miss Rose Lee?" Jeff asked.

"Actually, Mr. Jeffrey, I'm not comin', I'm goin'."

For some reason beyond the stretch of Cassie's imagination, Rose Lee tittered again at the humor of her reply.

"I'm returnin' to Virginia. My daddy feared for my well-being, so he sent me to live with my auntie Rose Marie in Santa Fe until the war ended." She rolled her eyes in dismay. "Ah can't tell you, Mr. Jeffrey, that between her name being Rose Marie and mine being Rose Lee, how distressin' it was for everyone?"

"It certainly must have been," Jeff said, hanging on to her every word like an awestruck schoolboy. Cassie thought he had to be the most naïve person on earth.

Cathy must have had the same reaction, because she kicked Cassie's leg.

"Ouch!" Cassie yelped. To cover the outburst, she quickly said, "Yes indeed, it must have been very distressing. Just think, while the Civil War raged in the South, you and your Auntie Rose Marie waged another War of the Roses right here in New Mexico."

Colt, who had maintained an enigmatic expression throughout the conversation, chuckled loudly.

Obviously history was not Miss Rose Lee's forte, and Cassie's comment flew right over her head without even brushing the tip of the peacock feather in the flight.

The woman's long lashes whipped her cheeks again. "Dare ah hope that we'll be travelin' companions on the way back to Virginia, Captain Fraser?"

"Afraid not, Rose Lee. I'm headed in the opposite direction. I'm joining Garth and Clay in California."

She jerked her head around to him, and once again, only Colt's quick reflexes saved him the possible loss of an eye as he dodged the feather.

"Garth's in California!"

There was a long pause as everyone appeared to hold their breaths at the threatened spillover of her heaving breasts.

"Ah do declare," Rose Lee sulked, "with Garth, Clay, and you gone, there won't be a handsome man left in the whole county."

Colt cleared his throat. "You better not let Jed hear you say that."

Rose Lee's eyes brightened. "Of course! Ah do declare, that's quite astonishin' that I forgot about your brother Jed."

Much to Cassie's disgust, the woman batted her eyelashes at Colt again.

"He's as handsome a rogue as you and Garth."

Her hand flickered to his arm. "Of course, all of you Frasers were devils in disguise. Ah couldn't believe it when Daddy wrote me that my dear Miss Lissy ran off with a Yankee soldier. Ah was so shocked, poor Auntie

Rose Marie had to give me a tonic to prevent me from succumbin' to the vapors."

She shook her head, then patted his hand. "Far be it from me to besmirch dear Miss Lissy—and one of my dearest friends—Colt, but you must admit your sister was always headstrong and outspoken."

"I always found her to be mild-mannered and even-tempered," Colt said. "And I've never heard any of my brothers say anything to the contrary. We all adored her."

"Ah agree that you and your brothers never could see any fault in Miss Lissy's actions. Y'all spoiled her rotten, as Daddy always said. Ah hope she's not been sufferin' for her hastiness."

"Quite the opposite; Clay wrote that he's never seen Lissy happier. She has a healthy son and a wonderful husband who adores her."

Rose Lee snorted. "A Yankee! How could she be happy married to a Yankee?"

"I'm not the one to ask. Maybe you should ask Clay—he married one, too."

The smile slipped from Rose Lee's face, and she appeared to be slightly piqued. She turned her head to Cassie.

"Ah hope I'm not offendin' you, Miss Cassandra, but ah notice your manner of dressin' is quite unusual for a lady."

"Do you think so, Miss Rose Lee? I find it preferable when I ride."

"Why would you want to be garbed as a man for ridin' in a carriage?"

"I meant on horseback, Miss Rose Lee."

"Oh, so you ride to the hounds, too. In Virginia, we ladies wear a ridin' costume on such occasions."

"Rose Lee, you won't find anyone fox hunting these days back home," Colt said.

"Oh, dear, don't tell me those Yankees have spoiled that simple pleasure, too."

"Actually, Miss Rose Lee, I wasn't referring to hunting. I'm too busy herding cattle to chase down a little fox."

Rose Lee gasped in shock. "Herdin' cattle? Are you suggestin', Miss Cassandra, that you indulge in such masculine endeavor? Why, that would be considered most shockin' in Virginia."

"Well, in New Mexico it's considered survival."

"Well, ah never would," Rose Lee declared. "It's so unfeminine. Ah do declare, I'd surrender my virtue before I'd give up my femininity."

Colt began to choke on his coffee. Rose Lee bolted to her feet and began to pound him on the back.

Leaning over, Cassie whispered to Cathy, "No doubt his reaction is due to how often Miss Rose Lee has proven that theory."

As soon as the brief incident was over, Cathy quickly tried to steer the conversation to a safer topic.

"The war ended a year ago, Miss Rose Lee. What delayed your return to Virginia?"

"Daddy insisted ah remain in Santa Fe. He said when the war ended, it wasn't safe for a decent woman to walk the streets."

"Why was that?" Cassie asked.

"Can't you guess? Why, it must have been terrorizin'," she said with disdain. "Daddy wrote the streets were full of nothin' but Yankee soldiers, carpetbaggers, and hundreds of homeless slaves."

Cassie could not bear another moment of the woman's haughtiness and insensitivity. "I can't speak for the carpetbaggers, Miss Beckenridge, but I'm sure that most of those Yankee soldiers were decent men who would have liked to return to their homes and families. And thanks to the war, those *slaves* you referred to are free men who have the same right to be on the street as you or your daddy. And *that*, Miss Beckenridge, ah do declare!" Cassie said as she shoved back her chair and strode out of the dining room.

"What a despicable person," she muttered as she headed for the livery.

Entering its cool darkness, she made straight for Midnight's stall. "I really did it this time, Midnight," she said to the horse as she saddled him. "I played right into her hands. Why didn't I just excuse myself quietly instead of making a scene? Instead I made a fool of myself in front of Colt Fraser. And you know as well as I that Jeff will never let me live it down. Not that I care, considering the way he was slobbering all over that heartless flirt."

Sam and the James brothers came in as Cassie was on the verge of mounting.

"Where are you going, Cassie?" Sam asked.

"To the ranch." She climbed into the saddle. "Will you tell my dad and Cathy for me?"

"How come you didn't tell them yourself? Is something wrong, Cassie?" Sam asked worriedly. "Did the deputy say something to upset you again?"

"No, dear, I just feel like being alone for a while. Besides, there are a few things I want to get done there. I'll probably be gone for a couple of days, so tell my family not to worry."

"What do you think's wrong, Sam?" Bowie asked. "Ain't like Cassie to ride off for a couple days and not tell Cathy or the sheriff where she's going."

"It's very suspicious."

"Yeah, 'speechis," Petey seconded with the same worried frown as his companions.

Sam said, "I bet my best pair of bloomers the deputy has something to do with it."

Cassie leaned back against the tree to enjoy the view and reflect on her situation. Here at the Lazy B she could always find peace.

Why couldn't people understand that just because she'd rather wear pants instead of fancy gowns, and herd cattle instead of bake a cake, she wasn't less a woman than that worthless Rose Lee Beckenridge, whom the men so admired?

It didn't mean she didn't want to marry and have children with the man she loved. She adored children and knew in her heart she would make a wonderful mother.

But what kind of wife would she make?

She hadn't been much older than Petey when her mother had died. Maybe if her mother had lived longer, she would better understand the role a woman played in a man's life. Yet Cathy had grown up in the same situation, and it hadn't affected her. Cathy was perfect in all ways—that's why it was so easy to love her. Many men had proposed marriage to her sister, and Cassie had no idea why her twin had always turned those offers down.

Cassie gave a deep sigh. No, the problem had to be her. But she'd rather die a spinster than throw herself at men like Miss Rose Lee Beckenridge.

She glanced heavenward. Overhead the leafy green spires of the trees intermingled with the blue sky and the white, drifting clouds. Awed by God's majesty, Cassie realized her woes seemed insignificant. Relaxing, she closed her eyes and let her senses dwell on the sounds around her.

The soft plod of approaching hooves didn't alarm her; she didn't even open her eyes. She knew who it would be. Had known he would come. Perhaps that's why she, too, had come here.

"Cassie, what are you doing out here alone?" Colt asked.

Cassie opened her eyes. He looked handsome and virile looming above her on Bullet.

"I enjoy being alone. I'm surprised to see you. How did you ever pry Miss Sugarplum's fingers off your arm?"

Colt threw back his head in laughter and dismounted. She couldn't help but admire the smooth motion. He was a superb horseman, born to the saddle. She had observed that the few times she had seen him ride.

"Do I detect a note of jealousy, Miss Braden?"

Cassie snorted. "Now why would I be jealous, Deputy Fraser?"

"Because you were faced with a woman who's not ashamed to expose her sensuality."

"That's not the only thing she exposed. She made quite a point of flaunting what she exposed."

"Perhaps so, but unlike you at least she doesn't try to deny it."

Cassie jumped to her feet. "Are we back to that again? Don't you dare criticize me by comparing me to that insensitive, heartless woman who—"

"Cassie, you're getting carried away now. And it's not becoming to you."

"Are you trying to deny what she is?"

He expressed his impatience in an audible sigh. "I'm not denying anything. I don't give a damn about her morals. Frankly, I think the woman's an incredible bore, and at this moment I find you to be the same way. So get over this childish tantrum and we'll change the subject."

"Why is it, Colt, that every time I don't agree with you, I'm being childish? I'll be truthful with you. Since most of the war was fought in the South, whenever I thought about the hardships the women and children were going through, I couldn't help feeling sorry for them. But now, after listening to poor Miss Rose Lee Beckenridge, I have to say it was wasted sympathy."

She might just as well have fired another volley to set off the war again.

"Do you actually believe the Rose Lees are examples of all Southern women? Are you suggesting her type can't be found elsewhere? Granted, we Southerners may have a different culture. But don't doubt for a moment, Miss Braden, that throughout this country's history there has always been a breed of women, be it with rifle *or* plow in hand, calluses *or* lacy gloves over iron fists, who have stood side by side with the men they love. And those women's fortitude, that inner strength and courage to face any adversity, is what gave the men who loved them greater strength.

"So I'll tell you about the *real* women of the South—the thousands like my mother, my sister, and my brother's wife. Many of them saw their homes destroyed—*all* of them lost loved ones. But they didn't run off to a safe harbor or remain unscathed, like many of the women in the rest of this country. Our women buried their dead, went to bed hungry at night so their children wouldn't have to, and prayed to the Almighty that the war would end.

"They were the unsung heroes of the late war. God bless each and every one of them. And instead of pinning medals on the chests of the men, they should have been pinned on the women of the South!"

He spun on his heel and strode to his horse.

Chapter 19

Cassie stood, stunned. She had hit a raw nerve, and he'd revealed the emotions he kept so well in check under that smooth Southern veneer. To someone like herself at the mercy of her own emotions, it was a relief to see it happen. He appeared less calculating and more human to her than ever before.

He was magnificent!

His outburst proved that he was a big sham. All this strutting around pretending he wasn't involved, with "no dog in the hunt," but he wasn't fooling her anymore. He was just as emotional as she, and from now on they were on even ground—no more mouse to his cat.

Cassie climbed on Midnight and rode after Colt. She owed him an apology for what she had said—and the thought of apologizing to someone she knew was as tenderhearted as herself made it so much easier.

She found him walking, leading Bullet by the reins. The horse was limping.

"What happened?" she asked, dismounting.

"He threw a shoe."

"He can't hobble all the way back to town. Let's get him over to the barn and I'll put a new shoe on him."

Colt nodded, and she continued to walk alongside him. "I'm sorry, Colt. I have no right to pass judgment on women like your family members because of a woman like Miss Beckenridge."

"You've got that right, lady." His grim expression never altered.

"Well?"

"Well, what?" he snapped.

"Do you accept my apology?"

"You never seem to learn, Cassie. You always run off half-cocked without any thought as to the danger, or what you're going to do or say."

Who did he think he was? She'd had the decency to apologize, but he wasn't gracious enough to accept it. How could she ever have thought he was a sensitive person?

"The truth hurt, Miss Braden?"

She stopped abruptly. "Truth! I'll give you some truth, Colt Fraser. You're the smuggest, most arrogant man I've ever met. It's a miracle you can find a hat to fit over that swelled head of yours. You and Miss Sugarplum make a perfect couple. And as far as I'm concerned, you can go straight to hell and try to convince Satan what a nice guy you are." She snatched Bullet's reins out of his hand. "I can take care of our horse without your help."

She took about two steps before he caught up with her. "Am I supposed to walk back to town?"

"Try flying back on that inflated ego of yours."

Once again she didn't get more than two steps before he grasped her by the arm and spun her around to face him.

"You are one bad-tempered lady," he said, more astounded than angry. "I think you could use some cooling off."

"Put me down," she cried when he picked her up and carried her to the nearby pond.

"That's just what I have in mind," he said as he tossed her into the water, then waded in ankle-deep and stood over her with his hands on his hips. "You've had that coming for a long time, Miss Braden."

When he turned his back on her, Cassie leaped at him and shoved him off balance. Colt landed on his backside with a gigantic splash.

Water dripping down her face from her sodden hair, Cassie now stood over him.

"Since you've come this far, maybe you should attempt swimming back to town, Deputy."

Her victory was short-lived. His hand grasped her booted ankle and pulled her down. She surfaced and kicked water at him. He splashed her back, and suddenly they were laughing as the water fight continued until, wringing wet, they recovered their sodden hats and sought firm ground.

"I'm afraid you can add stupid to those descriptions of me," Colt said as he removed his gunbelt and slung it over the saddle. Then he pulled off his boots and shook the water out of them.

"Impetuous of you, wasn't it?" She grinned.

"To say the least. Seemed like a good idea at the time, though."

Cassie shook out her hat and plopped it over her head.

"Now you know how the other half lives, Deputy Imperium."

After they got as much water as they could from their clothing and hats, they took the reins of their horses and moved on, trailing water behind them. By the time they reached the barn, their clothes had ceased dripping but were still wet.

"I'll unsaddle the horses," Colt said as Cassie headed for the house.

"And I'll check out whatever clothes Jeff and Dad have left here. I'm sure we can piece together something for you to put on while your clothes dry."

"Don't go to any trouble, Cassie. I went through four years of war and had the clothes dry on my back many a time."

"There's no reason why they have to now." She gave him a glance over her shoulder, her eyes alight with devilment. "Even if it's your fault they got wet in the first place."

As she continued to the house, Colt's gaze shifted to one of his fondest diversions lately: the jeans, now wet, that clung to her trim little ass and hips even tighter.

With a deep sigh, he took the horses' reins and led them to the barn. "You know, fellas, a sight like that sure makes a man glad he's alive."

After stabling the horses, Colt hung his gunbelt over a hook in the barn, then removed his shirt and strung it over a nearby shrub of chaparral to dry. He sat down and pulled off his boots and wet stockings. There was nothing more uncomfortable than wet socks, and they could rub a blister quicker than a size nine boot on a size eleven foot.

Colt began to whistle as he returned to the barn. He picked out a couple of horseshoes that hung on the wall, then he collected a hammer, rasp, tongs, nails, and a bellows, and carried them over to a small forge in the corner.

By the time Cassie joined him, Colt was fanning the flames with the bellows to intensify the fire in the forge. Her heart lurched at the sight of his strong, bronzed body, and her own body responded with a raw lust that sent a heated wave of arousal throughout her.

Barefoot and clad only in wet trousers that hugged his slim hips and long legs, Colt was covered with perspiration that glistened on his arms and the muscular brawn of his chest.

Mesmerized, she watched the ripple of muscle across his wide shoulders and the bulge of his bicep as he pounded the white hot horseshoe, shaping it to fit Bullet's hoof.

He glanced up at her. His gaze sought her face, then the length of her in a slow, sensual sweep that fueled the fire already ignited within her. An invisible web of desire spun between them, but who was the spider and who was the fly?

His grin broke her reflection. "I'll soon be through here."

Still shaken by her carnal thoughts, Cassie stepped closer. "I didn't have much luck finding a pair of trousers that will fit you, but I think this shirt of Dad's and these socks should do."

Had her voice always sounded so unsteady? Had her hand always shaken? Her body always trembled? No one had ever caused this feeling within her. She had to get a grip on herself, or her battle would be lost and his won.

"I don't need a shirt, Cassie—mine is about dry. I'll take the stockings, though."

He plopped the shoe into a pail of water, resulting in a loud sizzling and sputtering that vaporized into a puff of steam. Wiping off his brow with his forearm, he said, "I'll be done soon. I may not know how to herd cattle, but I've shod more than my share of horses."

"Then I'll go back into the house and drudge up something for us to eat."

"Sounds good."

Colt paused to watch Cassie return to the house. She had brushed out her hair to dry, and it lay across her shoulders like an auburn-colored mantle. She had shed the delectable wet pants and changed into a skirt and blouse, but he liked this new look, too. She sure was a cutie, with her hair bouncing on her shoulders as she walked. Any way she packaged herself, Cassie Braden was one good-looking female—and she stoked a fire in him hotter than the one in the forge.

And tougher than the nails he was about to use to pound on the horseshoe, he reflected, turning back to his task.

He lifted Bullet's leg and gave the hoof a final scraping, then nailed the shoe to its rim. A few strokes with the rasp to smooth the edges and the shoe was replaced.

"Good boy," he said with several pats to the horse's flank, then he led him back to a stall.

He tossed some hay in the stalls and filled the troughs, then doused the fire thoroughly, returned the tools to where he had found them, and closed the stable doors.

The sun had set by the time he grabbed his gunbelt and clothing and headed for the house.

"Mmmm, what smells so good?" he asked when he entered.

"I don't have much to offer you other than trout and fried potatoes."

"Trout?"

"Yes, there's a trout stream at the bottom of the hill behind the house. This time of year the fish are practically jumping out of the water, so it was easy to catch a couple."

"So did you use your hands or a pole?"

The grin on his face was too appealing. "Dinner will be ready in a few minutes," she replied. "I heated a kettle of hot water for you to clean up before we eat."

"Thanks."

Colt washed his face and hands, slicked his hair back with water, and put on his shirt and the stockings.

"Hope you won't be offended if I come to the dinner table without boots."

With a theatrical fluttering of her hand to her chest, she said, "But ah do declare, Deputy Fraser, I've never been so insulted. Why, my Daddy would never tolerate such outlandish behavior."

He rolled his eyes. "Are we going to fight the Civil War again?"

"Not on an empty stomach. Sit down and eat before the food gets cold."

There was a gingham tablecloth, and the candle surrounded by white yucca blossoms in the center of the table cast a warm glow.

"I've never tried to pass myself off as a cook," Cassie warned when Colt pulled out her chair for her.

Remembering the dessert competition, Colt prepared himself for the worst. After a few bites, he was pleasantly surprised to find the truth was just the opposite.

"Cassie, this is very good."

"Well, anyone can fry fish and potatoes," she said, but she couldn't help smiling with pleasure at his words of praise.

When they finished eating, Colt lit a fire to get the night chill out of the living room while Cassie cleaned up the dinner dishes. Then they sat down on the rug in front of the fireplace to relax with their coffee cups.

"Don't get too comfortable," Cassie said. "It's getting pretty late and you should think about getting back to town."

Looking at her lying there with the fire's glow turning her auburn hair to copper, he felt anything but comfortable. Rising passion had begun to cloud his brain. Getting back to town was the farthest thing from his mind.

"I've decided to stay here tonight," Cassie continued. "Will you tell my family so they won't worry?"

"How can they not worry about you being out here alone?"

Her tempting lips curved into a smile. "Colt, if you intend to live in the West, you've got to learn that the women aren't clinging vines. We're quite capable of taking care of ourselves."

"Sounds like we're getting back to our earlier South versus West argument."

"I'm referring to physical strength, not an inner one. Out here we have to learn pretty early how to do a man's job. As feminine as Cathy is, she's as good a rancher as anyone."

"I'm sure she is."

He saw her eyes deepen in reflection. "You know, Colt, Cathy would be the perfect woman for you. She has the qualities to fit into your world, as well as mine."

"My world, your world. Do you really feel they're so different, Cass?"

"Of course they are. So why pursue me instead of Cathy?"

"It's a male thing. When I look at Cathy I immediately envision marriage, gingham curtains on the windows, and loading up the children to take them to church."

"And when you look at me?" Cassie wanted to bite her tongue the moment she said it. Did she really want to know?

"Honey, I can't help envisioning the delights of that hayloft."

A blush heightened the color of her cheeks, and she lowered her eyes. "Do I appear that cheap to you?"

He reached over and grasped her hand. "On the contrary, Cass. You have a do-not-touch air about you that's enough to scare off braver men than I. But from the moment you landed on my lap in that stagecoach, and I looked into those blue eyes of yours, honey, you lit a fire in me that I can't put out—and Lord knows I've tried to. But as much as I want you, I can't fight the ghost of Ted McBride."

She looked him straight in the eyes. "And if there wasn't a Ted McBride?"

His dark eyes immediately deepened with a devilish gleam, and his mouth widened in a grin. "We'd *still* be in that hayloft."

The corners of her lips tucked into a smile. Sighing deeply, she stretched out on her side and pillowed her cheek on her hands. She couldn't condemn him for his honesty. It just made her realize how much she wished he would remain.

"I don't know if that was a compliment or an insult, Colt, but I'd like to think it was a compliment. And whether or not you intended it to be, I think it was quite romantic."

The warmth of his chuckle rippled her spine. With every moment they spent together, her memory of Ted faded more and more.

"I don't think you have any idea what a desirable woman you are, Cass."

"And I have to admit that being in that hayloft with you sounds considerably more exciting than the church pew and children. But, Colt, since you came to Arena Roja we've gotten to know each other pretty well. Is making love the only way you see me? Surely by now your view of me goes beyond merely having sex."

"Doesn't making love, by its own definition, go far beyond having sex? Men, prostitutes, animals have sex. It's an act of nature. *Making love* combines that natural act with an emotional one. So yes, when I first saw you, I wanted to have sex with you, and now—"

Dammit! He had backed himself into a corner. She was one beautiful woman, but he'd been around women enough to know it took more than that to fall in love. He liked being with her, he liked teasing her, he liked her sense of humor, her loyalty to others. He loved the sound of her laughter, her smile. He admired her courage and fortitude. He thought about her constantly. But that was because he wanted to go to bed with her—so that wasn't love.

"And now?" she asked expectantly. Despite the softness of her tone, the question echoed like the boom of thunder.

"And now I think of nothing but making love to you."

She felt an incredible joy, along with equal disbelief. "Are you saying you've fallen in love with me?"

"I've never been in love before, so I'm not certain what I'm feeling."

"Except that you're certain that you want to *make love* to me." Smiling, Cassie closed her eyes, the sound of his voice as soothing as a lullaby.

Well, he'd done enough damage for one day—and made a fool of himself doing so. Colt finished his coffee and rose to his feet. "I guess I better get going."

When she didn't move, he realized she had drifted into sleep.

He bent down and carefully lifted her into his arms, carried her into the bedroom, and gently lowered her to the bed.

For a few seconds, Colt stared down hungrily at the seductive picture she made, with her mass of auburn hair a spectacular contrast against the pillowcase. Unable to resist the temptation, he leaned over and pressed a light kiss to her lips. He remained bent above her sleeping figure, studying the serenity in the face that had filled his days and nights from the first moment they'd met.

"I looked, Cassie, but I didn't touch," he whispered tenderly, and pulled up the blanket and covered her with loving care.

He couldn't leave her alone here with the doors and windows unlatched, so he grabbed a pillow off the bed and returned to the living room. Then he latched the door, lay down on the rug, tucked the pillow under his head, and fell asleep—with visions of a hayloft dancing in his mind.

Chapter 20

Cassie slowly awoke, yawned, and drowsily swung her legs over the edge of the bed. She stopped short when she discovered she was still clothed in the same skirt and blouse she'd worn last night. Come to think of it, she couldn't even remember going to bed. She pinched her arm to make sure she wasn't dreaming and tried to recall what *had* happened. She remembered Colt being there and admitting he wanted to make love to her . . . "Good Lord!" she cried as she bolted to her feet and rushed out of the room.

The living room was empty, but there was a bed pillow on the floor in front of the fireplace. Then she smelled the unmistakable fragrance of freshly brewed coffee. A pot was sitting on the stove.

Apparently Colt must have spent the night on the floor in front of the fireplace and brewed the coffee before he'd left this morning.

The man was very thoughtful, but she wished he'd wakened her. She would have ridden back with him.

Cassie poured herself a cup and leaned back against the counter, thinking about their conversation last night.

There was no sense in trying to fool herself any

longer how she felt about him—she was in love with him. But she knew it would be a bittersweet romance, because the ending was inevitable. Apparently she was doomed to a life of watching the man she loved ride away. She should have had enough sense not to let herself get in this position.

Desolate, she strolled outside. It looked like another day of bright blue sky wih patches of white clouds. At least the earth hadn't turned topsy-turvy just because her world had.

"Good morning."

Startled, she spun around. Colt had just crested the hill, and he held up two trout. "Hate to say this, Miz Braden, but you make a pretty poor hostess. Not only do you fall asleep in the middle of a guest's sentence, but then you expect him to get up the next morning and catch his own breakfast."

"Thank you, Colt. Here, let me. That's woman's work," she said, when he started to scale the fish on a nearby stump of a tree.

"Really? And here you had me convinced that there's no division of labor between a man and woman on a ranch."

"I admit there are a couple."

"Such as?"

"I don't hunt b'ar and I don't chew tobaccy."

Laughing, he relinquished the fish to her.

And Cassie's world had just gotten a lot brighter.

Upon returning to Arena Roja, Cassie went directly to her house, and Colt took the horses to the livery.

"I see you met up with Cassie," Jeff said as he began to unsaddle Midnight. "Figured she and the kids would stay at the ranch for a couple days." He chuckled. "Or at least until Miss Rose Lee left town."

"The kids?" Colt asked.

"Yeah. Sam and the James brothers."

"They weren't with Cassie. What's wrong?" Colt asked at Jeff's troubled look.

"You're pulling my leg, right?"

"No, Jeff, I'm not. What's this all about?"

"Dan James was just here to see if Cassie and the kids were back yet. Sam left them a note yesterday saying they were worried about Cassie and were going out to the Lazy B to cheer her up. When Cassie and them didn't come back last night, nobody thought nothing of it. We figured they decided to spend the night."

Colt felt a knot tighten in his stomach. He shook his head. "They weren't at the ranch. How long have they been gone?"

"Sometime yesterday afternoon. They must have walked, because they didn't come here for transportation. The ranch is only five miles from town and they know the way blindfolded. Even Petey."

"Is it possible somebody might have given them a ride?"

"I don't know. You don't think anyone would hurt those kids, do you, Colt?"

"No human, at least. I better talk to Dan."

"I'm coming with you," Jeff said.

Dan James was behind the desk when Colt and Jeff entered the lobby.

"Morning," Dan said.

"Dan, Jeff tells me that Sam and your boys took off for the Lazy B yesterday."

"Yes, and those boys are going to get a good tongue lashing when they get back. Their mother is worried sick since we read the note. Sam's poor mother's in the same state of mind."

"Have they done this before?"

"No. They've always told us where they were going—even if it was just down to the creek to go swimming." Dan gave Colt a wary look. "What's wrong? Did something happen to one of them?"

"Dan, they didn't show up at the ranch."

The man kept his composure, but his eyes revealed his rising fear. "Sam wouldn't lie about where they were going."

"Do you have any idea of the actual time they left?"

Colt had ridden out there about an hour after Cassie had left. If the children had left before him, he would have passed them on the road.

"What difference does the time make?" Dan asked, his anxiousness mounting. "It doesn't take all night to walk five miles. I better go and tell Nina and Sarah."

"Tell Nina and Sarah what?" Nina James asked, joining them. "Good morning," she greeted with her usual friendly smile in spite of her worried state. "You boys come for breakfast?"

"No, Nina," Dan said.

At her husband's worried look, her smile faded. "It's about the children, isn't it? One of them's had an accident. Who? What happened?"

Dan put an arm around her shoulders and led her over to one of the chairs in the lobby. "Sit down, honey."

"Tell me what happened! Which one of them is hurt?" The three men exchanged meaningful glances. "Tell me," she cried.

"The children never reached the Lazy B," Dan said.

"Never . . . oh, dear God!" Her knees buckled, and she sank down on the chair. "I thought they went with Cassie."

"No, they went alone, Nina," Colt said. "We're riding out to look for them now. They might have just gotten confused and wandered off in the wrong direction."

"There are wild animals out there. Indians."

"Nina, the Apaches moved west a month ago."

"There's always a few strays, and if they came upon the children they might have—Oh, God! Oh, dear God!" She broke down and started weeping. "My babies. My babies."

"We better get started," Colt said. "Will you tell Sarah?"

Dan nodded. "Yes, but I'm going with you. Don't leave without me."

"Perhaps it would be better if you remain here with Nina and Sarah, Dan."

"My boys are out there somewhere," he said. "I'm going with you."

"I'll go get my sisters to stay with them," Jeff said, and ran out of the hotel.

Colt went into the kitchen with the Jameses to find

Sarah Starr. The woman had buried her husband and five children, and now he had to be the one to tell her that her remaining child was missing.

Upon hearing the news Sarah sank down on a chair and sat in silence, staring into space.

It seemed an eternity, but it was actually only a minute before Cassie and Cathy showed up. They rushed over to embrace the distraught mothers.

Feeling there was nothing more he could do for them at this time, Colt prepared to leave. Cassie grabbed him by the arm when he started to go.

"Colt, I want to go along."

"It's better you stay here with these women."

"Colt, I know every rise and hollow of these woods."

"Honey, I don't doubt that, but Cathy's going to need your help with Nina and Sarah."

Her hand slipped from his arm. "I suppose you're right." She looked up at him, and for the first time he realized the personal anguish she was suffering, too. She adored those children and had to be heartbroken.

"Go with God, Colt," she said softly and returned to grasp Sarah's hand between her own.

Word of the missing children spread rapidly through town. There were a dozen and a half mounted riders waiting when Colt got to the livery. He was just about to lay out his intentions when Kit Carson and twelve of his Navajo entourage joined them.

"As you've all heard," Colt said, "Sam Starr and Bowie and Petey James are missing. They left town yesterday to go to the Lazy B Ranch. We have no idea if someone offered them a ride, or if they went on foot. We know for certain they didn't leave in anything from the livery.

"I think the best approach is for us to split into two groups. General Carson, you can take one group and spread out on the right side of the road. I'll take the other group and do the same on the left. Don't spread too far apart; stay close enough to each other so that you don't miss anything. We'll cover every inch between here and the Lazy B. General Carson, your experience far exceeds mine; if you have a better idea, I'm glad to hear it."

"Your plan is sound and practical," Carson said. "I suggest, though, that we send out a couple of my Navajo scouts in the event there are hostiles in the area."

"As you wish, General. I rode down this same road this morning and encountered no problem. And I'm told that the Apaches have moved to higher ground for the summer."

"How about the gang that shot my dad?" Jeff said. "They could still be in these parts. Or even have come back to hit the bank again."

If the kids had stumbled upon them, the malicious murderer wouldn't hesitate to kill the children. Then Colt thought of a ray of hope. "Or the children might have seen them and are hiding."

Carson spoke in Navajo to his men, and two of the Indians rode away.

Progress was slow, and even though Colt tried to maintain a positive attitude, it was obvious that the general opinion was that they wouldn't find the children alive.

After thirty minutes of plodding, they hadn't even covered a quarter-mile when the two Navajo scouts came riding back at a full gallop. Colt's spirits plummeted. He could tell by their serious miens as they conversed with Carson that the scouts had discovered something. He glanced at Dan James and knew the worried man was of the same opinion.

The general frowned grimly and turned to them. "The scouts said there's a large group of Apaches headed this way. They're sure they saw three white children among them. One was a girl with red hair they remembered seeing in town."

"That's got to be Sam," Dan said excitedly. "Were the other two children boys?"

After a short exchange with the scouts, Carson nodded. "One with dark hair and a yellow-haired younger one."

"That's them. Bowie and Petey. Thank God, thank God," Dan cried joyously.

"I wouldn't celebrate too soon, gentlemen," Carson warned as the men cheered and offered back slaps to Dan.

"What do you mean?" Colt said. "It would appear the Apaches are bringing them to town."

"The Apaches are Arizona Chiricahuas, my friend," Carson said. "They were a peaceful tribe until '62, when a half-assed government official ordered the hanging of several of their tribesmen. The Indians had been innocent of the crime they'd been executed for, and the Chiricahuas went on the warpath. They've been raiding and killing soldiers and settlers ever since. The people of Arizona are terrorized because the army hasn't been able to stop them for the past four years."

"So what are they doing in New Mexico?" Colt asked.

"That's what surprises me," Carson said. "Their chief, Cochise, has vowed his people will not be driven from their hunting grounds."

Carson's words started a scramble, as the group turned to ride back to town to protect their women and children.

For many years, Indian attacks had not been uncommon to the residents of Arena Roja. As soon as the group arrived back in town, the church bell rang out the alarm, and people dropped whatever they were doing and hastened into action.

The merchants closed their shutters to protect their glass windows. The banker shoved all the cash into the safe and locked it up. Mothers grabbed their children and headed for the church; women without children grabbed rifles and took positions among the men. Colt saw that Jethro had abandoned his sickbed and had taken a position at the jail. His son and two daughters were at his side, rifles in hand.

"Jeff, get your sisters and dad out of here. The Apaches are coming in from this direction, and this is the first place they'll hit when they ride in. General Carson wants everyone up at the other end, because we don't have enough firepower to spread out the whole length of the town."

At that moment, Bob and Glen Callum rode up in a gallop. "They're about a half-mile behind us. At least a hundred, heading straight for town."

"Glen, ride up and warn the others. Take Cathy with you." Colt lifted her behind the man, and Glen galloped away. "Bob, give your horse to Jethro; he's still a little shaky on his feet. Cassie, you crawl up behind him."

They helped Jethro mount, and Cassie swung up behind her father. Colt, Jeff, and Bob ran behind on foot, rousting any stragglers who were too far from the others.

At the other end of the town, some of the men and women had taken positions on rooftops and the balcony of the hotel near the church. Others were opposite the hotel on the other side of the street. General Carson ordered armed residents to take their positions behind a barricade of wagons and sandbags, which he and his Navajos had erected in front of the church as the final line of defense.

In passing the livery, Colt saw that the stagecoach had been on the verge of pulling out. Gus was trying to unhitch the team and get the horses into the stable as Rose Lee Beckenridge yanked at his arm, screaming at him for the stage to leave before the Indians arrived.

The minute Rose Lee saw Colt, she threw herself into his arms and clung to him. "Oh, Colt, help me! You've got to save me! Ah don't want to die!"

"Rose Lee, get to the church with the other women."

"I'm too petrified to move. Ya'll have to carry me."

"Too bad she ain't too petrified to stop that squealing," Gus grumbled. "Keep that she-cat off my back so's I can get these horses off the street."

With rifle in hand, Sarah Starr came over to them, her shoulders squared, her back ramrod straight.

"Lady, get moving to that church right now, or I'll kick your worthless ass all the way there myself."

Stunned, Rose Lee gaped at her. "Ah do declare, no lady ah know would ever use such language—"

"Rose Lee," Colt warned, "the lady means what she said."

Sobbing and threatening collapse, Miss Rose Lee Beckenridge stumbled toward the church.

Nary a sound could be heard among the defenders as they watched the Indians ride up slowly. This unexpected approach surprised them all. Whenever the Indians raided, they always rode in yelping, a bone-chilling, petrifying sound.

"Hold your fire," Carson ordered when the Indians halted near the town limits. "They aren't wearing paint, so maybe they've come in peace."

The stagecoach driver snorted. "Cochise come in peace!" He spat a stream of tobacco juice into the dirt.

The Indian leader rode forward on a magnificent chestnut stallion. Two others rode behind him, one on the right, the other on the left.

"I am Cochise, chief of the Chiricahua Apaches. Cochise has been told that Kit Carson, the famous scout of the white man, is among you."

Carson stepped out from behind the barricade.

"Carson's eyes are pleased to see the great chief of the Chiricahua again."

He had often spoken with this chief, whose mere name struck terror in the hearts of Arizona settlers, and for the next few minutes the two men spoke together in Apache. Then Carson stepped back to the townsfolk.

"I've agreed to a powwow in the center of town, with Cochise, Mangas Coloradas—the father of his squaw—and his war chief, Goyathlay, or Geronimo as we whites call him."

"Sure you're not walking into a trap, General?" Colt asked.

"Cochise said he does not come with the paint of war or a raised war club."

"The children. What about the children?" Dan cried out.

"That is the purpose of the meeting, Mr. James. Colt, I want you"—his gaze swept the crowd—"and young Braden to accompany me."

"Me?" Jeff said, astounded. "Why would you want me?"

"Because your father's the sheriff. This town has no mayor now, so the sheriff and deputy represent the leading authority here. Since your father is still weak, it will honor the chief to have the sheriff's son represent him. You two will have to shuck your gunbelts."

"I bet it's a trap," Gus said, and several of the people around the driver nodded in agreement.

Colt glanced at Cassie. Her face was stretched tight with anxiety, her body taut with tension.

"Cochise is a man of honor," Carson declared. "He wouldn't disgrace his honor under a flag of truce."

"We ought to shoot him and that murderous Geronimo while we have the chance," Gus said.

"And that would result in everyone here being slaughtered and the town burned to the ground."

"We've got enough firepower here to wipe out him and that scum with him," Gus continued to argue.

"What makes you think we can do what the cavalry has failed to do? Cochise is too smart to take such a risk. He's one of the greatest military strategists I've ever known. If you doubt me, ask the army officers who have attempted to capture him. Right now, there are probably a hundred more Apaches concealed around us and watching our every move."

Carson turned to address Dan. "Mr. James, if you want to get your children back, I'd advise you to keep an eye on this hotheaded stagecoach driver." Fear gleamed in the eyes of the Bradens as they looked at Jeff, then Cassie came over.

"Be careful, Colt, Gus could be right."

Colt grasped her shoulders and gazed into her worried eyes. "Whatever happens, Cass, I wouldn't want to have missed knowing you."

"Ready, gentlemen?" Carson asked Colt and Jeff.

They removed their gunbelts and followed him down the street toward the three approaching Indians.

"Show Cochise respect, and let me do the talking," Carson said.

The parties halted in the middle of the street in the

center of the town. Cochise and Carson raised their hands in a sign of peace.

"It has been many years since I've had the pleasure of speaking to the mighty chief of the Chiricahua," Carson said. "I welcome you, and my old friend Mangas Coloradas, and the fearless warrior Geronimo."

"Cochise is glad to see Kit Carson, friend of the Chiricahua."

"I thank you for the honor. I bring with me Deputy Colt Fraser and Jeffrey Braden, who is the son of the town's sheriff."

Colt nodded his head. "I am honored to meet you, Chief Cochise." Jeff followed Colt's lead and did the same.

Carson and Cochise began to converse again in Apache. As they did, Colt took the opportunity to study Geronimo.

The Indian had a fierce gleam in his eyes and seemed to hate the white man as bitterly as the stage driver hated the Indians. It was clear there was much to be resolved before there would ever be peace between such people.

The powwow ended, and Geronimo wheeled his horse and rode back to his tribesmen. Colt had no idea what was happening until the three children stepped out of the crowd of Apaches. Appearing unharmed, they started to walk toward the townsfolk. Sam paused when Cochise spoke to her as she passed him.

"So long, Chief. Thanks for everything," she said

when he finished, and walked on with a wave of good-bye.

The enigmatic expression the great chief had worn throughout the powwow changed to a near grin.

"Blazing Hair has much courage. She make good squaw someday," Cochise said to General Carson.

Jeff leaned over and said sotto voce to Colt, "Did he say good squaw or good squawk?"

Then Cochise and his escort wheeled their horses and rode back to their tribesmen. Yelping, the thundering horde rode away and disappeared over a hill.

Only a cloud of dust remained to mark their passage.

Chapter 21

Still stunned by the scene that had unfolded before them, the residents moved slowly back to their houses and businesses. Shutters were removed, the bank replaced its cash drawer and reopened for business, the restaurants relit their ovens.

Many of the religious went into their respective churches for prayerful thanks.

Under the loving care of his three children, Sheriff Braden was transported back to his bed.

Gus Burk reharnessed the team to the stagecoach, hoping to make up the hour already lost. He had gained several passengers now determined to leave town, and much to his relief he had lost his former passenger, who'd been carried back to the hotel with a case of "vapors" by the reluctant deputy.

After depositing Rose Lee on the bed of her room, Colt joined the Jameses and Sarah Starr in the hotel lobby, where they listened as Sam related their harrowing experience.

"We stopped because Petey had to pee, and Bowie and I were taking a drink of water when four Indians suddenly jumped out at us from nowhere and took us to their chief. I told him he better let us go, or he'd be in worse trouble than us when our parents found out."

Sarah drew a shuddering sigh. "Sam, Cochise is the most feared Indian chief in the country. He might have killed you right there on the spot."

Sam's eyes rounded in surprise. "That's the same thing he said, Mama."

"Go on. What happened then?" Dan asked.

"I said if he was so great, how come he had to pick on three little kids?"

"I bet he liked that," Dan said. "What did he do when you said that?"

"He said my tongue was as blazing as my hair. Then that ugly guy Geronimo started to argue with him. I didn't understand them 'cause they were talking Apache, but I could tell Ugly Face wanted to kill us and the chief said no. They took us away, and when it got dark they tied our hands and told us to go to sleep."

"What brave darlings you were," Nina said, hugging her sons tighter to her sides.

"I wasn't as brave as Sam, Mom," Bowie said. "It was kind of scary."

"Yeah, scary," Petey said. He slipped his hand into his brother's.

Seeing that his wife was on the verge of tears, Dan James said, "I don't know what we're going to do with you boys. You've got punishment coming for running off the way you did, but we'll decide that later. You go and clean yourselves up now."

The boys scampered away, and Sarah left, hugging

Sam to her side. As Dan put his arm around the trembling shoulders of his wife, Colt slapped him on the shoulder and left.

Outside, as he helped clear away the hastily constructed barricade in front of the church, Colt reflected again on the hazards of getting too involved with the townsfolk.

There was a lot more to being a deputy than just wearing a badge.

Cassie brushed out her hair and tied it back with a yellow ribbon. Tonight General Carson was joining them for dinner, and she had overhead her father tell Cathy to set an extra plate for Colt, as well.

With all the excitement over the Indians, she hadn't gotten around to telling her sister about last night. Neither of them were much good at keeping a secret from each other, and as soon as Cathy saw her in a dress, her sister would figure it out immediately.

She stepped back and viewed herself in the oval-shaped floor mirror in the corner. She'd worn this yellow gown on special occasions for the past five years—not that there'd been that many. The color was becoming, but maybe the time had come to make a new dress.

Cassie spun around several times, striking a different pose each time, and then slumped in dejection. She just didn't look comfortable in a dress like other women did. Her legs were as long as a horse's, and her breasts seemed too small for her height, which was too tall for most of the men in town. She always felt lanky and awkward.

And why couldn't she have beautiful, honey-blond hair like Cathy? Instead, hers was neither brown nor red, but an in-between shade of both.

Doggone it! She loved her sister dearly, more than life itself, but how did Cathy always manage to look dainty and feminine? While she . . .

Yet last night when she'd been alone with Colt, she had felt attractive and desirable. She wasn't just another girl he wanted to have sex with—he wanted to make love to her. It had thrilled her to hear him say that.

He had to be in love with her, even if he didn't realize it. Her knight on a white horse had a tin badge on his chest instead of armor, and a Colt on his hip in lieu of a lance. And she was in love with him. And tonight she would tell him so.

Cassie heard the sound of male voices and knew the guests had arrived. Her heart started thumping at the prospect of seeing Colt again.

She hurried from her bedroom just as he threw back his head in laughter at something the general had said to him.

At the sight and sound, Cassie could barely keep from throwing herself at him.

"How lovely you look," Cathy said when Cassie joined them.

"Yeah, what got you into a dress?" Jeff said. "You trying to impress the deputy?"

She would kill him. She would wring her brother's neck the next time they were alone.

"We have a distinguished dinner guest, Jeffrey,"

Cassie replied with a sugary smile that was more threatening than sweet.

"And dinner's ready," Cathy interjected quickly. "Jeff, will you help Dad to his seat? General Carson, please take the seat at the opposite end of the table. Colt, you and Cassie can sit on that side, and Jeff and I will sit on this side. If you'll all be seated, I'll serve dinner."

"You've done the cooking, so you sit down, Cathy," Cassie said. "I'll serve dinner."

Colt remained on his feet until Cassie was ready to sit down, then he pulled out her chair to seat her and sat down beside her.

"I've been anxious to hear what you and Cochise discussed, General Carson," Colt said.

"I know the Chiricahuas very well," the general said. "As I mentioned to you the other night, Cochise advocated living peacefully with the white man until those hangings in '62 caused him to go on the warpath.

"Since then, my attempts to convince Cochise to bring his people to live on a reservation have been unsuccessful."

"I'm not implying that he should take the government's blunder lightly," Cassie said. "But with all the slaughtering over the past four years, they've certainly had their revenge. If Cochise was such an advocate of peace, General, why wouldn't he be willing to cease fighting and do what you suggest, if the government admits their mistake and makes some kind of restitution?"

"Because the government wants to move them to a reservation. Cochise refuses to do so. He says that Arizona is the home of the Chiricahua."

"If it would end this slaughter, why won't the government let them stay where they are?"

"They want the Indians where they can control them on their terms," Carson said. "It doesn't take much to set off an Indian war, and it would be impossible to restrain them if the Indians are on their familiar grounds. The government wants to make room for the influx of settlers."

"By moving peaceful Indians out of their homes?" Cathy asked.

"Unfortunately, Miss Braden, that has been the case. Have you heard of The Trail of Tears? In '38 and '39, the government forced the Cherokee nation in Georgia and Florida to move their people to Oklahoma. More than four thousand of them perished from starvation and exposure on that move. They forced the Florida Seminoles to do the same thing in '42."

"I've read what they did to the Five Civilized Tribes," Colt said.

"Five Civilized Tribes?" Jeff asked. "What's that?"

"In the southeastern part of this country there were five tribes: the Cherokees, Choctaws, Chickasaws, Creeks, and Seminoles. They formed a confederacy, somewhat like the Iroquois Confederacy farther north, and lived together peacefully. The difference between these five nations and the Iroquois is that these Indians were civilized. They planted crops, built houses and even schools. They had newspapers and even a written constitution, like this country does, to govern them. Sadly, they had the misfortune of having land that their white neighbors wanted in order to expand. So like so many others, they were deemed a threat and were shipped to the west, to an environment so foreign to them that fifty percent of them perished," Carson explained.

"Those members of the Five Civilized Tribes who remained in the South pledged their loyalty to the Confederacy during the war," Colt added.

Carson nodded. "Because their bitterness wasn't toward Southerners, but to Washington, who forced them to abandon their own constitution and live under the white man's rules. As the government is now forcing the Western Indian to do."

"Sounds like the Indians are fighting for the same cause as the Confederacy did," Colt said. "Southerners settled our states, lived in them a couple hundred years, then fought a war to protect them when the Yankees in the North told them they had to live by their rules."

"Colt, my friend," Kit Carson said, "I don't wish to refight that war with you. I have enough on my hands right here with the Indians."

"And I've had enough of war to last me for a lifetime." Colt winked at Carson. "Unless it's the battle of the sexes."

"Well, I enjoyed the history lesson," Jethro said gruffly, "but I wanna know what the Indian chief has on his mind."

"Cochise said he has no fight with the white man in New Mexico, because they have made their homes away from the land of the Chiricahua. They crossed into New Mexico because the cavalry was pursuing them, but they are returning to Arizona."

"Did he tell you why they took the children prisoners?"

"He said the children were in danger. A bear had picked up the children's scent and was following them. The flesh of a bear will feed many, so Cochise believed the children were a good sign to his people. He had no thought of killing or taking them with him. That would have brought dishonor to his tribe in the eyes of the god who sent them the good fortune."

Colt said, "If those three sprouts are lucky charms, I'm the king of England. They've brought me nothing but bad luck since I met them, and I even had to get shot to do that." He winked at Cassie to let her know he was joking.

After dinner, Cassie's hopes of confessing her love to Colt were thwarted when he was called to duty over a fistfight in the Alhambra.

The Braden house was in darkness the next time Colt passed it.

Kit Carson and the Navajos left at dawn the next morning. True to his character, Carson departed the way he preferred to live, with no cheering crowd, no flags waving, and no brass band.

Four hours later, Colt walked to the stage office to say good-bye to the the departing Miss Rose Lee Beckenridge, whom Dr. Williams had fortified with a mild sedative in the event she felt another impending attack of the vapors.

"When you get back to Virginia, Rose Lee, say hello to my family and tell them I think of them often."

"You should leave this unpleasant town, Coltran, and come back with me to Virginia."

"I expect to leave for California next week. By then the sheriff should be well enough to resume his duties."

"Ah do declare, Coltran Fraser, ah don't understand why you feel an obligation to these people. Why, they're just a lot of overbearin' Yankees. There's not a gentleman among them, except for the doctor. And women! Why, the slaves on Pheasant Run dress finer than the women in this town. It must be plumb painful for you to tolerate it."

"I manage, Rose Lee."

"We're pulling out, Colt," the driver said.

"Have a pleasant trip back, Rose Lee."

"What can be pleasant about being jostled about in this stagecoach like a sack of grain?"

He kissed her cheek and helped her into the coach.

"Goodbye, Coltran." She dabbed at her eyes with a handkerchief. "Ah do declare, this is so painful, my heart is breakin'."

The flutter of a lace-trimmed white handkerchief was his final glimpse of Miss Rose Lee Beckenridge.

Upon seeing Cassie hitching up the wagon outside the livery, Colt walked down to her. He groaned when the three sprouts ran up and climbed into the back of it.

"You aren't actually driving out to the ranch again, are you?"

"It has crossed my mind," Cassie said in amusement.

"Defying the gods again. Regardless of what you think, you all need supervision. That includes you, Miss Braden."

"You know, Colt," Cassie said, "I've been thinking about the subject of bad luck, which you mentioned at dinner last night, and I have a theory about all the accidents I've been having lately. Remember what General Carson said about Cochise believing the children brought his tribe good luck? Think about this: your bad luck started when you were shot—which was before you arrived here."

"Debatable," he countered.

"Well, so is this: the children have been to the Lazy B hundreds of times, but since your arrival, it's been one disaster after another. I'm beginning to think you could be responsible for all this bad luck I've been having lately. The Hindus call it bad karma."

"You're having fun with this, aren't you, Miss Braden? First Indian superstition, now Hindu philosophy. What's next?"

"How about some good, old-fashioned faith in the Almighty, Deputy Fraser? This is just a quick trip out to the ranch. If we're not back by noon, send out a posse.

"Hi, ho! And away we go!" She flicked the reins, and with the children laughing uproariously, the wagon rolled away.

They had been gone less than two hours when Colt decided to ride out to the ranch, and there he found Cassie packing up some clothing.

"Why, Deputy Fraser, what a surprise. What brings you to the Lazy B?"

"With all the bad *karma* I generate, I've been concerned about you and the children out here alone."

She grinned. "Battling broken ladders and vicious skunks."

Chuckling, he said, "Okay, so I'm not very convincing."

"The other day, when I was looking for something for you to wear, I realize many of these clothes would never be worn again, so I decided to pack them up."

"And that's important enough to come out here the day after an Indian scare?"

"Is it if I want to donate them to the church's fund-raising drive tomorrow," she said.

"So where are the sprouts? I didn't see them when I rode in."

She nodded toward a window. "At the bottom of the hill, picking bouquets of wildflowers for their mothers. Isn't that sweet?"

"They're probably doing it because it gives them a chance to do something destructive—even to Mother Nature."

"Colt, do you really think that they're as bad as you make them out to be?" she scolded.

He broke into laughter. "Of course not, but I'd never let them know that. So, maybe they kind of grow on you. What about you, Cass? When are you going to admit your true feelings?"

"I always have. They know I adore them."

"I'm not talking about the children."

He turned around and went outside.

Cassie watched him start down the hill. If someone were to ask her what she admired most about him physically, aside from his handsome face, strong body, and the warmth of his chuckle, she would have to say his walk. He walked tall, with neither a swagger nor a slouch. The kind of walk that said, This is what I am, who I am.

Sam and Bowie came running over as soon as they saw Colt. "I s'pose you came to snoop on what we're doing," Sam said.

"Just making sure you're not trying to start any more Indian wars," he said.

"I swear, Deputy, we didn't do nothin' to those Indians."

"You thinking again of jailing us, Deputy?" Bowie asked with a worried look.

"I was thinking of it on general principle, but I lost the vote."

"I betcha this is more of your teasing." Sam grinned.

Her eyes suddenly widened, and she pointed to the ground. "Yipes! Look, it's a snake! Let's get out of here."

Colt paled when he saw the brown-and-yellow reptile slithering through the grass, its forked tongue darting out. He froze at the sight of the horny rings on the end of its tail.

"Come on, Petey," Bowie called.

"Slinky!" Petey cried out with joy and ran toward the snake.

Colt's blood ran cold, and perspiration broke out on his body at the snake's chilling, lethal rattle. His

heartbeat was as loud in his ears as the ominous rattle. Coiled to strike, the snake's flat head and glistening eyes were fixed on Petey, the nearest threat to it.

Colt jumped forward and shoved Petey aside just
as the snake struck, and his shot blew the snake's
head off.

Transfixed, Sam and Bowie walked over and stared
at the remains of the snake. Then, mouth agape, Sam
looked up at Colt, who stood silent, still holding his
drawn pistol.

"That was the fastest draw I've ever seen," she said,
reverence in her voice.

Cassie came running down the hill. "I heard a shot.
What happened?" Upon seeing Petey lying on the
ground, her eyes darted from him to the dead snake.
"Dear God, was he bitten?"

The panic in her voice snapped Colt out of his
trance, and he slipped his gun back into its holster.

"No," Sam said as Petey stood up and ran into
Cassie's arms. "The deputy saved Petey from being
bitten."

Cassie hugged the boy tighter, tears glistening in her
eyes as she glanced up at Colt. "Thank you."

Breathless with excitement, the two older children
described the whole scene to her. When they finished, she looked around and saw that Colt had
moved away and was sitting off alone. "Sam, you
and the boys go back to the house. I put out some
cookies and milk for you. I want to talk to Colt for a
few minutes."

Chapter 22

As the children ran off, Cassie walked over to Colt and sat down beside him, smiling tenderly. "You once told me you were petrified of snakes, Colt, yet you risked your life to save Petey's. That was very noble of you."

"Don't remind me," he grumbled, visibly shaken by his own actions. "Dead or alive, I still hate snakes."

"I think most of us do," she said, putting a consoling hand on his arm. "But I've never seen you like this. There's something greater behind your hatred of them. What is it, Colt? Did someone you love die from a snakebite?"

"I wasn't much older than Petey when I saw my fourteen-year-old brother being bitten by a copperhead. He was the eldest of us, and we all loved him so much. I sat at his bedside holding his hand, sobbing and praying that he wouldn't die."

Cassie's heart ached. "Colt, I'm so sorry. If it's painful for you, don't go on."

Lost in the memory of that moment of terror, he didn't seem to hear her. "In those deadly seconds today, that long-ago scene flashed through my mind, and I relived the horror of it. Only then it was my older brother Will who had shoved aside his four-year-old brother and taken the strike himself; the bite that had been meant for me."

"Then he didn't die," Cassie said, relieved. "You said your brother Will lives in Virginia."

"He didn't die, but neither did the memory. I still can't bear to look at snakes."

"That makes what you did for Petey even more courageous."

He shook his head. "I still can't believe I faced down a rattlesnake."

"I can. I think you'd face down Lucifer himself to try and save someone's life."

"You're giving me a lot more credit than I deserve, Miz Braden. I'm no saint."

"But you're a man who puts other people's interests above your own. Like my father's, and it's wonderful what you're doing for Jeff, too. I've never seen him so comfortable in his own skin. We're all beholden to you."

"I'm surprised Jeff told you. He swore me to secrecy."

"He didn't. I followed the two of you one morning."

"Have you told anyone else?"

"Only Cathy. We don't keep secrets from each other."

"Well, it's Jeff's secret, so let's keep it to ourselves and let him reveal it when he's ready to."

"You have my word on it."

Colt stretched out with his head in her lap, and felt the tension ease from his body. He felt at peace as he gazed at the majestic mountain peaks in the distance. The laughter of the children carried to their ears on the summer breeze.

"Oh, oh. They're plotting something," he said.

"Do you like children, Colt?" Cassie asked as she lightly stroked her fingers through his hair.

"Never thought about it much. And I can't say I've been around too many in the past five years." He paused for a short moment. "I like the sound of a child's laughter, and their incredible tiny little fingers and toes when they're born. I like their awe and excitement, whether watching the progress of an ant or the antics of a circus clown. And I like the curiosity in their eyes when they discover something new. But most of all, I like that they believe there's a Santa Claus.

"So yeah, I guess you'd say I like children."

"You'll make a great father someday."

"Who knows? Maybe someday." His gaze swept the far horizon. "This is beautiful country, Cass. It's no wonder you love this ranch so much."

"What? You mean as beautiful as those rolling green hills of Virginia that you miss so much?"

"Virginia's green, pastoral. Everything here is stark and dramatic. Look at those mountain peaks, the rock formations, the passages carved out of granite by time and erosion. Two completely different environments, but both of them splendorous."

"Do you think you could be happy settling down here? You've got the makings of a good rancher."

"I'd be happy anywhere with the woman I love."

She was silent for a minute and then said, "This is a

good time to bring up a subject that I've been thinking about a great deal."

"Is this a proposal?"

"Now why would I propose to a California bound Southern gentleman like you, Deputy Fraser?"

"Obviously you can't resist me, Miz Braden."

"Obviously I've done a pretty good job up to now, Deputy Fraser."

"Uh-huh: up to *now*, Miz Braden."

"Were you serious when you said you might be falling in love with me?" Cassie asked.

"I don't know. I've never been in love before."

"Well, I've been thinking that maybe you're right."

He sat up. "Hallelujah!"

Cassie chuckled. "I mean you've made a believer out of me; there *is* a decided difference between making love and having sex."

"The choice is yours. I'm ready anytime you are."

"Colt, please be serious. You know I'm referring to the discussion, not us actually . . . that is, I mean—"

"I know exactly what you mean."

"Then you know that our making love will probably never come to pass."

He arched a brow. "How can you be so certain?"

"I can't, but I'm relying on your integrity."

He snorted. "Ho, ho, lady. That's a big mistake."

She smiled, amusement in her eyes. He was relaxed now, which was good. She had succeeded in taking his mind off his most dreaded subject in favor of his favorite one.

"How can I be mistaken, when I've put my trust in

the town's knight in armor? When they hear about you saving Petey today, your head's going to swell to the size of a pumpkin."

He feigned indignation. "You calling this knight a pumpkin head, my lady?"

"Admit it, Fraser, you can be kind of *seedy* at times." She chuckled at her own joke.

He gently pushed her to the ground and leaned over her, his mouth so close she could feel the warmth of his breath. "I fear you must pay the price for that cruel thrust, my lady. So what shall it be, fair maiden: a kiss, or do I recite another of my poems?"

"Nay, nay, not another, Sir Knight," she groaned.

"I was hoping you'd say that."

He pressed his lips to hers in a kiss intended to be quick and light, but they'd fought to keep their hunger checked for too long. Cassie parted her lips and his kiss deepened, sending delightful thrills throughout her body. She moaned, wanting far more than a kiss.

Then the sound of laughter carried to their ears, and they sat up as the children came racing down the hill.

"Methinks the fair maiden has dodged the bullet again." Colt stood up and reached out a hand, pulling her to her feet.

The snake incident ended any further plans for remaining at the ranch. Colt loaded the trunk of clothing that Cassie had packed up onto the wagon, and then followed them back to town.

* * *

After dropping the children off at the hotel, Colt followed Cassie to the church and unloaded the trunk of clothes. "I'll take the wagon back to the livery for you."

"Don't bother," she replied. "I still need it. Colt, you're welcome to join us for dinner tonight."

"I appreciate the offer, but I thought I'd try getting to bed early. I don't think I've had a decent night's sleep since I arrived in your so-called 'quiet' little town, Miss Braden. Need anything else right now?"

"No, Deputy Fraser. I think you've done enough for us for one day." He started to leave, and Cassie put a hand on his arm. "Colt, I don't have to tell you what your action means to me. If Petey had . . ." She felt the rise of tears and choked back her words.

"I know what you're trying to say, honey. It's over; put it out of your mind."

He tipped up her chin to get her to look at him. "You know what, Cassie Braden, engaged lady? Right now I have a tremendous urge to take you in my arms—but I'm afraid the town would never recover from the scandal."

She smiled and said softly, "You know what, Deputy Fraser? Right now I have a tremendous urge for you to do it."

The merriment slowly faded from his eyes, and for the longest moment their gazes locked in an unspoken message. Her whole being filled with a need for him as she waited in anticipation for his next move.

He reached out and gently brushed her cheek. "I better get the hell out of here before I make a damn fool of myself." He quickly mounted Bullet and rode away.

Cassie folded her arms across her chest and leaned against the church door until he disappeared into the livery.

Yes, she knew now beyond any doubt that she loved Colt Fraser from the depths of her heart.

Darkness had long since descended when Colt made his final round of Arena Roja. As he passed the Williams house, he saw the doctor sitting on the porch, smoking a pipe.

"Everything quiet for the night, Deputy?"

"All clear, Doc."

The doctor took a draw on his pipe and glanced up at the sky. "Nice night."

"Yes, it is. Breeze feels good."

"How's your shoulder feeling?"

"Great. I've already forgotten about it. What's your prognosis about Jethro?"

"Looks good. No fever or infection."

"He was pretty weak the other day when those Indians showed up. How soon do you think he'll be strong enough to get back to work?"

The doctor shrugged. "Hard to say, Colt. At his age, taking a bullet in a lung takes longer to recover from than it would for a young buck like you. The old coot ought to give up sheriffing and leave it to one of you boys half his age." Williams eyed him. "You getting tired of us, Colt, or just bored?"

Colt laughed. "When would I have time to get bored

around here? Something's always happening. But I've got kin in California who I'm anxious to see."

"So you're headed to a better life in the land of milk and honey, hoping to hit a bonanza?"

"After four years of war, I guess I'm just restless. Have to know what's on the other side of the mountain, so to speak."

"Sometimes it ends up being worse than what you left behind."

"Doc, nothing could be much worse than the South right now."

"There's no Utopia." The doctor's face fell into a frown. "Colt, you saw that tribe of Indians that rode in here. They're a good example of what's between here and that land of milk and honey. Only next time, they'll probably be wearing paint and trying to cleave your skull with a war club. Sometimes a man can't see the forest for the trees. Arena Roja is a good place to settle down."

"I won't deny you have a good little town here, Doc. And it's full of fine people. But the advancement of civilization's busting loose. It no longer can be contained on the other side of the Mississippi, and these Rocky Mountains aren't going to stop it, either. Before the migration is over, Doc, you'll see a fleet of prairie schooners pass by searching for the one thing man has always coveted—a place to call the land under his feet his own."

Williams nodded. "I won't give you an argument about that."

"So they'll come West, Doc. If not by foot or stage,

they'll come by shiploads, and by trainloads—because one of these years, there'll be railroad track stretching from the Atlantic to the Pacific—they've already laid track as far west as Nebraska.

"Nothing's going to stop it—not rivers or mountains, not the Apaches, the Comanches, or the dozens of other tribes that might get in the way. Because you can't stop the advancement of civilization. The Mohawks, Mohicans, Cherokees, Seminoles, and dozens of Indian nations just as great found that out in the East and South.

"So be prepared, Doc, because the world's moving in on your little town, and life as you know it will be over—the same way it's over in the South."

"I can only hope that I'm not alive to see it happen."

"It already is." Colt tipped a finger to his hat. "Good night, sir."

"Good night."

Dr. Williams took a deep draw on his pipe as he watched Colt walk away, then he nodded slowly. "All the more reason why the town needs a young man like you, Deputy Fraser."

Dan James had retired for the night, and the dimly lit hotel lobby was empty. Colt went behind the desk, took his key from its pigeonhole, and went upstairs to his room. The moment he opened the door he was hit with a blast of hot, stuffy air.

After locking the door, Colt crossed the darkened room and opened the window; then he sat on the edge of the bed, tossed his hat and gunbelt to the side, and removed his boots.

As always, at night, his thoughts were on Cassie. He wanted her so badly that he was wound up tighter than a spring ready to pop.

"Get over it, Fraser," he muttered in disgust. He stripped down to his underwear, propped the pillows up against the headboard, then leaned back against them. He knew it would be useless to try and sleep. Suddenly he sensed a movement at the window and reached for his gun.

A figure stepped through the open window and paused, adjusting to the darkness. Colt had no such problem; he could see the invader clearly, silhouetted by moonlight.

"That's a good way to get yourself shot," he said as he slipped the gun back into its holster and leaned back against the pillows again. "Get out of here, Cass." He could feel the sweat that had begun to dot his brow.

She moved to the bedside and stood above him. "Is that what you really want, Colt?" Her hushed breathlessness in the darkness made him more acutely aware of his need for her. "I don't believe it is," she said. "We've both thought of nothing else for too long. It's time we fish or cut bait."

"Dammit, Cass, you may be sexually innocent, but you're not that naïve."

"You have accused me of taking too many risks."

"And now you're really on thin ice. So turn that cute little ass around and get out the same way you got in, while you still have the chance."

Cassie's gaze never wavered from his as she sat on the side of the bed.

"You're going to have to help me, Colt. This is all new to me. I don't know what I'm supposed to do next."

Colt curved his hand around the nape of her neck, then slowly drew her head down until their mouths were only inches apart.

"The kiss today was a mistake. I don't want any regrets, Cass." His breathing was labored with desire.

"I know what I'm doing."

"I don't think you do, but it's too late now. The negotiations just ended."

The warmth of his breath was a tantalizing torment to her senses. She closed her eyes and, with a sigh of surrender, parted her lips. Any reservations she might still have were incinerated by his kiss.

Her breathing turned to breathless gasps when he parted her shirt and his mouth and tongue began to toy with her nipples.

"Colt, I can't think when you do that."

His eyes were heavy with desire as he raised his head. "This isn't the time for thinking, Cass. It's the time for feeling."

When he undressed her and stretched out on top of her, and the curves and hollows of her body conformed to the hard muscles of his, all became whirling imagery. The warmth of him, the scent of him, the touch of his hands on her womanhood, the feel of his mouth on her breasts all became merging sensations;

as did the memory of doing the same to him, the feel of his corded muscle under her fingertips, and the sound of his groans when her lips explored him.

She felt a jolt of pain, mingled with rapture, when he entered her. Then only rapture remained, building and building to an ecstatic burst of release.

His lingering kiss drew the remaining breath from her lungs, and he raised his head and gently traced the delicate curve of her chin.

"Once you commit yourself there's no half measure with you, is there, Cass?"

She didn't understand how he still had enough breath to speak; her body and senses were still throbbing with sensation.

They lay quietly, allowing their breathing to resume its natural rhythm.

After several minutes, she turned her head and saw that he had drifted into sleep.

For a long moment Cassie stared at his face, relaxed and almost boyish-looking in its innocence. In the short time she had known Colt Fraser, they had gone through more together than most people experience in a lifetime. She had run a gamut of emotions ranging from frustrated anger to this incredible passion, and now only love remained.

She couldn't help smiling. They'd ended up in that hayloft, figuratively speaking, just as he'd said they would from the beginning.

Cassie leaned over and kissed him gently on the lips. "I love you, Deputy Fraser." Then she slipped out of bed and dressed.

The house was in darkness when she returned home and stole soundlessly into her bedroom.

Once in bed, she stretched and tested a purr of contentment. Liking the sound, she purred again. Then she giggled. All he would have to do would be to discover that he had her purring, and she'd never hear the end of it.

Chapter 23

Colt felt better than he had in weeks. The sexual tension that had been building within him was finally satisfied—yet he already wanted her again. Cassie was incredible. Her passionate response had been greater than he'd even imagined. She'd been wrong when she'd said that underneath those mannish clothes she was as much woman as any other; she was more than any other woman he'd ever known. He'd opened a Pandora's box, and it wasn't possible to close it now.

He went downstairs and was hit with a hot blast of sunshine the instant he stepped outside. It was too damn hot to even eat breakfast. The three sprouts were sitting in the shade of the porch and jumped to their feet when they saw him.

"Morning, kids."

Bowie and Petey grinned broadly.

"Good morning, Deputy," Sam said. "Ain't you gonna eat breakfast?"

"Too hot to eat, Belle." He was anxious to see Cassie, but she was probably catching up on the sleep she'd missed last night. He headed for the jailhouse, and the sprouts followed him.

"Mama makes me eat breakfast," Sam said. "She says it's just as important to eat in hot weather as it is in cold. You just shouldn't eat too much."

"I'm sure your mother's right, Belle. By the way, I hope Bowie and you have convinced Petey that snakes don't make good pets."

"You bet we have. Especially since Mama told us that Slinky ate Cocker."

Figuring that one out was a challenge at this hour of the morning. "Cocker was the pet cockroach?" he said.

"Yep. Petey decided he didn't want no pets that eats his other pets."

"Sound thinking, pal," Colt said, patting the grinning boy on the head. "Maybe Slinky ate Leaper, too. Isn't he among the missing?"

"No, we found Leaper in the hot water tub," Sam said. "Sure glad there weren't no hot water in it."

"Yeah, old Leaper woulda been cooked alive," Bowie said.

"Well, I've heard that frog legs are pretty tasty."

Appalled, Sam stamped her foot. "Oh, that's so gross!"

The three children dashed away before he could tell them he was only joking.

A loud cloud of dust from the north indicated an approaching stagecoach. Funny, it wasn't too long ago that he had yearned to climb on a stage and ride out of the town. Now . . . well, now he wasn't in that much of a hurry. California would still be there when he was ready to leave Arena Roja.

He sat on the bench in front of the jailhouse, and

within minutes the stagecoach pulled up in front of the hotel. Gus jumped down from the box and opened the door.

"You've got thirty minutes, folks," he said to the couple that stepped out. Two more men disembarked and followed the couple into the hotel.

Colt felt a sudden premonition when he saw the last passenger get out of the stage. The man stood about six feet, and a well-worn black suit covered his thin frame. His left sleeve was folded up and pinned above the elbow.

Buck crawled to the top of the coach and tossed a worn carpetbag down to the man, who caught it with his one arm.

Colt's suspicions were confirmed when the sprouts raced past him shouting, "Mr. McBride!"

The name hit Colt like a cannon blast. So Ted McBride had returned to Arena Roja.

Colt watched with interest as McBride greeted the children. Then they raced away, headed for the Braden house.

For several seconds McBride took a long look around him, then he walked down the street toward the schoolhouse.

So I was wrong. But why had McBride stayed away so long?

Colt continued to watch as McBride entered the schoolhouse. Why in hell would he go there first, before going to the woman he supposedly loved? The woman to whom he was engaged?

Maybe he was being too cynical, but he sure didn't

understand these wartime romances. Maybe the outcome of his brother Clay's relationship with the
woman he'd loved all during the war had jaded Colt's
belief in wartime romances.

Cassie, with the sprouts trailing, came running up
the street. She looked around anxiously and drew up
sharply when she saw Colt.

"Where—"

"In the schoolhouse. You kids stay here," he ordered
when they started to follow her.

The sprouts looked annoyed but ran to the hotel,
most likely to spread the news.

Seeing that Cathy had arrived, Colt walked over
to her.

"Is it really true?" she asked.

"I guess so. Did they tell you that he lost his left
arm?"

She paled. "Oh, dear God." Her eyes misted with
tears, and she turned away and ran back to her
house.

Colt knew this was none of his business, but he
cared about this family. And he cared about Cassie
more than he was willing to admit. So he couldn't help
wonder how the return of Ted McBride would affect
the family . . . and himself.

Cassie's heart was pounding when she reached the
doorway of the school. She froze when she saw Ted in
the center of the room, unaware of her.

His blond hair was longer and shaggier, and he
looked taller, maybe because he was much thinner—

even gaunt-looking. Then she saw the pinned-up sleeve of his coat. She sucked back the gasp before it could slip past her lips.

"I knew you'd be back."

Ted turned around and smiled at her. "Hello, Cassie."

He held out his arm, and she ran across the room and flung herself into his embrace. He kissed her on the cheek and held her as she sobbed.

"Everyone said you were dead, but I didn't believe it. I knew you were alive. Where were you, Ted? Why didn't you send us word that you survived?"

"It's a long story, Cassie." He released her and sat down at one of the desks. "It hasn't changed much, has it?" he said, glancing around the room.

"We kept it just as you left it. I did put a fresh coat of paint on the walls recently."

"And the children. How are the children?"

"Well, they've changed. Five years makes a big difference in growing children."

"How many students are there now?"

"Twelve regular ones."

Once again he smiled, but it wasn't the smile she remembered from the past. It was more sad than happy, and it never reached his hazel eyes.

"You'll see a few new faces that have replaced the older ones. I'm so glad you're back, Ted. The children need a full-time teacher badly. You do intend to resume teaching them, don't you?"

"If the town wants a one-armed teacher."

"Of course the town wants you back." Tears glistened in her eyes as she looked into the sadness of his. "We all love you, Ted. Losing an arm doesn't make you less a man in the eyes of anyone who knows and loves you."

He reached for her hand on his cheek and slipped it to his lips. Then he pressed a kiss on her palm.

"It's been so long, Cassie."

"I know, dear. I know." She rose to her feet. "You must be exhausted. There's so much to say, and I have so many questions, but they can wait. The important thing is you've come back to us."

"I am tired. It was a long trip."

"We'll go back to the house. You can rest there, and I know Cathy and Dad are anxious to see you."

"Has Cathy married?" he asked, rising to his feet.

"No. She's had plenty of offers but refused them."

"It's hard to believe that she—or you—haven't wed in the past five years."

"I promised to wait for your return."

"I thought you might have grown tired of waiting."

His words seemed stilted, formal. The whole conversation seemed strange to her, as if they were two strangers trying to strike up a conversation.

Word of Ted's return had spread rapidly through the town, and as soon as they stepped outside, several people came hurrying up to them.

Cassie stepped aside as the people crowded around Ted, shaking his hand and welcoming him home. Glancing toward the jail, she saw Colt sitting outside, watching the welcome. Instantly a flush flooded her body as she recalled last night's passionate lovemaking. How could she face him now? Especially since Ted's return. What was she going to say to him?

When they reached the house, Cathy came out to greet them. Her eyes held tears of joy when Ted took her hand and stepped back to admire her.

"You're looking lovely, Cathy."

"I can't believe it's really you, Ted. We all were convinced you perished in the war."

"I came close a time or two," he said with a crooked smile.

"Ted's tired, Cathy. I told him he could come here and rest for a few hours."

Flushed with pleasure, Cathy smiled. "Of course, Ted, come inside. Dad's waiting to talk to you. Did Cassie tell you he's recovering from a wound?"

"What happened?"

Cathy quickly related the whole story.

"I've always thought of Jethro as being invincible," Ted said.

"You wouldn't have thought so if you'd have seen him then."

As Cassie followed them into the house, she listened to the exchange between Ted and Cathy. She and Ted had acted more like strangers than a couple in love, whereas Cathy and Ted had practically picked up their conversation where it had left off five years ago. She just didn't have Cathy's knack for putting people at ease.

Fortunately, it being Saturday, Colt's duties kept him busy throughout the day and evening; that helped put his concern for Cassie's situation temporarily aside. But the topic of McBride's return was on everybody's lips to remind him.

On Sunday morning he caught sight of the Braden family on their way to church, accompanied by McBride. Jeff had told him earlier that morning that the man was staying with them until he and Cassie were married.

For the past two mornings Colt had purposely avoided making his daily visit to Jethro, hoping to avoid any contact with Cassie until she'd had time to adjust to this unexpected turn of events. But it didn't keep her out of his thoughts, a constant reminder of how much he wanted her.

Colt was just releasing the Callum brothers, whom he'd locked up last night to sleep off their drunkenness, when Jethro entered the jail.

"Mornin', boys."

"Mornin', Sheriff. Good to see you up and around," Bob Callum said as he and Glen shuffled out.

"I'll echo that, Jethro," Colt said. "You must be feeling pretty good."

"Plumb tired of sittin' around and figured it was about time I get my legs under me. I'm comin' back to work tomorrow."

"Can't keep a good man down, Sheriff. What does Dr. Williams say about that?"

"Said I'm healin' fine and should be up and around by the weddin'."

"So they've set a date."

"Yeah. Ted's got no money or place to live and

wanted to put it off 'til he got better situated, but Cassie wants to get it over with so's they can live on the ranch."

"Sounds like the logical thing to do."

"I can't figure out if she's that anxious to get hitched, or just wants an excuse to go back to living on the ranch." Jethro grimaced. "Between you and me, son, somethin' just ain't right about the whole thing."

The sheriff's words piqued Colt's curiosity. "What's bothering you, Jethro? I thought it was the bride who's supposed to be nervous before the wedding."

"Everyone in the house is walkin' 'round with long faces whenever it's mentioned. You'd think they were plannin' a funeral instead of a weddin'." He shook his head. "They sure don't act like my Maudie and me did when we were gettin' ready to tie the knot."

"They haven't seen each other for five years, so—"

"More reason for them to be wantin' to be alone—if you know what I mean. The war sure changed that young fella. He walks around now like he's pickin' his way through a passel of rattlers."

"I've noticed that. Thought maybe that was his natural way. So he used to be more confident and outgoing than he is now?"

"Well, he never wuz no life of the party. And I can't say I ever saw him likkered up. But he wuz always agreeable to be around. I always figured he was kinda shy. For damn sure, he wuz more educated than the rest of us. My three kids wouldn't be as smart as they are if he hadn't taken them under his wing."

Jethro leaned closer and lowered his voice to almost a whisper. "And I'll tell you one thing, son. Cassie's always been headstrong about havin' her way, but if she thinks she's gonna make a rancher of Ted McBride, it ain't gonna happen."

"I guess she'll have to find that out for herself. Looks like you'll have some excitement on your hands when she does. Are you sure you're up to coming back to work?"

"I can rest here just as good as at home—probably better, with all that weddin' talk goin' on. Cathy will probably be bangin' pans all week in the kitchen. I know you're anxious to get out of here, but I'm hopin' you'll be stayin' for the weddin'."

"When is it?"

"Next Saturday."

"That would mean almost another two-week delay, if I can't get out of here until a week from next Thursday."

"'Fraid you'd say that."

"But I'll be here until next Thursday, for sure." He winked at Jethro. "Besides, I always cry at weddings. I'm sentimental."

Though in this case, Colt figured, his tears would be more lamenting than tender.

"You figure on comin' to the Welcome Back party for Ted this afternoon?"

"Yeah, I'll try to drop in if things don't get too busy."

"Well then, I best get back home before them hound dogs come sniffin' for me. Pretty sad when a man can't find some peace and quiet under his own roof."

"I'll walk with you back to your house," Colt said. He was too restless to sit still. He couldn't believe Cassie intended to go through with the wedding, even though she no longer loved McBride. What was the woman thinking of?

The sound of Cathy's and Ted's voices carried to Cassie's ears as she stared out the window. She had never felt so miserably unhappy in her life. She wanted to scream aloud to keep from bursting apart. And sharing Cathy's bedroom while Ted was using hers, she didn't even have a room of her own where she could escape to cry in the hope of easing some of the tension. She could find the solace she needed so desperately at the Lazy B, but running from her problems would not solve them.

Her heart seemed to stop when she saw the tall figure walking toward the house with her father.

From the moment she had realized she was in love with Colt Fraser, she'd known that the moment would come when she would have to say good-bye to him. Yet her heart had held out the hope that the dreaded moment would never come—that some divine intervention would keep it from happening. But now that could never be.

Having lain in his arms and known the wonderment of his touch, having basked in the warmth of his eyes and the sound of his laughter, how could she ever hope to find it with any other man? How could she deceive a man as fine as Ted into believing she had found it with him?

The Reverend MacKenzie had often preached the danger of retribution for the sins one commits. Why hadn't she heeded that warning?

God forgive her, she still wanted to run to Colt, to beg him to take her to California with him, to plea for his help in escaping from this web she had woven for herself.

But what one sows, one reaps, and the time had come to pay the piper.

Her gaze lingered on Colt as he and her father exchanged a few words. Then Colt laughed and patted Jethro on the shoulder before moving on.

Chapter 24

Most of the town's residents turned out for the return of their favorite son, Colt observed.

McBride appeared to have adjusted very well to functioning without a left arm, and the loss wouldn't interfere with resuming his teaching career.

Cassie seemed to be merely going through the motions at his side. She didn't have her usual vibrance as the couple was bombarded with questions about the wedding.

Jethro was certainly right about one thing; neither one of them appeared excited about it.

As Colt perused the crowd, he spied Cathy helping serve the refreshments.

When the reception line finally thinned, Colt went up to Cassie and Ted, and she introduced Colt to her future husband. It was the first time Colt had talked to her since the brief encounter the previous morning, and he could tell she was uncomfortable. Colt welcomed McBride home, then extended his regrets that he'd be leaving town and would miss their wedding.

McBride was polite and thanked Colt for filling in as deputy while Jethro was recovering. Colt had to give the man a high score for tact and diplomacy, but there was a nervous reserve about McBride that Colt sensed immediately. He appeared uncomfortable and avoided eye contact with Colt as much as possible. Was it a self-consciousness due to the loss of his arm, or had Cassie told her future husband about the previous relation-ship between her and the town deputy? All in all, Colt was glad to move on.

He walked over to where Cathy was pouring coffee and dispensing desserts. "Good afternoon, Miz Cathy. Thought I'd get it straight from the chef's mouth. Which dessert should I try?"

"I think a growing boy like you should try them all. But knowing how you like apple pie, I recommend the apple pandowdy."

Even though her tone was cheerful, her eyes were swollen, as if she'd been crying.

"Jethro tells me there's so much excitement at your house that he's tempted to bunk in the jail."

The sound of her giggle was delightful. "Did he really?"

Colt chuckled. "Not really. He did say that he's com-ing back to work tomorrow. Do you think he's well enough?"

"Dr. Williams said he was, and the old darling's chomping at the bit to get back." Her face shifted into a soft smile. "But that means we'll be losing you, Colt."

"It's just as well. I've enjoyed my stay here, but it's time to move on. And I bet it'll be different for you when Cassie gets married."

Once again, he saw a glint of sadness in her eyes.

"Yes, it won't be the same. I thought I might travel East. I've heard so much about cities like St. Louis, Chicago, and New York, and I've never seen them. What about you, Colt? Do you intend to remain in California or return to your home in Virginia?"

"I expect to go back home again. There would have to be something extraordinary to keep me from doing so."

"Or someone," she said.

He raised the cup he held in acknowledgment. "True. Would someone special keep you from ever returning to Arena Roja?"

"I would like to believe so." She glanced over to where Cassie and Ted were talking to Dr. Williams. "But I doubt it."

The three sprouts came up to Colt, and Bowie said, "Is it true you're leaving on the stage next Thursday?"

"News travels fast."

"Well, are you?" Sam asked.

"Reckon so, Belle."

"Boy, you leaving Thursday and Cassie getting married next Saturday—this town won't be the same."

"Oh, you'll still have Jeff to fight with, and Cassie's just getting married, she's not leaving town."

"Well, pretty soon she'll have a passel of babies and won't have no time for us."

"By that time, you might not have any time for her. And that's the very time she'll need you the most."

"Hmmm," Sam contemplated, "maybe you're right."

"Belle, I'm speechless. You mean you actually agree with me?"

"Ain't agreeing for sure, but I suspect you could be right."

"I suspect so, too," Bowie agreed.

Colt glanced down at Petey, who was grinning up at him. "What about you, pal?"

"Yeah, I 'spec so, too."

Colt winked and walked away. Those kids had really grown on him. How could the people in a town come to mean so much to him in such a short time?

After three failed attempts to slip away, Colt finally decided to stick it out to the end. As he sat at a table with Jethro and Dr. Williams his eyes swept the room, seeking Cassie. He saw her talking with several women.

She appeared more animated now than when she had stood with a forced smile beside McBride greeting well-wishers. He couldn't keep putting off talking to her, so he excused himself. As he started to walk over to her, his attention was drawn to the open door.

McBride and Cathy were outside, engaged in a conversation. Their expressions were serious, and when McBride swiftly walked away, Cathy dabbed her eyes with a handkerchief.

What had McBride said to bring her to tears? Though it was none of Colt's business, he hated to see her so unhappy.

McBride joined Cassie and her frozen smile returned, along with another missed opportunity to speak to her. Colt turned to see if he could offer some consolation to Cathy, but she had disappeared.

Some kind of undercurrent was going on here, and

he intended to get to the bottom of it. Since Cathy's motives were the only ones he trusted at this time, he stepped outside to find her.

Cassie *had* to speak to Colt. She needed to have a long talk with Ted, too. Other than that brief reunion when he'd arrived, they hadn't been alone. And there were so many questions that remained unanswered: the biggest one being why he had stayed away as long as he had. This man was almost a stranger to her. Whatever he'd endured during the war had created a wall around him, and she didn't know how to penetrate it.

Perhaps it would have been wiser not to rush into getting married, but she knew the longer she delayed, the greater the temptation to return to Colt's arms.

When she had finally accepted the belief that Ted wasn't returning, her betrayal of him had been done in innocence. But Ted had come back to her bearing the scars that the war had wrought on him, and she would never betray that love and trust again, no matter how she felt about Colt.

Cassie glanced longingly at him. How she yearned for Colt's touch, to feel his arms around her just one more time. Four more days and he'd be gone forever. She would never see him again. Four more days— then maybe she would be able to put that temptation behind her.

She watched Colt go outside, and then, with a deep sigh, she turned to the man who loved and needed her.

* * *

Colt saw no sign of Cathy, but Jethro came outside, tired from the festivities, so Colt walked him home.

On the way, Colt allowed Jethro to convince him to stay for dinner. Colt needed to satisfy his curiosity, and this would be a good way to do so, since Cassie and Ted would arrive soon as well.

By the time they reached the house, Cathy had dinner almost ready, which was clearly why she'd disappeared earlier. The atmosphere around the dinner table wasn't much better than it had been at the reception other than Jeff, who appeared oblivious to what was going on around him. The positive change in him was as evident as the gloomy one in the rest of them.

But Colt was able to make some observations, and it soon became obvious to him what the problem was. He couldn't believe no one else had realized it.

When McBride went outside to smoke a cigar, Colt followed him.

"I have the impression you don't like me, Mr. Fraser," McBride said.

The last thing Colt had expected was for McBride to go on the offensive. "What gave you that idea?"

"You've been scowling at me all through dinner. Have I offended you in some way?"

"That's nonsense; I barely know you."

"I realize I'm not very good company. I haven't been for a long time."

"For God's sake, McBride, don't apologize for being alive."

"I suppose the loss of my arm has contributed to making me bitter."

"Is that what it is, or is it guilt?"

"What do you mean?"

"Your real reason for staying away all this time. I don't mean to denigrate the tragedy of losing your arm, McBride, but many men return from war missing limbs, and I don't believe that's what kept you away. But I *have* been watching you—and Cathy. When did you realize you were engaged to the wrong woman? That you were in love with Cathy?"

McBride started to deny the accusation, then paused and said softly, "I stayed away because I couldn't bear to hurt Cassie."

"And you think marrying her, when you're in love with her sister, isn't going to hurt her when she finds out the truth?"

Ted flared angrily, "She won't find out if you don't tell her."

"So you're going to martyr yourself and marry the devoted little fool you think loves you because you can't *bear* to hurt her? Bullshit! What about Cathy, the woman who truly loves you? The woman you really love? Can you bear to hurt *her*?"

"For God's sake, Fraser, why do you think I stayed away? When I realized it was Cathy I loved, I made up my mind not to come back to Arena Roja."

"Have you told Cathy this?"

"Of course not. I love them both and didn't want to hurt either of them. I thought if I stayed away long enough, Cathy would be married by now, and I hoped that Cassie would be, too."

"Then why did you come back?"

"Because I was too weak to stay away. Have you ever tried to stay away from the woman you love? I had to know."

"That's the only intelligent thing you've said. So face it like a man now, and tell Cassie the truth."

"And break her heart."

"You aren't going to break her heart. You're going to relieve her of her burden of guilt."

"Guilt?"

"She's not in love with you, McBride. I doubt if she ever was. There's a big difference between love and hero worship. She was infatuated with her schoolteacher, but she's had five years to grow out of it. She's no longer that dewy-eyed girl you said good-bye to. She's a woman now and deserves a damn sight better than marriage to a man who's in love with her sister."

"If that's true, then she should be the one to admit she doesn't love me," Ted said.

Colt looked at him in disgust. "Are you so wrapped up in your own self-pity that you can't figure it out? After five years, you've finally come home from the war with a serious injury. Believing you love her, Cassie's too tenderhearted to tell you the truth. If she suspected for a moment that she was standing in the way of your and Cathy's happiness, she wouldn't hesitate to tell you."

"So you're implying that if I'd come home uninjured, she would have told me her true feelings at once?"

"You're damn right. You have no idea of her depth of

character, do you, McBride? Even if she'd still been in love with you, she would have stepped aside if you were truthful about you and Cathy."

"Why should this matter to you, Fraser? You said yourself that you'll be leaving town in a few days."

"You're right. I really don't have a dog in this hunt. Matter of fact, my stomach can't take any more of this Greek tragedy."

Colt spun on his heel and departed.

Later that night, unable to sleep, Ted paced the floor and finally went outside in fear of disturbing the household. Since his talk with Fraser, he had thought deeply about what the deputy had said about Cassie not loving him. If it was true, there was no purpose in marrying her; it would only make both of them miserable. The situation was hopeless. The best thing he could do was leave Arena Roja once and for all. Perhaps then they could all get on with their lives. As hard as it would be, he would tell them tomorrow that he was leaving.

He turned to go back into the house and discovered Cathy standing in the doorway.

"I'm sorry. Did I wake you?"

"No, I couldn't sleep." She stepped outside.

"I couldn't either," Ted replied.

"We all seem to be a little on edge. I guess none of us will relax until after the wedding."

"About the wedding—I had a rather unusual talk with Deputy Fraser earlier."

"Is that what's disturbing you?"

"Yes. You know, plans often don't work out like people hoped they would. I think Fraser was right; I should have been honest with Cassie when I returned."

"Honest about what?" Cathy asked.

"About my feelings for her. I love her dearly and she'll always hold a special place in my heart, but I'm not in love with her, Cathy. I realized that during the war. And that's what kept me away—not the loss of my arm."

Cathy paled. "Are you in love with somebody else?"

"Very much so," he said softly.

"Then why didn't you tell Cassie? Why let her continue to plan a wedding?"

"I didn't want to hurt her. I thought I could go through with it, but I can't."

"How can you do this to her? She loves you."

"If I'm to believe Fraser, she doesn't."

"I don't believe it. She and I never keep secrets from each other."

"Why would he lie?"

"I don't think he would, but perhaps he misinterpreted something she might have said. Maybe she was momentarily attracted to him—he's charming and handsome, and she had waited five years for you. Naturally she was flattered by Colt's attention, but you're the man she's always loved."

"A schoolgirl crush, Cathy. You can't build a marriage on that. I'm telling her tomorrow, and then I intend to leave."

"Why? Arena Roja is your home. Your work is here and the children need a teacher like you."

"Can't you guess, Cathy? I couldn't remain here

knowing I could never have the woman I really love."

"Why not? Isn't she willing to come here and live?"

He sighed deeply. "Cathy, my dear, beloved Cathy. Don't you realize *you're* that woman? I love you, Cathy. I've loved you for years."

She stared at him in disbelief. "I don't understand. Then why did you tell Cassie . . . Why did you promise to marry her?"

"I was blinded by her vivaciousness, by the boundless energy that makes everything around her seem more exciting. It wasn't until I went away that I realized I wasn't in love with her—that it was the affection a teacher feels for a prized student, a personal pride in her accomplishments.

"That's why I was never shocked by her prancing around in boy's trousers and her daring recklessness. Underneath all that bravado, I saw the mind of the girl, the student every educator dreams of encountering. Her thirst for knowledge opened to everything I fed it like a sponge, as if it were water."

His voice lowered in remorse as he dredged the words from the depths of his conscience.

"As her teacher, I thrived on that energy. I misled myself—and her—into believing I was in love with her, when it was the student I actually loved, not the woman."

Ted gently cupped Cathy's chin in his hand. Her eyes were misting as she looked into his.

"But in war, a man has time to think, Cathy. In war, the face he envisions in his daydreams is that of the woman he loves. That face was always yours, beloved.

The warm smile in my darkest hours and the soft voice soothing my worst moments were always yours. The gentle hand soothing my fevered brow was yours. Never Cassie's."

He smiled tenderly at her. "Gentle, sweet Cathy. You'd always been there standing in Cassie's shadow, and I never recognized it. I love you."

Tears streaked her cheeks. "And I love you, Ted. I've always loved you. I used to watch you and Cassie together, and wish it were I. I lived with the guilt of coveting the man my sister loved."

He pulled her to his chest. "Oh, my darling, if only you had told me. I might have realized the truth about myself sooner."

She stepped back. "But now it's too late, Ted. I would never do anything to hurt Cassie."

"What if Fraser is right, Cathy? What if Cassie doesn't love me? If she's perpetuating a myth out of loyalty and sympathy? Should we deny our love for one another to sustain that pretense? Darling, listen to me. We can leave here. Start a new life somewhere else."

"No, I'd never betray Cassie like that, no matter how much I love you. Don't you see? We'd both be plagued with guilt. We can't buy our happiness at the expense of hurting the people we love."

"And what of our love? Doesn't that matter?"

"It appears we've both learned to live with that heartache."

She ran tearfully back into the house.

Chapter 25

Colt wasn't surprised when Cassie showed up at the jail later that evening.

"What are you doing here at this time of night?" he asked.

"I want to talk to you. Ted went to bed, but he mentioned that the two of you had a conversation about my marrying him."

Why had the man even brought up the subject with her if he hadn't intended to fully pursue it?

"Actually, it was more about him marrying you," Colt replied, trying to grin but not quite able to carry it off. "I've always told myself not to get in the middle of other people's personal problems; I should have heeded my own advice."

"Colt, I'm serious. I trusted you. Now I feel betrayed."

"Why should you feel betrayed?"

"I was naïve to believe you meant what you said that night at the ranch."

"Cass, if sex was all I wanted, I could have gotten it that night from you. Didn't I make it clear that as much as I wanted to make love to you, I wanted your friendship, too? I did not mention one word to your intended about the relationship between us. If he implied I did, then maybe he suspects it and is feeling you out."

"No, he didn't say anything like that. I guess it's my own guilty conscience, reading something that wasn't there."

Colt knew that this would have been a good opening to tell her the truth about McBride's feelings for Cathy, but hearing it from him would only stir up more heartache. The truth would have to come from McBride or Cathy.

"What do you think of him, Colt?"

"I'm sure he's an excellent teacher."

"That's not what I mean. What's your opinion of him personally?"

Colt had reached the end of his patience with the whole damn situation. They were acting like children; no one was being honest or saying what they thought. Himself included.

"What in hell does it matter, Cassie? I'm curious about one thing, though. Did he tell you what delayed his return home?"

"No, other than he was in the hospital for a couple of months."

"Yet no letters or telegram to let you know he was alive?"

"I didn't pursue it, Colt. There's so much on his mind. We've barely been alone."

"And no one else thought to ask?"

"You don't understand, Colt. Ted's very withdrawn right now. It must be the effects from the war—his injury."

"When did he lose his arm?"

"He said during a battle at Fort Stedman in Virginia."

"If I remember right, that was in March of '65. General Lee surrendered the following month, and General Kirby-Smith held out until May. So McBride should have been on his way home over a year ago."

"If only he'd come back a day sooner, we never would have—"

"Here come the regrets, just as I said there would be."

"I feel guilty for betraying him, but I'll never regret the other night. That's what I came to tell you."

"Then you don't intend to tell him about us."

"I can't say I'll never tell him, but not right now."

"Do you still intend to marry him?"

"Of course."

"Then my advice is you damn well better tell him now—or never."

She turned away and stared out the window.

Colt walked over to her. "Cassie, look at me." He turned her to face him. "How can you marry a man you don't love? You're too honest to live with that kind of deceit."

"How can I *not* marry him now? No matter what I say, he'll think it's because he's maimed."

"If he believes that, then he doesn't know you."

"He's a fine and sensitive man, and a dear friend. I know he'd be a good husband to me."

"And what kind of wife will you be to him? Fine and sensitive are sufficient for old age, Cass, but you're young. Don't harness yourself to a life that will destroy your spirit. When you marry, it must be to a man who can tap into that wild streak in you."

"You don't know Ted, so what makes you think we're not suited for each other?"

"I know more about him than you think. You can tell a lot about a man by the set of his shoulders and the way he holds his head. Ted McBride apologizes for being alive. May the day never dawn that you do, Cass."

"And you can tell all this about him just from a brief meeting?"

He released her and stepped back. "Damn right. And from one other important thing: he never made love to you."

"Because he believed we should wait until we were married."

"That's a noble sentiment, Cassie, but it's not human nature. A man *has* to make love to the woman he loves. He's physically consumed with it."

"Maybe he found a release with one of the women at the Alhambra."

"Honey, that's like giving a sugar pill to a man with a fever. His head might tell him he's cured, but his body never gets the message."

"This conversation is ludicrous. You're condemning a man just because he doesn't share your carnal appetite."

"And doesn't share yours."

She stared at him, stricken. "That was an ungallant remark, even for you, Colt."

He felt like a bastard. She was the last person on

earth he'd meant to hurt. He gently clasped her cheeks between his hands and looked into her wide blue eyes.

"I meant it as a compliment, Cass. You're all woman," he said tenderly. "You're spontaneous, you have a zest for life, and you meet a challenge head on, whether it's driving cattle in the rain or making love. Honey, you're going to wither on his noble vine, married to a man unprepared to stick his face in the wind and spit back."

"Well, thank you for your analysis of him, Colt. I might have expected it, considering having sex is so important to you, but love is not."

She walked to the door. "But why should I have expected any more from a stranger just passing through town?"

Maybe it's just as well that we avoid each other, Colt reflected the next morning as he watched Cassie enter the schoolhouse. She was right; as someone who intended to move on, he'd gotten too involved with her—with the whole family.

He glanced at Jethro, who was half asleep as he tried to read the newspaper. Colt hoped that Dr. Williams was right about the sheriff being well enough to work, because it was high time that he got on that stagecoach.

"Jethro, why don't you lie down and grab a nap," Colt said, plucking his hat off the wall peg. "I'm going out to stretch my legs."

"Might do that, son. Ain't no news worth readin' in

this paper." Jethro went over to the cot and was asleep before Colt was even out the door.

Monday mornings were always quiet, and as Colt neared the hotel, he met the three sprouts.

"Where are you three off to so early?"

"School," Petey exclaimed.

"Your buddies don't look too happy about the idea."

"Neither would you, if you were in our boots," Sam grumbled. "Now that Mr. McBride's back, he said we gotta go back to the old schedule."

"Yeah, six hours a day, five days a week," Bowie said.

Colt shook his head. "Inhuman."

"Exactly," Sam agreed.

"Yeah, zactly," Petey declared.

"Maybe if you took the teacher an apple, he might ease up on you."

Sam reached into her pocket and pulled out an apple. "I've already thought of that."

"I tell you, Belle, a person's gotta get up pretty early to outthink you. Six straight hours of you kids, you say? The guy must be a glutton for punishment. Be good."

Colt walked on down the street and sat down by Jeff in front of the livery.

"How's Dad doing?" Jeff asked.

"He's lying down. I think it'll take him a while longer to get back into the routine. He's been used to sleeping most of the day for the past couple of weeks. I'm not certain I should be leaving in a few days."

"Wish I were going to California with you. I've never been farther than a hundred miles from this town."

"Have you thought about going away to college, Jeff? You're bright, and there's a lot to learn."

"I've been thinking about it. Cathy was talking about going East. Maybe I'll go with her and enroll in one of those big universities."

"Have you thought about what you want to do for a living?"

"Not ranching. I wouldn't mind being a lawman like you, but if you promise not to laugh, I'll tell you what I'd really like to become."

"What is that?"

"A doctor. Doc Williams has let me read some of his medical books, and he told me if I ever consider medicine as a profession, he'd help get me into medical school."

"Then go for it, Jeff, if that's what you want. Have you mentioned this to your father?"

Jeff shook his head. "He'd only laugh."

"I'm not so sure about that."

The sudden blast of gunfire caused both of them to jump to their feet.

"Sounded like it came from the bank," Colt said, drawing his pistol.

People on the street began scrambling for the protection of doorways as four men came running out of the bank firing their pistols.

"It's the Pike gang," Colt shouted. "Where in hell did they come from? Get down to the jail and help your dad; I'll cover you."

Jeff raced down the street as Colt shot the closest outlaw, who fell to the ground. The other outlaws directed their fire at Colt, giving Jeff the chance to get to the jail.

The gang mounted their horses and galloped off with a hail of bullets. As they rode past the jail, Jeff's shot took down another of the gang.

Down the street, Cassie and Ted chased after Sam when she ran outside to see what was happening. Recognizing the young girl, the vengeful Pike aimed a shot at her, but Ted threw himself at her and knocked her down, covering her with his body. The shot caught him in the back of the shoulder, and he slumped over her, unconscious.

Cassie screamed and raced over to them. With two of his gang shot, Pike seized the opportunity to save his own life.

"Rein up," he shouted to Keeler.

They jumped off their horses and Pike grabbed Cassie, using her as a shield. Colt and Jeff were forced to cease firing.

Holding a gun to Cassie's temple, Pike shouted at the top of his voice. "We're ridin' out of here. One more shot in this direction and this bitch gets it. Keeler, cut off a hunk of your rein and tie her hands behind her back."

By this time, Jethro had joined his son. "You harm one hair on that girl's head, Pike, and there'll be no hole big enough for you to crawl into."

Pike snorted. "Thought I got rid of you, old man. Call off your flunkies, Sheriff, or her blood'll be on your hands."

With sinking hearts, Colt and Jeff lowered their

weapons and watched helplessly as the two outlaws rode off with Cassie as a hostage.

Colt and Jeff dashed back to the livery. There was no time to wait as Jethro rounded up a posse.

Precious minutes were lost as the two men saddled horses and rode off in pursuit of the outlaws.

Colt stopped where Dr. Williams and Cathy were kneeling over McBride.

"Is he dead?"

"No. The doctor said he should be okay," Cathy said.

"And Sam?"

Sam's head popped up. "I'm okay. Don't you let that varmint hurt Cassie."

Colt galloped after Jeff.

After a short distance, they halted on a rise to view the terrain.

"There they are," Jeff said, pointing to the riders in the distance.

"At least they haven't . . . disposed . . . of her yet," Colt said, unable to say the real word hovering in both their minds.

They urged their horses onward.

Chapter 26

Cassie was scared. Her thoughts raced frantically. Was Ted still alive, or had this murderer, who even shot down children, claimed another victim?

She knew that as soon as Pike felt they were safely away, he would kill her, too. She had to think of some way to stall him until Colt caught up with them. She knew he would find her—but would it be too late?

She continued to work at the knotted rein around her wrists. If she succeeded in freeing her hands, she might be able to pull his gun and shoot him. Even if she couldn't get Keeler, at least this vicious killer would no longer harm innocent people.

"Pike, if we don't stop and rest these horses we're gonna run them to death," Keeler said.

"You want to swing from the end of a rope? They've had plenty of time to mount up a posse."

"If you weren't so damn quick to gun down folks, we wouldn't be in this fix. You had no call to shoot that fella back there—and he only had one arm, to boot—just because you wanted to shoot down a kid."

"That wuz the brat that almost bit my hand off the last time we tried to hold up that bank."

"You're gettin' crazier by the day, Pike. Snatching this gal puts a posse on our tails for sure."

"If I hadn't snatched her we'd be layin' in our own blood on the street right now, just like Colby and Benson."

Keeler shook his head. "Ridin' with you is gonna get me on the wrong end of a rope for sure."

"If you don't like it, go join Colby and Benson."

Listening to their quarrel, Cassie thought of a possible way to save herself. If she could convince Keeler to help her, she might have a chance. But how could she get him alone? She was running out of time.

Pike pulled up on his reins and stopped. "Keeler, my horse's been carryin' a double load long enough. Time you carry this bitch for a while." He dismounted, roughly pulled Cassie down from the horse, and shoved her in Keeler's direction.

"She's slowin' us up, Pike. You oughta just let her go."

"Right now, she's our ace in the hole. Long as we got her, they don't dare try to move in on us. So just shut up and do as I tell you."

This was the opportunity Cassie had been hoping for. As soon as they remounted and got underway, she whispered, "Keeler, can you hear me? I must talk to you."

He didn't respond but dropped back behind Pike.

"If you help me escape, I can prevent you from getting hung."

"Yeah, sure you can."

"It's true. My father's the sheriff. If I tell him you helped me to escape, he won't let them hang you."

"You must think I'm stupid, gal. Now shut up, or I'll tell Pike you're the sheriff's daughter. Then he'll make sure you don't die easy."

Of course I think you're stupid—you're riding with this crazy killer. But Keeler was her only hope, and she wasn't giving up on the idea.

"We got company, Pike," Keeler said later when they stopped at a stream to fill their canteens and water the horses. He pointed to a distant cloud of dust. "That cloud that's been followin' us is gettin' closer."

"A posse couldn't have picked up our trail that fast."

"Don't have to be the whole posse. From the size of that cloud, I figure it's only two, maybe three riders."

Cassie's heart leaped to her throat with new hope. The Callum brothers! They were the best trackers in town, and her dad always sent them on ahead while he organized a posse. And she would stake her life that Colt would have come with them.

"Well, Mr. Pike, it appears you have a problem," she said. "If Bob Callum's on your trail, you don't stand a chance. He has Apache blood, and he could follow an ant in a sandstorm. So what are you planning to do now?"

"Put my fist in your mouth if you don't shut up," he snarled. "I ain't afraid of no 'breed, bitch. They're as easy to kill as any redskin."

"Look, Pike, ridin' double is slowin' us down too much. If they get the girl back, they'll hold up and wait for the posse, or even turn back. That'll give us more time to get away."

"Or one of 'em might stay on our trail. I ain't givin' up the gal. I told you: they don't dare try anythin' as long as we got her."

Pike's cold-eyed stare darted to Cassie, then back to Keeler. "I'll ride on with the gal. They're sure to stop here to water their horses; find yourself some good cover in those rocks up there and bushwhack them when they show up," Pike said.

"Why don't you stay behind, and I'll ride on with the gal," Keeler replied.

"'Cause I don't trust you. You're too willin' to let her go. Just get up in them rocks and do as I say. You can pick 'em off with your rifle as they ride in, like shootin' fish in a barrel."

Pike's mouth turned up in an evil smirk. "Wouldn't mind stickin' around to see it, but the rest of the posse probably ain't far behind 'em, and like you said, ridin' double slows us up."

Cassie watched with a sinking heart as Keeler led his horse to higher ground.

Pike grabbed her and lifted her up on the back of his horse. "Sorry we can't stick around for the fireworks, bitch."

"Do you figure they spotted us by now?" Jeff asked.

"They'd have had to. We've been following their dust; they'd have to be blind not to see ours," Colt said.

"Night closes in fast in these mountains. It's going to be dark soon," Jeff warned.

"We should catch up with them before then; there can't be more than a mile between us. They've been riding hard and their horses are tiring from carrying Cassie's extra weight, even if they switch off." Colt reined up and wiped the sweat off his brow. "You know, Jeff, if I were in their boots, I'd start thinking of ambushing whoever was following me. It might be wise to proceed more cautiously."

The crack of a rifle shot sounded, and a bullet hit Colt's horse. Several more shots followed, and Colt barely managed to clear the saddle before the horse keeled over. Colt dropped to the ground and shielded himself behind its dead body.

Jeff's horse bolted into the nearby trees. He dismounted, and a hail of bullets kicked up a trail of dust at his feet as he scampered behind a nearby rock to get closer.

"Where are the shots coming from?" he shouted to Colt, who was returning the gunfire.

"From those rocks up the right of you."

"Are you hit?"

"No, I'm okay. It must be a single shooter, or they'd have tried to take both of us out at the same time."

Several bullets ricocheted off the rock that Jeff was concealed behind, and the two men returned the fire.

"Cover me," Colt shouted and crawled over to the rock as Jeff sent a hail of shots toward the rifle flashes.

The rifle firing stopped as suddenly as it began. After a long pause, Colt said, "I think he's pulled out." The thud of retreating hoofbeats confirmed that belief. They cautiously waited a few more minutes, then

Colt went over to Bullet and removed the saddle from the dead horse. "Sorry about Bullet. He was a good horse."

"What are we going to do now? We're so close to them, but if we ride double we'll never catch up," Jeff said.

"We'll run if we have to."

"Take my horse, Colt—you're a better shot than I am. I'll start walking back toward town. I'm sure to meet up with the posse."

"How do you know if they stayed on our trail?"

"I figure Bob Callum will be leading them. He can sniff a trail better than a hound dog. They're probably not more than half an hour behind us. Now get going before you lose sight of them. Good luck, Colt."

Colt mounted the horse and rode away. He turned his head and looked back. Jeff raised a hand and waved.

It was funny how often the people you figured were the weakest could turn out to be the strongest.

"How'd you make out?" Pike asked when Keeler caught up with them.

"Just as we thought," Keeler said. "There wuz two of 'em. The deputy and the sheriff's kid."

"Did you kill 'em?"

"I ain't sure. Wounded the deputy maybe, but I shot the horse out from under him."

Pike looked at him with contempt. "That's real good, Keeler. At least now we don't hav'ta worry about the horse attackin' us."

"If you think you could have done better, then why didn't *you* try, Pike? Both of 'em were pumping lead at me. I wuz lucky to get out in one piece. At least losin' a horse'll slow 'em down if they hav'ta ride double," Keeler said. "And if one of 'em's wounded, they might even hav'ta wait for the posse to catch up with 'em."

"Well, let's get movin'. It's turnin' dark."

Cassie's body was stiff, and her fingers ached from trying to free her hands, but as long as they were on the move, she had a chance of remaining alive. Lord knows what would happen to her when they stopped.

Cassie continued to work at the knot on her wrists as they rode along. It was a slow and painful process, but she was making progress. The rope felt a little looser.

The sun had long set by the time Pike called a halt. He insisted on not lighting a fire in case they were still being followed, so they had a cold camp with only a few bites of deer jerky to eat. Cassie began shivering. Keeler gave her a blanket, but she was still cold.

"Keeler, take the first watch and wake me in a couple hours," Pike ordered as he lay down to sleep. "Just make sure you stay awake."

As soon as Cassie heard Pike snoring, she shifted over and whispered, "You know they're going to catch up with us, Keeler. Let me go and I swear I'll speak on your behalf."

"Pike would kill me if I let you go."

"He's sleeping. Untie my hands, and we'll get his gun and I'll help you tie him up."

"You make it sound easy. Pike ain't stayed alive this long by bein' stupid."

"You know I'm right, Keeler, or you would have told Pike I'm the sheriff's daughter. Use your head. Once that posse shows up, it'll be too late for me to help you."

Keeler glanced nervously at Pike, then back at her. "Okay, I'll help you, but you—"

"You're a fool, Keeler." Pike rose to his feet with a drawn pistol pointed at the man.

Keeler backed away. "Don't do it, Pike. I wuzn't gonna listen to her. She's been tryin' to get me to let her go whenever she had the chance."

"Tell the devil the last person to see you alive wuz Bill Pike."

Keeler drew his pistol as Pike fired, but the gun slipped through his fingers when he clutched his stomach and slumped to the ground.

Pike walked over and kicked Keeler's gun out of reach. "Nobody crosses me, Keeler. You oughta know that. It takes longer to die when you're gut shot, so you've got plenty of time to remember that."

Glaring malevolently, he turned to Cassie. "Get on your feet, bitch. We're gettin' out of here. At least now we won't hav'ta ride double." He turned away and headed for the horses.

Cassie desperately yanked her wrists apart with all her might. The bond cut into her flesh like a knife, but the knot finally snapped. She lunged for Keeler's gun, but before she could reach it, Pike was on her. He smacked her in the jaw, sending her stumbling backward, and she slammed against a tree and fell to the ground.

Pike came over and yanked her to her feet. "I oughta kill you right now," he snarled. He tied her bleeding wrists behind her back again then shoved her toward the horses.

"You ain't gettin' away, and by the time I finish with you, you'll be beggin' me to kill ya."

"Let her go, Pike."

Keeler had crawled over to his gun, but he was so weak from pain and the loss of blood that he could barely hold up the weapon.

Pike laughed in derision. "I wuz hopin' it'd take you longer to die, Keeler." He drew his gun and fired.

Smirking, he turned back to Cassie. "You didn't think I heard you tell Keeler that you were the sheriff's daughter, did you? Well, I did, and I wuz waitin' to find out what he wuz gonna do about it. I figured if he wuz gonna help you, he'd try when he thought I wuz sleepin'. And I thought of somethin' else, too: I don't need you no more. Now that I've got two horses, I can outrun a posse." He went over and got the lasso that was hanging from his saddle.

Cassie guessed his horrible intent when he formed one end into a noose and tossed the other over a high limb on a nearby tree. He adjusted the length of the rope to his satisfaction, then tied it in place and led his horse over to the tree.

"Your daddy's mighty anxious to see me swingin' from the end of a rope. Wish I cud see his face when he sees his daughter the same way."

Cassie tried to run, but he caught her at once. She struggled to free herself as he carried her over to the horse and slammed her onto the saddle. Then he slipped the noose around her neck and tightened it. "Any last words you want me to pass on to your daddy?"

Cassie lifted her head. "Yes. When he's slipping the noose around your neck, tell him I'll be watching."

With maniacal laughter, Pike slapped the horse's flank.

Chapter 27

The soft plod of his horse was the only sound Colt heard as he slowly moved through the darkness. He dismounted and looked around with defeat and frustration. He dare not continue on in the dark, for fear of overshooting Cassie and her captors.

He had held onto the foolish hope that they might build a campfire, but he should have realized that Pike was too wily to make that kind of mistake. It would have been a beacon in the dark.

A gunshot suddenly shattered the stillness, flushing a bevy of quail from a nearby copse. Colt's heart pounded in his chest. It had to be them—had the bastard just shot Cassie? Colt tethered his horse and moved quickly in the direction of the shot, then faster when another shot sounded.

Pausing again, Colt looked around hopelessly. In his anxiety he was forsaking caution for haste; if Cassie was still alive, he wouldn't do her much good by stumbling recklessly into the camp.

Then he heard voices. Drawing his pistol, he moved toward the sound.

Colt couldn't believe his eyes when he saw Cassie on the horse with a noose around her neck. The son of a bitch was going to hang her! Just as Pike slapped the horse out from under her, Colt's shot severed the rope.

When Cassie dropped to the ground, Colt fired at Pike, catching him in the shoulder just before the outlaw disappeared into the thick cover of trees.

Colt ran to Cassie's aid. She was bruised and dazed, but alive. He drew the knife out of his boot and quickly freed her wrists, then took her in his arms. "Are you all right, honey?"

He felt the salty moisture of her silent tears against his cheek. "I knew you'd come. I knew you'd come," she murmured over and over. Her voice was gruff, and he knew that the rope had done some damage. He wouldn't need a rope when he caught up with Pike; he'd strangle him with his own hands.

Cassie was shivering, and Colt wanted to find some blankets to wrap her in, but she clasped him around the neck and wouldn't release him.

"It's okay, baby. You're safe now. I won't let anything happen to you," he whispered as he pressed gentle kisses to her forehead and cheeks.

It was too dark to see her face clearly, but he could tell it was swollen. She held on to him tightly.

"Just sit here, Cass, while I check Keeler."

"He's dead. Pike killed him."

The quicker he got her away from the spot, the safer it would be. He picked up Keeler's pistol and the blankets, then led Pike's horse over to her.

He bundled her in the two blankets he'd found. "Look, honey, you'll be better off away from here. Besides, I can smell rain moving in, and we should get you under cover where you can stay dry. My horse is tethered a short distance away. Do you think you're up to moving?"

"Sure. I'm feeling a lot better now."

He tipped up her chin and stared into her eyes. "You're a great little soldier, Trooper Braden. I'd want you in my company anytime."

"Captain Fraser, whatever would I be doing in the Rebel cavalry?"

He grinned. She'd taken a knockout blow, but she was climbing back onto her feet.

Distant streaks of lightning and the rumble of thunder indicated a rapidly approaching storm. He quickly saddled the horse, then lifted her gently onto it.

"Keeler said Jeff was with you. Is he—"

"He's fine, Cass. Bullet was killed, though."

"Bullet and Midnight were always stabled together; he'll miss him, too. But where's Jeff now?"

"We didn't want to lose your trail, so he gave me his horse and said he'd head back to meet up with the posse."

"On foot? Alone? Colt, he's still a boy."

"He's a man, Cass. It's time his family starts treating him like one. Now let's get to my horse and find some decent cover. Then we can get a fire going." He took the reins and started to lead the horse away.

The bullet that whizzed past his head missed by a mere inch. Colt yanked Cassie off the horse. "Stay down," he warned. "That was a rifle shot." He handed her Keeler's pistol. "That bastard must have found Keeler's horse, and now he's between us and my horse.

Or else he's found that one, too. We'll have to get back by a different route. Are you able to walk, Cass?"

"Yes, I'm okay."

"Good. You'd be a sitting duck on the back of a horse."

Colt pulled Pike's rifle out of the saddle holster and slung the saddlebags over his shoulder. "I'm sure there's something in these that will be useful to us later. Do you have any idea how much ammunition Keeler still had in his saddlebags?"

"I never heard it mentioned."

"That's our greatest danger, because come daylight, Pike can pick us off from a distance with a rifle. We can only hope the posse catches up with us before then. For now, we stay low and find some cover. He can't see us any better than we can see him, so there's no sense in trying to pick him off in the dark."

"I'm surprised he didn't take off," Cassie whispered as they moved away cautiously.

"So am I. I know I winged him, so he most likely has a bullet in him."

"He's crazy, Colt. Mad with killing. I saw it in his eyes when he killed Keeler and tried to hang me." She shuddered.

Colt was worried about Cassie. He could tell she was in pain, but he needed a fire to see the extent of her injuries. Since there were no further shots as they traveled, he figured Pike had either lost them in the dark or was waiting for daylight so he could get a clean shot. If Pike trailed them seeking revenge, the man would be as crazed and as dangerous as a wounded wild animal.

They hadn't gone more than a mile when the sky exploded with a thunderbolt and rain poured down upon them.

Jagged lightning streaked across the sky, and deafening booms of thunder echoed through the mountains. Water streamed down the walls of granite buttes and dripped from the edges of overhanging cliffs, turning the earth into muddy quagmire or slippery rock too difficult to traverse.

Colt hugged Cassie to his side to shield her as much as possible, but he knew she was hurting and exhausted. He had to get her out of this storm.

A bolt of lightning struck a nearby tree, and the sheared top fell to the ground in flames. Colt peered through the darkness, and before the rain extinguished the fire, he was certain he saw an opening in the rocky wall.

They hurried over and ducked just inside the entrance. They dared not go any deeper in case a bear or other wild animal might have had the same thought, but it was a relief just to be out of the storm. Another lightning bolt cast enough light for a quick glimpse of the interior of the cave. It appeared to be empty, but Colt remained cautious. After several more flashes of light, he discerned a woodpile in one of the corners.

"You got that gun I gave you?"

"In my pocket," she said.

"Now's a good time to get it out. And stay here."

"Where are you going?" she asked, alarmed.

"To check out that woodpile, in case a snake's

crawled into it . . . or a skunk," he added, trying to lighten the mood.

"Colt, be careful," she warned as he moved away.

Using the lightning flashes to see, he poked at the pile with the end of the rifle until he was satisfied it was safe. Then he returned to the entrance and riffled through one of Pike's saddlebags.

"He must have a flint in here."

After some additional groping he victoriously held up a flint. He shaved some dried bark off a log, then struck some sparks with his knife and flint. The sparks ignited the shavings, and within minutes he had built it into a fire.

Cassie was shivering so badly that her teeth were chattering, and she hurried over to the fire.

Let's get out of those wet clothes," Colt said. "I'll see if there's some in the saddlebags."

"I'd rather freeze than put on anything Pike wore," she declared.

He pulled off her boots and stockings, and she stripped down to her underclothes while Colt dug out another blanket he'd stuffed into the saddlebags. He wrapped it around her, then he knelt down and rubbed her legs and feet vigorously to restore the circulation, until the color returned to her cheeks.

Her face was bruised and swollen from where Pike must have struck her. Her neck bore an ugly red rope burn from the noose, and her wrists were bloody.

Colt slit his bandanna in half and bandaged her wrists. "I wish I had something to ease your pain, honey."

"My back hurts the worst," she said. "When he hit me, I slammed against a tree."

"Let me take a look at it." He removed the blanket and gently turned her over on her stomach. He pushed up her camisole and lowered the top of her drawers, then gently felt her back. It had started to bruise, but there appeared to be no other injury.

"Honey, I'm no doctor, but my guess is that you won't want to do much riding for a while."

He slipped his hand under the camisole and lightly massaged her shoulders and neck. "We need to loosen these muscles or you'll be so sore by morning, you won't be able to move."

She closed her eyes and sighed. "Oh, that feels so good, Colt."

He continued until he felt her muscles relax, then he helped her sit up. She leaned back against the wall.

"That bastard did a real job on you, honey. Maybe there's something in the saddlebags to soothe the rope burns."

"They don't hurt that much. I'm just glad to be out of that storm."

"Looks like we won't have to go hungry. There's coffee and jerky here," Colt said as he searched the one side of the saddlebags. "And here's a coffeepot, a tin cup, a couple cans of beans, and even a plate and fork." He filled the pot with rainwater, then put the coffee on to brew. "We can dine royally tonight."

Colt opened the other saddle bag and pulled out a few items of clothing, then let out a long whistle.

"No wonder Pike didn't take off. He wants this." He held

up a money bag from the Arena Roja bank and dumped it on the ground. "There's hundreds of dollars here."

Colt took off his boots and stockings, then shucked his gunbelt, shirt, and jeans.

"How can you put on that man's clothing?" Cassie asked when he pulled on a pair of jeans and a shirt he'd found in the saddlebags.

"They're clean and dry. I stop at underwear and stockings, though."

"Pike will trail us to get the money back." Fear had replaced her previous relief.

"Cass honey, he's not going to hurt you again. He's wounded, he's out in that storm, most likely with nothing to eat. We'll be dry, rested, and well fed. If he catches up with us, we'll be ready for him. We've got a rifle, my gunbelt, and Keeler's pistol." He held up a box of shells he'd dug out of the saddlebags. "And ammunition. A lot of ammunition."

He pried open a can of beans with his knife and set it near the fire to warm while he wrung out their clothes and spread them around the fire to dry.

"You're a pretty handy fellow to have around, Deputy Fraser."

"Thank you, Miz Cassie."

He walked away and peered deeper into the cave. Branching off from the front chamber were long underground corridors with stalactites hanging from the ceilings and twisted columns and spears of stalagmites reaching up from the floor.

"From what I can see, there seem to be passages that go on for miles."

"They probably do," she said. "There are a lot of limestone caves around here. They're formed by water dripping through from above."

"This chamber isn't dripping."

"Someone probably lived in it and sealed the ceiling."

"You mean Indians?"

"Or maybe a limestone miner," Cassie said. "It brings a good price."

"That would explain the firewood. But from what I can see, there's still plenty of limestone available."

"The Indians probably drove him away."

"Or something worse happened to him. Who knows, his remains might be back there in one of those passages."

"Colt, please. Must you always bring up an unpleasant subject?"

Colt went to the fire and poured a cup of coffee, then scraped the beans onto a plate and cut up the jerky. He came back and handed her the plate and fork.

"Here—this will keep your mouth too busy to pick fights with me."

As gruff as Colt tried to sound, Cassie could tell from the amusement in his eyes that he wasn't angry. He could be the most pleasant man in the world when he wanted to be.

She ate some beans and a bite of the jerky, then handed him the fork. He did the same. They continued to pass the fork and cup back and forth between them until the plate was empty. Then he refilled the coffee cup.

"That was delicious," she said.

"We must extend our thanks to Mister Pike for his generosity if we see him again."

"There you go again, Colt Fraser," she sassed. "Every time I begin to relax, you bring up an unpleasant subject." She took a sip from the proffered cup.

"Can you think of a pleasant one?"

She paused, then said, "I would think the thought of leaving next Thursday would be pleasant to you."

"It's more bittersweet. You've all grown to mean a lot to me."

"We feel the same about you. It'll be very hard to say good-bye. So don't be surprised if I don't show up when you leave; you know how emotional I am."

"What with your wedding plans and all, I'll soon be forgotten."

Their fingers touched as she handed him back the cup, and they both stared for a long moment at their joined hands.

Tears misted her eyes as she looked at him. "I'll never forget you, Colt."

"For God's sake, Cass, don't look at me like that."

He snatched the cup away and went over to the fire. "The only thing that's keeping me from making love to you right now is knowing how much you're bruised and aching. Unlike you, I don't give a good goddamn about Ted McBride. Armless or not, he's getting far better than what he's giving."

"I'm not going to marry him, Colt."

He jerked his head up in surprise. "When did you decide that?"

"I don't know. I think I've always known in my heart."

"So what's changed?"

She shrugged, then winced in pain from the movement. "I feel it would be worse to deceive him by marrying under false pretenses."

"Good for you, Cass. Have you told him?"

"Not yet. I intended to tell him this morning."

"Playing devil's advocate, what makes you now believe he won't think you're rejecting him because of his injury?"

"Because I'll tell him I'm in love with you."

The statement caught Colt totally unprepared. "And what makes you think he'd believe that?"

"Because it's the truth," she said, looking him straight in the eyes.

"Cass, you know I'm—"

"Colt, I know how you feel; you've been honest from the start. I can't be any less honest with you."

A coldhearted laugh sounded through the cave, and the hair on Cass's neck stood on end when she saw Pike at the entrance with a rifle pointed at Colt's back.

"What a sad story. It's enough to set a man to weepin'," Pike taunted. "But don't worry. Ole Pike here is gonna put you both out of your misery."

Colt moved away to get Cassie out of the line of fire. "Can't we talk about this, Pike? You can see I'm unarmed."

Cassie inched her hand closer to the pistol concealed under her blanket.

"You shoulda kept your gunbelt on, Deputy. No tellin' what mighta stumbled in here to get out of the storm."

"I figured a snake like you would find a hole to crawl into. Give it up, Pike. You've lost too much blood. Give me the rifle, and I swear I'll help you."

"Too late—thanks to you, I ain't gonna make it. But I'm gonna take you and that bitch with me."

"Shoot him, Cass."

Pike snorted. "That's the oldest trick in the book, Fraser—if I turn my head, you'll jump me. And she ain't in no condition to shoot anyone even if she had a gun. I seen to that."

"You must be real proud of yourself. There aren't too many who'd take pleasure in hanging a woman. *Shoot him, Cass,*" Colt ordered calmly.

"I ain't feelin' up to no more polite conversation, Deputy, so it's time we part company."

Before he could pull the trigger, Cassie's shot rang out. Pike's eyes widened in shock, then he pitched forward.

Colt ran over and picked up his rifle, then examined the body.

"He's dead."

"Are you sure?" she asked.

"No doubt about it."

Colt went over to Cassie and knelt down. The dazed look had returned to her eyes.

"I've never shot a human being before," she murmured.

"You still haven't, honey. Pike was a deadly wild animal." He carefully pried her fingers off the gun and put it aside.

"You saved our lives, Cass. He would have killed both of us." She began to tremble again, and he pulled her into his arms. "He's finally dead. He can never hurt you or anyone else again."

"I had to do it, didn't I, Colt?"

"Yes, honey, you had to do it." He cradled her and pressed her head to his chest. "You did right, baby. You did right."

Colt had no idea how long he held her before her trembling ceased and she finally slipped into slumber.

She felt so good in his arms. Soft, clinging. He would have liked to continue holding her and feeling the warmth of her. Reluctanly, he slipped away, made sure she was covered, then went back to Pike's body.

Colt didn't want a corpse lying around when Cassie awoke, and since the rain had stopped, he decided to take the body outside. He dragged it over to a copse of trees, and as he turned to go back he heard a horse neigh. He was delighted to discover Keeler's and Jeff's horses tied to a tree. If Cassie was able, they could ride back to Arena Roja. He led the horses to the cave, where there was plenty of room to take them inside.

After adding some wood to the fire, he lay down next to Cassie, gathered her into his arms, and then, exhausted, closed his eyes and fell asleep.

He didn't open his eyes until the next morning, when Jeff Braden gently shook him awake.

Chapter 28

Ted sat at the table as Cathy finished up the dishes. A pall had hung over the house ever since the posse, shivering and wet, had returned near dawn. They had met up with Jeff and found Keeler's body, but there had been no sign of Pike or Cassie and Colt.

From the spent shells on the ground it was clear there had been a gun battle. A severed rope hanging from a limb and a discarded noose on the ground confused them, since Keeler had been shot, not hung. It only made people's imaginations run rampant.

Jeff and the Callum brothers were still searching, but the rain had washed away any evidence of a trail.

"Cathy, why don't you sit down," Ted said. "You've been on your feet for practically two days."

"I've got to keep busy or I'll go out of my mind. And I think Dad's on the verge of a relapse. He never should have ridden out with that posse. He isn't strong enough yet, and Cassie's kidnapping is weakening him more."

"I just checked on him. Dr. Williams gave him a strong dosage of medicine to get him to sleep. By the time he wakes up, maybe we'll have some news."

"That doesn't mean it will be good news."

"All we know for certain is that all of the gang is dead except Pike, and he may be dead, too. I have a feeling that Fraser caught up with them and Cassie's with him, now."

Cathy filled two coffee cups and sat at the table. "I wish I had your confidence."

Her eyes were red and swollen from crying. Ted reached across the table to hold her hand.

"They're probably just lost, Cathy. They'll show up, I'm sure."

"Cassie doesn't get lost, Ted; she's always had an incredible sense of direction. Maybe she's wounded and needs help, or maybe Pike—"

"Or maybe they're holed up somewhere to get out of the storm," Ted said firmly. "I believe in my heart that she's still alive."

"You sound like Cassie. For the past year, she insisted the same was true about you."

"And she was right, wasn't she? Now, you won't do yourself or your dad any good by exhausting yourself. Lie down and try to get some sleep. I promise I'll wake you if there's any word."

"I can't sleep, Ted. I think I'll go for a walk."

"May I come with you?"

"I'd like to be alone right now. Will you keep an eye on Dad while I'm gone?"

"Of course."

Outside, Cathy drew up when she saw Sam and the James brothers huddled under a tarp.

Sam looked up hopefully. "Any news?"

Cathy knelt down. "No, dear. Not yet."

"She'll be back, Cathy. I know she will," Sam said. "You know how she always got herself out of predicaments."

"She'll get out of this one too," Bowie said.

Petey nodded. "Yeah." His little mouth puckered up and he began to sob.

"Oh, darlings," Cathy cried. She gathered them into her arms, and the four huddled together and shed their tears.

Hours later, their sorrowful tears turned to those of joy when the Callum brothers rode in with the news that Cassie had been found, and she, Colt, and Jeff were following two or three hours behind.

Word of the rescue spread rapidly, and a crowd quickly gathered to listen to the Callums' report.

"This is a day of rejoicing," the Reverend MacKenzie declared. "Sam, run to the church and ring the church bell."

Cathy was hugging and kissing everyone in sight, and the news had an amazing recuperative effect on Jethro, who jumped out of bed to await Cassie's arrival.

Practically everyone in town was there to greet the three riders when they arrived a few hours later.

People listened with grim faces and muttered oaths when Cassie described her treatment at the hands of Pike. Colt received awed glances and pats on the back when she related her near miss with death and his timely rescue of her. Jeff received kudos for his relentless determination to find his sister.

Then they cheered and applauded when they heard how Cassie had shot Pike as he'd been about to kill Colt.

The end of Pike's reign of terror was a relief to everyone, but probably one of the happiest was the bank president when Colt handed him the recovered money bag.

After examining Cassie, Dr. Williams felt that she had suffered no serious damage. He dressed the wounds on her wrists and gave her a mild sedative to make her more comfortable.

Heeding the doctor's advice, she soaked in a hot bath under Cathy's devoted, watchful eye, then went to bed.

The last thing she remembered was the thought that nothing felt as good as stretching out in your own bed—unless it was sleeping curled up in Colt's arms.

Colt resumed his deputy duties and made his rounds. Had he accepted the many offers to buy him drinks, he would have staggered to bed drunk instead of merely exhausted.

After a full night's sleep, Cassie awoke early the following morning. Cathy was preparing breakfast when Cassie joined her in the kitchen.

"Good morning," Cathy greeted. "Did you sleep well?"

"I don't think I moved all night. What about you?"

"The same," Cathy said.

"You look tired, Cathy, and your eyes are swollen. You've been crying." She walked over and put her arm around her sister's shoulders. "It's all over now, honey. There's nothing to cry about."

"I guess tears of joy make one look just as bad as those of sorrow," Cathy said gamely.

Drawing her over to the table, Cassie sat her down.

"Tell me what's bothering you. You haven't been yourself ever since Ted came back."

"Don't pay any attention to me, Cassie. It's all the excitement of the wedding, and then fearing what would happen to you. It seems like everything kind of ganged up on me, and I'm still concerned about Dad's health, too."

"I'm so sorry, Cathy. I know you carried most of the load when Dad was sick."

"You know, I've been thinking that after the wedding, I'll take a trip East and see one of those cities I've read so much about."

"There's not going to be a wedding."

Cathy looked at her in disbelief. "What did you just say?"

"I know that I should tell Ted first, but you and I have never kept secrets from each other. Cathy, I can't marry Ted. I'm not in love with him. And I doubt that he's in love with me. We're just going through the motions."

"You're in love with Colt, aren't you?"

"Is it that obvious?"

"I once suspected it but then when Ted came home and you planned your wedding, I thought I'd been mistaken."

"What am I going to do, Cathy? I have to tell Ted the truth and say good-bye to Colt in two days."

"Maybe if you told Colt your feelings for him—"

"I did. It doesn't matter; his mind is made up. He's going to California. But please don't say anything to the family until I tell Ted."

"Tell me what?" Ted asked, entering the room.

Cathy got up to leave, but Cassie put a restraining hand on her arm. "Please stay, Cathy."

"What's this all about?"

"It's about us, Ted. I'm calling off the wedding."

He looked at her calmly. "So Fraser told you that I'm in love with Cathy?"

Whether out of relief or finally out of awareness, she laughed and shook her head. "I can't believe I never saw that for myself."

"Because we never admitted it to each other until the night of your party," Cathy said.

"You mean you feel the same way about him?" Cassie asked her sister, amazed.

Cathy nodded. "I love Ted, Cassie, but I never cheated behind your back."

"I know you didn't, darling." They got up and hugged each other.

"Wow!" Cassie continued. "The other night sure was busy for all of us. Colt ran to Ted. Ted came to me. I went to Colt. Then you and Ted confronted each other. The whole thing was more convoluted than a Shakespearean play."

They all broke into laughter.

Cassie put an arm around each of them. "I love you both so much. And I'm so happy for you that I want to cry."

Tears welled in Cathy's eyes. "I didn't think I had any tears left, but I guess I do."

"If you two are going to stand around weeping, I'm getting out of here," Ted teased.

Cassie wiped a tear away and bit her lip. "But I still have a serious problem. Colt is leaving Thursday. How do I convince him to say, I do?"

"Tell him you're in love with him," Ted said.

"I've told him that already. It doesn't work if the other person isn't in love with you." Cassie hurried from the room.

Perplexed, Ted looked at Cathy. "I may be minus an arm, sweetheart, but your sister is blind."

Well, she said she wouldn't come to see me off. As the stagecoach pulled out of Arena Roja, Colt looked back for a last look at the town. The three sprouts stood in the dust from the departing stage, looking sorrowful.

Yesterday, when Jeff had told him Cass had called off the wedding, and Cathy and Ted were getting married instead, Colt had considered remaining in town for a few more weeks. He had a good excuse, since Jethro still wasn't up to returning to work.

Then last night Cass had come to his room. They had made love and she had begged him to take her with him to California. He had refused, but he'd promised her he would come back after he saw his sister and brothers. One word had led to another, and the headstrong little fool had told him not to bother coming back, because she never wanted to see him again. So they had parted in anger, and he'd given up any thought of remaining.

Now he was having second thoughts. He should have remained and worked out a compromise when she cooled down. But dammit, he didn't take to prodding. Even if he'd agreed to take her with him, that would have meant marriage. And in his book, you had to be in love to get married.

Sex had always been the name of the game with him, love them and leave them, his philosophy.

And then Cass had come into his life. From day one, he hadn't been able to keep his mind off the woman. And when she'd been at the mercy of that crazed Pike, the thought of losing her had driven him wild.

Was he fascinated with her because she was so different from any other woman he'd ever known? She could do practically anything a man could do, yet she was all woman.

And the sex! Sex with Cass was the greatest he'd ever known. Her mere touch set him on fire. But was it the sex itself—or was it because it was with Cass?

If you wanted to be with a woman day and night; if thoughts of her monopolized every waking hour and all your dreams—was that love?

You're damn right it is!

She was no fragile piece of china; whatever hardships faced them on the way to California, she was the best trail partner a person could hope for. They could get married and catch the next stage to California.

He'd just yelled to Gus to stop the stage when a shot rang out and the coach come to a halt.

A masked bandit on a black horse rode up with another horse tied to the saddle horn. "Hands up and everybody out."

The rider may have been masked, but there was no disguising the black stallion. It was Midnight.

"What in hell is Cassie up to now?" Gus grumbled to Buck.

When one of the men inside the coach reached for his pistol, Colt put a restraining hand on the man's arm. "That's not necessary, sir. There's nothing to be alarmed about," Colt said calmly to the three passengers. "The poor woman's a little deranged. She imagines herself to be Belle Starr, but she's harmless, so just humor her."

Arms above their heads, the four passengers climbed out.

Cassie tossed a pair of handcuffs down to one of the male passengers.

"Put these on that tall, ugly one," she said, pointing to Colt.

Grinning, the man clamped the cuffs on Colt's wrists and winked at him.

"Okay, you three passengers get back in the coach."

"Cassie, we ain't got time for this," Gus groused. "We've got a long ride ahead of us."

"So get going," she said.

"Cass, what are you doing? I had to keep one of those men from shooting you," Colt declared as the stagecoach rolled away.

Pulling off the bandanna, she dismounted and came over and unbuckled his gun belt. Then she untied the other horse and tossed the gun belt over Midnight's saddle horn.

"Mount up, Deputy. You're coming with me."

"How do you expect me to ride with my hands cuffed behind my back?"

"Please—I've seen you ride."

"Don't you think this joke's gone far enough?" Colt grumbled, and swung into the saddle.

Chapter 29

After several minutes they turned off the road, and Colt knew where they were headed. He continued to go along with her plans.

"Where are we going?" he asked, feigning innocence.

"The Lazy B. I can hardly take you back to town without making a lot of explanations. This way, no one will know you're even here until Gus shows up next week."

"And what is the purpose of all this, Cass?"

"You'll find out when we get there."

They reached the ranch ten minutes later and went into the barn. Dismounting, she kept her pistol pointed at him as she motioned to a far corner. "Get over there and don't try anything dumb."

"I wouldn't think of it, Miz Braden."

He waited, amused, as she unsaddled the horses, put them in stalls, tossed in hay, and filled their troughs.

"You planning a long stay, Miz Braden?"

"Get moving," she said, with a menacing gesture of the pistol.

Once inside, she directed him to her bedroom. Then she pressed the gun against his stomach. "Now, no quick moves, Colt; I'd hate for this gun to go off."

Colt frowned. "This joke's losing its humor, Cass. Up to now I went along with it, but sticking a gun in a man's gut is dangerous."

"Then you know better than to try anything stupid." She unlocked the right handcuff. "Slip your shirt off your arm."

As soon as he finished, she attached the right cuff to the iron rail of the headboard. Then she unlocked the left cuff, pulled his shirt down that arm, and recuffed him so he was tethered to the bed.

"Good, you can sit down now. Are you comfortable?"

Colt sat down and glared at her. As much as he loved her, that gun thing was just too dangerous to even consider. It was typical of her damn recklessness.

Cassie sat down on the edge of the bed and began to pull off his boots and stockings. "It was very smart of you, my love, not to try any foolish moves with a loaded gun shoved in your stomach. But the gun wasn't loaded." She picked up the weapon, pointed it at the ceiling, and pulled the trigger. Six times, it clicked on an empty chamber. "You don't actually think I'd stick a loaded gun into you?"

"You fired a shot to stop the stagecoach."

"One shot. I had emptied the chamber and put in one cartridge to do so.

"And now I've got seven days to convince you to marry me and take me to California with you."

"And you intend to do that by keeping me cuffed to this bed?"

"Well, what do you think of this idea?" she asked.

"There once was an innocent sprite,
Who loved a lawman beyond measure.
But she found herself in a plight,
when he spurned her offered treasure.
Determined to make it right,
She set off on a path of corruption.
So now, alas! Poor Cass
is forced to resort to seduction!"

Colt held back a laugh. Good Lord! Didn't she realize she seduced him every time he looked at her? At this moment, he wanted to take her in his arms and make love to her until they were both senseless.

"So you're going to try to seduce me?"

"Not try, my love—I *will*," she said confidently.

She straddled his lap, slipped her arms around his neck, and kissed him. Then she pulled back with an impish grin. "So, what do you think of my idea?"

What did he think of it! He'd already become aroused just at the thought of it, and as soon as the warmth between her legs hit his, he became so hard and hot, he thought he would explode. Since he was more sexually sophisticated than she was, he figured he could outlast her in this sex game. But he doubted he'd have to: every time he touched her, Cassie was like a wound spring ready to pop.

He reflected for several more seconds, then replied, "If that's your intention, Cass, it leads me to say:

"Well then, Miz Innocent Sprite,
Seems we're in for a long, sleepless night.

> *The question being: who will win?*
> *So, 'Let the games begin.'"*

"Yes, let them." She lightly traced the slope of his shoulders with her fingertips.

"I love your shoulders, Colt. They're so beautiful." She retraced the route of her fingertips with her tongue. "So broad. So muscular."

"I'm glad they please you." He could feel the perspiration beading on his brow.

"I love touching your body, Colt." Her eyes danced with merriment as she cocked a brow. "And there's so much of it to touch."

"That there is. You figure you'll get around to all of it in seven days?"

"Many, many times."

She dipped her head and teased one of his nipples with her tongue. He jerked, and she looked up in surprise. "Oh, you like that." She lowered her head and laved it again, then lightly took the tip between her teeth. A gasp slipped past his lips.

"I think I've found your Achilles Heel, tough guy."

"Wrong again, sweetheart," he bluffed. "My Achilles Heel is between my legs. It's been waiting a *long* time for the pleasure of meeting up with you."

Cassie pulled off her shirt and camisole. The twin peaks of her breasts loomed before him, so near that if his mouth hadn't gone dry, he'd be drooling.

With a smile as seductive as the one Cleopatra must have worn to get Marc Antony to shuck his armor, she murmured, "Do you like my breasts, Colt?"

"Oh yeah—I like them a lot."

He offered no resistance when she brought his free hand to one of her breasts. His fingers closed around its roundness and his thumb toyed with the peak.

"Does that feel good to you?"

"Oh yeah—real good," he said.

"It feels good to me, too. Would you like to taste them?"

His mouth was there before she even finished getting the words out. With ragged gasps, she threw back her head and closed her eyes. She'd bitten off more than she could chew, and the crazy little fool was becoming as far gone as he was.

With a smothered groan she leaned into him, and her taut peaks burned his chest. Clasping his face between her hands, she captured his lips, tracing the chamber of his mouth with hot, darted forays that charged every nerve end in his body.

"Who taught you to do that?" he asked when she broke the kiss. His voice was hoarse and his groin was on fire.

"You did," she murmured, and covered his mouth again. This time their tongues dueled. He slipped his free hand to the back of her neck and held her head motionless in a kiss that made a beeline straight to his groin and fueled the blaze. He figured he was good for about another ten seconds, then he'd lose it.

"I love you, Colt," she whispered, "I love you beyond words."

"Action speaks louder than words," he replied. He grabbed her hand and brought it to the swollen, throbbing mound of his penis. She palmed it and the pressure became an exquisite agony.

When he began to fumble at the fly of his pants to free it, she stood up and opened it, then pulled the pants off his legs. When she started to cast them aside, he stopped her.

"Hold on a minute. I need something out of the pocket." She brought the pants to him and he pulled out a small object.

"What is it?"

"The key to these handcuffs." He put the key in the lock and released his arm.

She stood, stunned. "You mean you could have unlocked them all this time."

"That's right. I kept the key to remind me of you when we're apart."

"And you let me believe that—"

"I was your helpless prisoner."

"That was a sneaky trick."

"Yeah, right up there with letting me believe you were sticking a loaded gun in my gut. We can argue ethics later—right now I have a little score to settle with you."

The angry glint in his eyes caused her to draw back in alarm. Before she could guess his intent, he grabbed her and clamped the handcuffs on her wrists.

"Now sit down and be quiet."

Colt began to pace the floor. "You're the most headstrong, shameless, conniving female I've ever met."

He spun on his heel and pointed a finger at her. "I told you when I left that I'd be back when I finished what I have to do in California. But no, that wasn't good enough for you. You had to have it *your* way."

"Can you blame me? The last time a man kissed me good-bye and said he'd be back, I waited for five years. I admit I'm all the things you've said. And I know I'm not a refined lady, like you'd prefer to marry. But Colt, no woman could ever love you as much as I do."

"You're also quick to jump to wrong conclusions. When did I ever tell you the kind of woman I *prefer* to marry?"

"Actually, you never said it aloud, but your actions indicated as much." Cassie eyed him warily when he removed his belt. "What are you doing to do?"

"I told you; I have a score to settle with you."

He looped the belt around the chain linking the handcuffs and pulled her arms over her head; then he buckled the belt to the railing of the iron headboard.

"Comfortable, sweetheart?" he said mockingly. Bending over, he placed a light kiss on her lips.

"At least I let you have one hand free," she said.

He pulled off one of her boots and the stocking. "Cass, I fell in love with you the moment I met you." The other boot hit the floor, along with the other stocking.

Then he unbuckled her belt and started to work her jeans past her hips. "You're courageous, energetic, tireless, stoic when it comes to pain . . . Lift your hips a little, will you, honey?"

With a combination of fear and anticipation, she did what he asked. He pulled the pants off her and tossed them on the floor.

"You've got a good sense of humor, you handle a horse superbly, and you've got the best little ass I've ever seen in or out of pants. What more could a man want for a wife?"

She gasped when he grasped the neckline of her camisole and ripped it down the center. Then he pulled off the torn pieces and tossed them aside. They landed in the heap with her jeans, as did her drawers.

"And did I mention how beautiful you are?" His gaze devoured her and he lowered his voice to almost a whisper. "So very beautiful." He leaned down and kissed her again.

"But, my beloved, once again your impetuousness has gotten you into a situation where you're in over your head. You see, as much as I enjoyed—and appreciated—your attempt to seduce me, you've ended up like the snake who caught its own tail in its mouth—and found it a hard dish to swallow.

"Perhaps when I told you the difference between making love and merely having sex, I failed to mention that being in love doesn't prevent two people from sometimes having just sex."

He bent his head and licked her earlobe, then darted his curled tongue into her ear. Tremors of passion rippled her spine and her breath quickened.

"So it's payback time now, baby. The velvet gloves come off," he whispered in her ear. "You know what that means? No sweet kisses, no tender caresses, no whispered words of love. Just hot, carnal sex that's going to make you beg for it. Whenever you can't take anymore, just tell me to stop."

"I can take anything you dish out, Colt Fraser. And *you'll* be the one left begging."

He dropped his drawers and stretched out on top of her. He began slowly with light, feathery kisses that aroused her need for deeper contact. She lifted her head to capture his mouth with her own, but he succeeded in avoiding her.

Then he slowly skimmed his hands along her sides until he reached her thighs. Parting her legs, he began to massage the heated flesh between them. Hot waves of sensation pounded at her brain, and she began to squirm. As he continued, she couldn't control her body's response, and he didn't stop until she felt the first ecstatic release.

Then his mouth and tongue moved to her breasts. When he began to suckle her taut nipples, his hand between her legs increased the tempo and pressure of the massage, his long fingers a mind-shattering probe that caused her to moan with ecstasy. Once again, her body imploded with exquisite, fiery tremors of release.

She struggled to draw ragged gasps of air into her lungs. She *needed* to touch him, to feel his flesh beneath her fingers, and she strained to release her hands.

"Please," she managed to plead. "Please, Colt."

He raised his head. "Are you asking me to stop?"

"No, release my hands. Let me touch you."

"That would spoil the point of this, now, wouldn't it?"

His hands and mouth continued their arousing exploration, finding every sensitive pleasure spot of her body. She writhed beneath him as each ecstatic gasp, each erotic moan, became a clarion call to the slide of his lips and mouth, the tantalizing pressure of his touch.

Floating in raw, sensual sensation, she lost awareness of time, of place. Time and time again he brought her to a body shuddering, soul-shattering climax where nothing existed except hedonistic sensation.

Somehow, through the erotic haze, she became aware that her arms were now free. Opening her eyes, she looked into his troubled ones.

"I can't take any more," he murmured. "This is killing me."

She smiled raggedly. "What do you think it's doing to me?"

"I'm sorry, love. I thought we could just have sex, but I can't do it. I need to make love to you. To kiss you, and caress you. I want to feel your touch, to smell the sweet scent of you. I want to whisper how much I love you, and hear you say the same to me. And then I want to lay beside you and reach out and pull you closer to me. To kiss you when I feel the need to. To have you kiss me when you have the same need.

"And I want our children conceived in love—not lust."

He kissed her passionately—a passion spurred by the love and need he'd spoken of. She responded with the same caresses of love, the same whispered expressions of her love.

When she felt the slide of his body on hers, she slipped her arms around his neck. Her body opened instinctively to him as she clung to him, and he entered her. Their bodies locked, their hearts beat as one, and they moved in the rhythmic dance of lovers to the melody of love. And when the dance was through, it ended as it began—with love.

Later, as she lay cuddled against him, Colt suddenly chuckled.

"What is it, my love?" she asked.

"I still can't believe your brazen attempt to seduce me."

"Attempt?" She sat up and poked him in the arm. "It only took about sixty seconds to succeed."

He pulled her down and kissed her. "Just the same, let's keep this between the two of us. None of this 'twins don't keep secrets from each other' kind of talk."

"Okay, but that's gonna cost you."

"I've already promised to marry you and take you to California with me. What else do you want from me?"

There was a devilish glint in her eyes. "Next time, my love, I get to cuff both your hands."

"You're such a brazen little hussy, it's no wonder I'm in love with you.

"But you were willing enough to leave me?" she said.

"I knew I was wrong about that as soon as that stage pulled out of town. I'd just told Gus to stop the stage when you held it up." He chuckled. "You saved me a long walk back here."

Cassie slipped her arms around his neck. "Oh, Colt, I love you so much," she murmured between kisses. "And you really *will* take me to California with you?"

"Guess I'll have to, or I'd always be worrying about

what you've got yourself into that I'm not here to get you out of. Honey, after we marry, you've *got* to promise you'll stay out of trouble. Trying to keep you alive can cut a lot of years off a man's life."

Her eyes filled with devotion as she opened her arms to him.

In his wildest dreams, he had never hoped to find a woman as incredible as Cassie. She was his soul mate, companion, lover, and all woman—more woman than he deserved.

"Now, let me see," he reflected. "The stage comes through again in seven days. That's not much time for everything I've got in mind."

With a sinfully seductive smile, she slipped her arms around his neck. "Then it's time to mount up, Deputy."

On Saturday, Arena Roja celebrated the double wedding of the Braden twins.

Jeff Braden, the new deputy, stood as best man for both of the grooms. Samantha Starr, glowing with the promise of the lovely young woman she would grow into, stood as the maid of honor for the two brides.

Jethro Braden wiped the tears from his eyes as he gazed proudly at his three children standing at the altar.

It seemed as if overnight his daughters had become women, and his son had become a man. On top of that, not only was he gaining two more fine sons that any father would be proud to have but he had also gained a deputy: his son.

Many of the spectators became confused when

Cassie Braden married Colt Fraser and *Cathy* Braden married Ted McBride.

Some had heard the rumor that Cassie had held a gun to the ex-deputy's head to get him to agree to marry her, but observing the love between the bride and groom, it was hard to believe. Cathy and her new husband seemed equally in love. But wasn't the schoolmaster supposed to be marrying Cassie?

It sure was confusing, but it didn't prevent anyone from having the best time at a wedding—ah, weddings—ever had in Arena Roja.

The following Thursday, Colt and Cassie prepared to board the stage. After a tearful good-bye to the three sprouts, Cassie said another parting farewell to her father.

"We're coming back, Dad, as soon as Colt sees his sister and brothers. Just think of this as a honeymoon. Then we'll move back to the Lazy B, just as you always hoped to do."

"We'll be waiting," said Cathy, who was standing beside Jethro. The two women hugged and kissed. "But I'll miss you so much."

"And I'll miss you, too. All of you," Cassie said, with a final kiss to Ted and Jeff. "Take good care of Midnight for me, Jeff."

"Time to pull out, Cassie," Gus yelled from the box.

"Let's go, honey," Colt said, helping her into the stagecoach.

Sam ran over to Colt and hugged him around the waist. "I love you, Colt Fraser. You're the best man I ever met," she said earnestly, tears welling in her eyes. "Promise you and Cassie will come back?"

"I promise, Belle." He hugged her, then climbed in and took a seat next to Cassie. Leaning out the window, he said, "Probably in a couple years, if not sooner. In five or six years for sure, because we don't want to miss your wedding."

"Wedding! I ain't never gonna get married."

Colt glanced at Jeff, who was standing nearby, shining the brand-new star on his chest with the sleeve of his shirt.

"I wouldn't bet on that, Belle."

As the stage started to roll away, she shouted, "My name ain't Belle!"

She hurried off to hide her tears.

Petey looked up at his brother. "Bowie, why's Sam mad?"

"She ain't really mad," Bowie said. "She's just pretendin', 'cause she feels sad." He put his arm around his little brother's shoulders. "Like I told you, Petey: women are complicated."

Petey nodded wisely as they followed in Sam's wake.

"Yeah. Very compli . . . cated."